**"You're beautiful, Winn, just as I pictured you."**

His palms contoured her breasts, sending currents of tension zigging downward to meet the fire between her legs.

"Right from the start, I wanted you. But even though I backed off that first night, I didn't stop thinking about you, wanting to do what I'm doing right now, wondering how to go about wooing a woman with another man's ring on her finger."

"Are you wooing me, Joseph?" Winn's voice was dark with desire.

His smile brought the devil's sparkle to his eyes. "What does it feel like to you?" He bent to probe her ear with the warm, wet point of his tongue...and sent rivers within Winn's body flooding their banks.

Dear Reader,

We at Harlequin are extremely proud to introduce our new series, **HARLEQUIN TEMPTATION.** Romance publishing today is exciting, expanding and innovative. We have responded to the ever-changing demands of you, the reader, by creating this new, more sensuous series. Between the covers of each **HARLEQUIN TEMPTATION** you will find an irresistible story to stimulate your imagination and warm your heart.

Styles in romance change, and these highly sensuous stories may not be to every reader's taste. But Harlequin continues its commitment to satisfy all your romance-reading needs with books of the highest quality. Our sincerest wish is that **HARLEQUIN TEMPTATION** will bring you many hours of pleasurable reading.

THE EDITORS

U.S.
HARLEQUIN TEMPTATION
2504 WEST SOUTHERN AVE.
TEMPE, ARIZONA
85282

CAN.
HARLEQUIN TEMPTATION
P.O. BOX 2800
POSTAL STATION "A"
WILLOWDALE, ONTARIO
M2N 5T5

# *Spring Fancy*

LAVYRLE SPENCER

*Harlequin Books*

TORONTO • NEW YORK • LONDON
AMSTERDAM • PARIS • SYDNEY • HAMBURG
STOCKHOLM • ATHENS • TOKYO • MILAN

For some wonderful friends
who enrich my life
with their refreshing humor
and love of fun...
Tyke and John Lapham
Meredith and Arvid Gafkjen
Jeanne and Larry Helling

---

Published March 1984

ISBN 0-373-25101-7



Printed in Canada

# 1

THE WEDDING REHEARSAL was scheduled for 7:00 P.M. Winnifred Gardner opened the door of St. Alphonsus Catholic Church at ten after. Hoping to slip in unobtrusively, she was dismayed when a howling gust of March wind caught the door and whipped it out of her hand, then sent it thunking against the brick wall before swirling inside the vestibule, announcing her tardiness to everyone. Muttering a curse, she tried to hold the hair out of her eyes with one arm while recapturing the stubborn door with the other.

There must have been fifteen people in the vestibule, and every face turned to note her late arrival. Bride, groom, priest, servers, parents, groomsmen, ushers and bridesmaids all watched her rush in, breathless, smelling like old Earl Evvsvold's garage floor and looking as if her hair had been styled with his air hose.

Sandy Schaeffer—tomorrow's bride and Winnie's dearest friend—left Father Waldron's side and hurried forward, smiling.

"Winnie, you made it!"

"Sandy, I'm so sorry I'm late, but my car—"

Sandy waved away the explanation. "It's okay. The organist isn't here yet, either, so we've just been talking over the procedure before we walk through it." Sandy reached impulsively for Winnie's hand but had barely touched it before it was sharply withdrawn.

"Don't touch me! I stink like gas. Oh, I hate those pump-your-owns!" Winnie sniffed her fingers, grimaced and hid the hand inside her coat pocket just as a stocky brown-haired man joined them.

"There she is! The maid of honor." He plopped a platonic kiss on Winnie's cheek.

"Hi, Mick. Sorry I'm late. Everything went wrong tonight."

"No problem. We just got here ourselves."

Winnie assessed Sandy's prospective groom—a sturdy convivial man of Polish descent, who'd made his fiancée the happiest woman in Brooklyn Park, Minnesota. There were times when Winnie envied them immensely for sharing "that certain something" so elusive and necessary to a truly special relationship. They laughed often, teased each other and shared so many common interests. Mick draped an arm around Sandy's shoulders and grinned down at her while Winnie began moving away toward the washroom.

But Mick stopped her and crooked a finger at someone. "Hey, Jo-Jo, come on over here." A man turned from his conversation with Mick's parents, raised an index finger, turned back to the couple to excuse himself and approached.

He clapped Mick's shoulder. "What's up, Ski, my man?"

Mick Malaszewski slapped his friend's shoulder and caught Winnie's elbow with his free hand. "I guess it's about time you two met. Jo-Jo, this is Winnifred Gardner, Sandy's maid of honor. Winnie, this is my best man and my best friend, Joseph Duggan."

*Jo-Jo.* How many times had she heard the name? A firm square hand captured Winnie's before she could warn him to beware of gas. But a moment later she forgot all about warnings, except that of her own heart as she heard again the pleasant tenor voice, rich with expressiveness.

"So this is Winnie. It's about time I met the woman I'm going to walk down the aisle with." He covered the top of her hand with his other and gave her a smile to match that in his voice.

He was nothing at all like what she'd expected. Not as tall, not as crude, not as brooding. Somehow the name Joseph Duggan had conjured up a tough thuggish sort, a longshoreman, maybe, with a wild Irish temper and a burly body. Instead, Jo-Jo was a toned and tapered five-feet-ten, had a head full of wild fluffy brown curls and the most twinkly eyes she'd ever encountered. His hand was dry, hard and very commanding. And as Winnifred placed her left hand atop his, she forgot the engagement ring upon it.

"Joseph," she said simply. "It seems as if we should have met years ago after all I've heard about you."

"I'll second that. I've heard plenty about you, too, and it appears none of it was quite true."

"Oh?" She cocked her head inquisitively.

"They've been holding out on me." For a moment his eyes flickered down to her mouth, then back up. Winnie suddenly realized how warm, personal and extended the handshake had become. She jerked free and leaped back a step.

"Oh, you're going to stink like gas! I'm sorry! I ran the pump over just a few minutes ago while I was filling my . . . my car, and I got it all over my hand and on my shoe and my cuff, and I was going straight to the ladies' room to get rid of the stench, but I never got the chance and—" she raked her hair with four fingers "—and the wind practically tore my hair out, roots and all. I have to . . . to comb it."

"A pity," he teased.

"A pity? Why, I look like a disaster, and I . . . I didn't—" She stumbled to a halt. *Winnifred Gardner, why ever are you prattling,* she thought while Joseph Duggan watched a becoming blush inch its way up one of the most charming chins he'd ever seen, then pass an exquisite mouth whose lips had dropped open in surprise. He lifted his eyes to her beguilingly disheveled hair. In the muted amber light it appeared to be the color of peanut butter. Large wide eyes stared at him momentarily before she did the most amazing thing: she blinked. . .but with only one eye! It was the most unusual nervous reaction he'd ever seen. And it *had* been a nervous reaction, and it *had* been a blink, not a wink. For a winking face uses more than an eye to flash its message. This was a blink, pure and simple, but he'd never in his life seen anyone do it so charmingly.

Her eyes flickered down to his Adam's apple, then away from him entirely, and he let his gaze wander downward. *Her name doesn't fit.* Winnifred Gardner sounds like a supercilious prude with lineage and laureateship. Instead, the woman before him seemed to blend the shyness of Winnie-The-Pooh with the conditioned body of Superwoman, and the whole bundle smelling like gas.

Joseph Duggan was enchanted.

"You have a few minutes yet. Father Waldron is still socializing over there."

Winnie clapped her mouth shut and whirled toward the hall leading to the washroom. Behind her, she heard Jo-Jo Duggan's voice chiding Sandy and Mick. "*Where* in the blazes have you been hiding her all these years?"

In the clean silent lavatory she doused her hands liberally with pink liquid soap and scrubbed furiously. After rinsing, she gave them a critical sniff and disgustedly began soaping again. This time she worked a thumb roughly over her knuckles in an effort to get rid of the smell. In the process she cut herself on her diamond ring. The swift sting of the soap in the cut brought her back to her senses.

*Winnifred Gardner, act your age. He's just teasing. And obviously a flirt. He probably said what he did just to see how you'd react, and you came through with classic feminine witlessness!*

Still, when she checked her reflection in the mirror, her cheeks held two bright patches of flustered blood, and her eyes were a little too sparkly, her lips quirked up in a grin that told how great it felt—witless or not—to be flirted with.

She removed her coat and caught it over one wrist, scrutinizing her dress. It was a pale mauve shapeless thing that came alive when its belt was cinched. She smoothed the wool over both hips and recalled Paul's words: "Well, well, a dress. What do you know about that?" If he hadn't prefaced his compliment with that wry remark, she wouldn't have become so piqued. But by the time he'd got around to adding, "You look great, darling," the effect had been ruined. Next he'd dropped his eyes to her high heels, given a mock-lurid grin followed by a growl as he buried his face in her neck, whispering his intentions, had she not had to leave at that moment. Still stung by his earlier remark, she'd pushed him away and given him a conciliatory kiss instead of the dressing down he deserved. It wasn't as if she *never* wore dresses!

Winnie pushed aside the memory, stooped to wipe the dull spot where the gas had splattered the toe of her black-patent high heel. She felt uncomfortable in both dress and heels, but what else was a woman supposed to wear in a church to practice walking on a white linen runner on the arm of a best man?

Back in the vestibule, Winnie felt his eyes following her as she slipped between Sandy's mother and father to greet them warmly, looping a hand through each of their arms.

"Why, Winnie, I didn't see you come in. Did the dress arrive?" Ann Schaeffer inquired.

"All hemmed properly and ready to go. And how about at your house? Any last-minute complications?"

"None. Everything's ready for tomorrow."

"But I'll bet you're both exhausted."

"I confess, we've—"

A shrill whistle cut through the vestibule and echoed in the cavernous nave beyond the open double doors: Mick calling attention to Father Waldron, who began filling everyone in on the opening part of the service. As he talked, he entered the main part of the church, and the wedding party followed.

Winnie moved toward the door, conscious that Joseph Duggan awaited there to escort her inside. She avoided his eyes until the last minute, then lifted her gaze to find him with a scintillating sparkle still in his eyes and the flirtatious expression on his lips. For the first time she realized why his buddies called him Jo-Jo. *That* name fit. While commandeering the coat from her arm, he gave her hair the once-over.

"I liked it better messy, Winnifred Gardner, and there was something a little offbeat and amusing about a girl wearing gasoline for perfume. But anyway, may I?" He presented his right elbow in courtly fashion, still grinning devilishly as they moved inside.

"Thank you, and no thank you, Mr. Duggan. I'm not certain if I've just been insulted, laughed at or both. But I can walk perfectly well without your elbow while I'm deciding."

His grin became dazzling, and without a glance aside he dropped her coat in the last pew, then took a rather deliberate grip on her elbow as they moved toward the front pews.

For the next five minutes Father Waldron outlined the procedures and rituals of the wedding service, explaining that both bride and groom had elected to walk up the aisle with their respective parents and have the attendants do so as pairs. Winnie had known this, of course, but had scarcely given it a second thought until now, seated on a hard wooden pew with Jo-Jo Duggan's knees sprawled wide, one of them only a scant inch from her own. He straightened, turned more fully in

Father Waldron's direction and hung his wrist on the pew behind her.

Not only a flirt, but an *accomplished* flirt!

The door at the rear of the church slammed, and scampering footsteps clicked up the aisle, causing every head to turn.

There stood a birdlike woman, pulling black gloves from her fingers, clutching a portfolio against her coat front. "I'm sorry, Father. I would have been here sooner, but somebody fed my cat beer and got it drunk and. . . ."

The rest was drowned out by laughter, and the twittery woman became more flustered. Father Waldron's voice echoed in the empty church. "Lent just being over, the cat probably needed it, Mrs. Collingswood."

Beside Winnie, Jo-Jo Duggan's chest shook with laughter, and his eyes glinted as if he himself might very well have pulled such pranks once or twice in his day and sympathized not with the cat, but with the prankster.

"We're ready for the music whenever you are, Mrs. Collingswood," Father advised benevolently.

"Oh. . . oh, certainly, Father." Her footsteps carried through the church again, then became a series of muffled thuds on the stairway at the rear. There followed a silence, the rustle of sheet music and a few testing notes.

Within minutes Winnie found herself walking beside Joseph Duggan toward the rear of the church. Father Waldron directed the proceedings like an elementary teacher at a school play, while everyone awaited instructions and cues.

Standing in the shadowed vestibule, Winnie covertly studied the best man more carefully. He was dressed casually, as were most of the men present. His Levi's were dark and new and creased. They fit snugly across lean hips and partially concealed clean new tennis shoes with a neat blue wave curling along their sides. Beneath a lightweight spring jacket he wore a button-down shirt of pale yellow. While listening to the priest, Duggan stood with feet widespread, firmly planted, both his hands slipped into his rear pockets. The stance pulled his open jacket aside, revealing a sturdy chest and hollow belly. Through the thin cotton of his right shirtfront she saw the dim image of a nipple. His other was hidden behind a breast pocket pressed flat against his chest. Father Waldron gestured, and Joseph Duggan's head swerved to follow the pointing finger. His profile was startlingly attractive, and she wondered why, for he had the kind of face that would still look seventeen when he was fifty, a vernal combination of features contrasting oddly with his physically fit five-feet-ten frame and the dense whiskers that must—she was sure—require two shaves a day if he had evening appointments. His nose was slightly upturned, rather short, and his forehead unmarked by frown line or blemish. The amber lights gilded the top of his girlish locks, which fluffed out just enough to obscure his hairline and touch the perimeter of his shiny forehead. For a moment Winnie wondered if she'd ever touched the hair of a man who possessed such curls. Not that she could recall. Paul's hair was feather cut to ultimate perfection, never out of place, always blow combed away from his face and held lightly in place with hair spray. She was accustomed to Paul's fastidious ways and found the breezy natural look of Joseph Duggan's unfettered curls arresting. She'd always thought curly-haired men rather effeminate looking. But there wasn't a square inch of Jo-Jo Duggan that was effeminate. Shorter by a good two inches than most men she'd dated, shorter than Paul by at least six, he had a sturdiness that compensated for the difference in height.

Perhaps it was the stance that caused her eyes to sweep his length and linger longer than was prudent: shoulders back, chest out, athletic, self-assured and perhaps a slight bit cocky.

Or maybe she gave him the twice-over simply because he was so different. Different from Paul.

He turned, caught her studying him and flashed a smile that transformed his face into a tableau of charm. He did it so effortlessly she wondered how many hearts he'd broken with no conscious intent. He smiled more with the right side of his mouth than the left, but with every volt of candlepower his eyes possessed. He had the most beautifully matched set of eyebrows she'd ever encountered, and when the lids beneath them lowered and crinkled at the corners, his smile was devastating. Bedroom eyes, some women called such as these, with their dark spiky lashes and that killing little flicker of teasing that would probably be present were he kissing the ring of the Pope of the Holy Catholic Church!

It glittered out of the nearly closed lids now as he turned and moved closer. "Looks as if you and I come fourth."

"Fourth?" She jerked awake, realizing she'd been preoccupied and had missed what Father Waldron was saying.

"In the wedding procession."

"Oh!"

"We head out when Jeanne and Larry get halfway up the aisle in front of us."

"Yes, I know." But she hadn't known. She'd been too busy assessing Jo-Jo Duggan to pay attention. "We'd better get behind them, then."

The vestibule was crowded, everyone conversing softly, when the talk was brought to a halt by the resounding chords of *Lohengrin*'s Wedding March. The traditional song was a surprise in today's upbeat world where everything from the Beatles to John Denver was used as wedding music. The staunch fortissimo chords had a legend of power and tradition that vibrated not only through the ceiling over Winnifred Gardner's head, but right through her body.

Her head snapped up, and her eyes met those of Joseph Duggan.

"I think that's our song," he said, offering his elbow. The grin had softened but was still on his face, disarming. "This time you have no choice."

Her eyes dropped down to the cream-colored sleeve of his jacket, and a queer premonition joined the body vibrations already scintillating along her nerves in time to the music. *Touch him, and you're a goner.* The flower girl and ring bearer were being coaxed up the aisle, then the first pair of attendants had reached the halfway spot. Winnifred looped her hand on the crook of Joseph Duggan's arm and let him lead her to the double doors.

It was disconcerting, being so drawn to a total stranger. The sleeve of his jacket was cool, but as her hand rested upon it, the warmth of his skin seeped up and made her aware of how solid his flesh was within. He stood with feet firmly planted, watching the couple ahead, waiting. Winnie was on his left, thus it was her right ringless hand resting on his elbow. She experienced a discomfiting jolt of guilt at the thought that she was glad she didn't have to expose her left hand just yet. There was a smell about him that she couldn't identify, something purifying, but not perfumed. A utilitarian soap, maybe, mixed with fresh air and the faint odor of dye, as if it were the first time he'd worn his blue jeans.

A twitch of his elbow made her look up into his face. "Ready?"

She nodded.

"On three, then, starting with the left."

They concentrated on the couple ahead. "One... two...three," she whispered. He pulled Winnie's hand against his ribs as they took their first step down the aisle.

It was the first time Winnie had been asked to act as a maid of honor. It was oddly disquieting. Why ever was she feeling so much like a bride? Programming, she supposed. Weren't all little girls programmed to respond to the song now beating upon her ears? Weren't they all taught to think of growing up in terms of "walking down the aisle"? Women's liberation had done virtually nothing to sway women's minds away from dreams of all that was traditional when it came to weddings.

She watched Jo-Jo Duggan's walk for the first time from the very distracting angle of top to bottom. His unblemished tennis shoes made not a sound, but his crisp jeans crackled slightly, and within them his thighs pressed as firmly as air against the inside of a balloon. To her surprise he strode not with the haughty athletic swagger she might have expected after his stance in the vestibule but instead moved with relaxed poise, almost as if strolling in time to the music instead of marching to it. He had superb rhythm.

"How am I doing?" he whispered.

Her eyes flew up to find him grinning down at her.

"You must be a dancer."

His grin shifted to a wince, and he whispered, "Hardly."

"Well, maybe you should be. You have impeccable timing."

"Thank you, Ginger. Next time I'll bring my top hat and cane."

She nudged his ribs and hissed, "Shh. Not here, Fred."

They'd reached the chancel rail and followed the verbal and hand directions of Father Waldron, separating and taking their places on either flank.

Turning to face the pews, Winnie watched Mick approach. She liked the fact that he and Sandy had chosen to walk up the aisle with their parents—Mick first, so he could be waiting when Sandy arrived to be given over from the arm of her father. She herself had never known a father and would be disinclined to walk up the aisle with her mother.

Just before Sandy reached the chancel, Winnie glanced across at Joseph and found his eyes resting steadily on her, as if they'd been there for some time. He smiled briefly, then looked away, and the rest of the instructions began. When they'd walked through the ritual of the bridal service itself, the attendants were instructed to file into the front pew, again in pairs, for the remainder of the Matrimonial Mass.

Winnie and Joseph were seated side by side, their hips separated by a few scant inches of hard wooden pew. His upper arm brushed hers, and she felt him glance at her when she crossed her arms to end the contact.

"Are you Catholic?"

She looked up in surprise. "Of course. Why?"

"Just wondering. I am, too, but I've never been too comfortable sitting through all this hoopla our church puts on at weddings. Reminds me of a carnival."

She smiled at her lap, trying to imagine him sitting through it dressed in a tux and ruffles. Somehow the picture didn't fit.

Just then Father Waldron raised his voice toward the choir loft. "And that will be my cue for you to begin the recessional, Mrs. Collingswood. Attendants, you'll come and take your places beside the new bride and groom before the final wedding march begins."

They lined up along the front of the church again, and this time when the organ boomed its call to exit, Winnie and Joseph met in the center aisle with a chuckle, a smile and the sense of growing familiarity such routine practices often generate.

They walked through the entire service once more before the entourage again clustered in the vestibule, and Mrs. Malaszewski reminded everybody that the groom's supper would be served at their house as soon as everyone got back there.

"So you drove, huh?" Winnie found Joseph Duggan again at her side, this time holding her coat. Slipping it on, she wished she could say no, just to see what he'd suggest.

"Yes . . . remember the gas?"

"Yes, I remember. Too bad, or we could ride over to Mick's house together."

"Well, in any case, I'll see you there."

He opened the exterior door, and a blast of wind nearly knocked her back against his chest. Instinctively he took her elbow as they ran down the steps together, her coat flapping back across his thighs, and her hair slicked straight back from her face. In the parking lot he stopped her with a forceful pressure of his thumb in the hollow of her elbow.

"If you get there first, save me a place next to you."

The wind worked its way inside his jacket and ballooned it out. He dropped her elbow and reached to raise the zipper higher up his chest. The curls on the upper right-hand side of his skull were forced flat, while her own collar-length hair blew across her mouth and eye. She stood in the wind looking up at him, wondering what to reply, knowing she wasn't permitted to encourage him, yet answering, "And if you get there first, save a seat for me."

"It's a promise. Only don't comb your hair this time!"

"I. . . ." A strand of it whipped into her open mouth. "What?"

He'd started jogging away but turned and jogged backward five steps while calling, "I said don't comb your hair this time. It looked great when you first walked into church!"

Some off-tempo warning slanted through her heart. *Beware. He's an inveterate flirt and a practiced flatterer. And you're only walking up the aisle with him by accident. In three short months you'll be walking up the aisle for real!*

THE GROOM'S DINNER turned out to be served buffet-style, but the dining-room table was extended as wide as it would go, and when Winnie took her plate and sat down, Joseph Duggan followed. He swung his leg over the seat of the chair as if it were a barbed-wire fence he was climbing over and deposited before himself a plate that needed sidecars to hold all the food he'd heaped upon it.

"Aw, you combed it," he chided, then sank his teeth into a slab of sliced ham.

"Mr. Duggan, do you always flirt with every girl you meet within five minutes of meeting her?"

"Was I flirting?"

"It's only a rough guess, because I'm really not up on the subject, but it felt like it to me."

"You're not up on the subject? A girl with your face and—" his eyes flickered downward, not quite reaching her breasts before starting up again "—hair?"

She ignored his continued flattery and commented, "Yes, I combed my hair. It looked like an explosion in a silo."

"Never." He assessed the subject of the discussion. "And it's pretty. A really pretty color and length."

She felt out of her league. "There you go again."

"You call that flirting?"

"Well, isn't it?"

He lifted a glass of milk, took three enormous swallows, ran a thumb along one corner of his mouth—and all without removing his eyes from her hair. When at last they dropped to hers, he replied, "No, just a compliment. I like your hair, okay? What are you so defensive about?"

It was the perfect opening. She lifted her left hand, pressed her thumb against the inner platinum band of the engagement ring so the stone stood out away from her fourth finger. "This."

His eyes dropped, and for a moment there was no

change in his expression. "Oh, I see. Well, you can't blame a man for trying." She rested her hand on the edge of the table, and without warning he picked it up, studied the modest diamond at very close range and surprised her by carrying it to his mouth, tilting his head and pretending to bite the rock. Drawing back, he continued holding her hand while grinning engagingly. "Damned if it isn't real," he said softly.

She burst out laughing but left her hand where it was. Inadvertently his tongue had touched her fourth finger and left a tiny spot of skin damp at the knuckle. It seemed to burn now as he studied the diamond and fingered it with thumb and index finger. He glanced up and bestowed that teasing little-boy grin. "Some guys have all the luck."

Reluctantly she withdrew the hand and began eating again. But she could feel his eyes on her time and again in between the moments of attention he gave to his plate.

"So, when's your big day?" he asked.

"Only three months away. The third Saturday in June."

"Ah, a June wedding, no less."

"Yes, we've had the date picked out for almost a year."

"You and—?"

"Paul Hildebrandt."

"Paul Hildebrandt," he repeated thoughtfully, then filled his mouth with potato salad. When he'd swallowed, he studied her askance. "So, what's he like?"

"Oh, he's. . . ." She drew circles on her plate with a celery stick. "He's ambitious and extremely intelligent, and very easy on the eye." She sensed that Joseph Duggan had stopped chewing, so quirked a quick peek at him from the corner of her eye.

"Naturally," he grunted sardonically, "he would be good-looking."

"But then, maybe I'm biased. You'll meet him tomorrow, and you can see for yourself."

"He'll be at the wedding?"

"Yes, though he only knows Sandy and Mick through me. He wasn't part of my old college crowd. I met him after I graduated."

"From the University of Minnesota?"

"Uh-huh. I went there, too, at the same time as Sandy and Jeanne and Larry and some of the others."

"That makes you. . . ." He squinted an eye while doing mental calculations. "Twenty-four years old."

"Twenty-five. And how old are you?"

"Twenty-seven."

"And I take it you're not married, nor considering it?"

"Absolutely not."

"And there's no. . . girl friend coming with you tomorrow?"

"There's a *girl friend—*" he mimicked her pause perfectly "—but I'm not sure if she'll make it back in time. She's gone to South Dakota for a funeral."

"Nobody close, I hope."

"An aunt."

"Mmm. . . ."

They fell silent for a moment. Their plates were empty. Winnie carefully wiped her mouth and more carefully avoided eye contact with the man beside her. But after some moments curiosity got the better of her, and she turned to find he'd been sitting with an elbow propped on the table, jaw to knuckle, studying her for some time. Discomfited by his close scrutiny, she groped for a conversational diversion.

"What's her name?"

"I have no idea."

A puzzled frown puckered Winnie's eyebrows. "You have no idea what your girl friend's name is?"

He laughed and seemed to force himself out of a deep reverie long enough to stop staring. "Oh, I thought you meant her aunt. My friend's name is Lee Ann Peterson, but I wouldn't really call her a girl friend. We've been seeing each other, that's all."

"And what's she like?"

He squared his shoulders and pressed them against the cane-backed chair. "Like all the rest." Did he pronounce that rather wearily, she mused. "A little bit smart, but a lot more dumb. A little on the ball, but often vague. Not quite as mature as she should be for her age and kind of scatterbrained." He glanced at Winnie sharply, as if owing her an explanation. "These are only impressions, of course. I don't know her well enough."

"And what does she look like?"

He flashed his devilish grin. "She's got a great body."

Winnie felt herself blushing. He hadn't passed his eyes down her torso, but she felt as if he had, for comparison's sake.

"You're a body man, then?" she ventured, trying to cut him down with a note of cool disdain.

A wicked glint sparkled in his eye. "Yes, as a matter of fact, I am. You see I have this—"

"Spare me, Mr. Duggan." She lifted both palms and held her eyes closed for a full five disgusted seconds. "I'm not interested in the graphic details."

"You didn't let me finish...Miss Gardner. I was about to say I have this little shop in Osseo where I refurbish old cars. Two of my brothers are in it with me, and sometimes when we buy a wreck, there's plenty of bodywork to be done."

She covered her eyes and groaned, then peeked from behind her fingers. "I think I've been adequately put in my place."

"No, it was my fault. I deliberately made the comment about bodies. I'm sorry."

"So, you own a body shop."

He tipped his head aslant and puzzled silently.

"Mmm . . .sort of, but not specifically. We do bodywork to earn money, but our labor of love is restoring classics."

"You mean like '57 Chevys?"

"No, mostly older, *classicker* than that. Right now I'm restoring a '54 Cadillac pickup."

"A Cadillac *pickup*? They never made pickups," she stated suspiciously.

"Oh, yes, they did. They used them as hearses for funerals. 'Flower cars,' they were called, and had rollers on the bed to roll the casket on."

"And where does one find such jewels?"

"In farmer's fields, at antique auctions, places like that. I bought this one from an old duffer up in Brooten, Minnesota, and it was in pretty decent condition. She's turning out to be a beauty—four hundred cubic inches and a V-8 engine, and—" Suddenly he cut himself off, then shrugged. "Well, you're not interested in that. I get carried away when it comes to cars."

She found it pleasant to be with a man who got carried away with something more understandable than computers. Duggan's eyes had danced with enthusiasm as he'd spoken of the collector's item he prized. But now he turned the conversation over to her.

"Tell me. What does the lucky Mr. Hildebrandt do?"

She was beginning to understand: flirting and flattery were second nature to this man. They scintillated from his eyes and rolled from his tongue with an effortless mindless ease. More than likely he was scarcely conscious of employing them so often. Ignoring his last ego tickler, she answered only the sensible portion of his remark.

"He's in computer work. They call him an 'optimizer.' He solves all the long-running problems nobody else has been able to solve. He's sort of a wizard, I guess you'd say."

"And how about you?"

But now she couldn't resist the temptation to tease. The subject was simply too opportune. "Well, I'm in bodywork, too." The grin had already begun climbing his attractive cheek when she hurried on. "But I work with human bodies. I'm a physical therapist at North Memorial Medical Center."

"An odd combination—a computer man and a physical therapist."

"No more odd than a body man and a—what is she again?"

"A hostess at a Perkins Pancake House."

"Ah," she breathed knowingly, laying a finger along her rounded cheek. "A hostess."

"Do I detect a supercilious note?"

Winnie was abashed to realize he had, so rushed to deny it. "Not at all. I was just. . .well, making small talk. After all, she. . . ." But suddenly Winnie had the surprising urge to tell the truth. She met Joseph Duggan's eyes directly, hoping she looked properly contrite. "Yes, I confess. I *was* being supercilious. I get it from my mother, whose main goal in life has been to succeed. And success to her is career. I find myself at times mirroring her—shall we call it, her middle-class disdain for the careerless multitudes? And when I catch myself at it, I hate it. But underneath I don't really think I'm as bigoted as I sound when I make comments like that. I sometimes think I've been programmed by mother to say things, whether I mean them or not."

It was one of the first times she'd seen Joseph Duggan's face neither smiling nor teasing. It reflected only deep thought, then a straightforward study of her own face, ending with a glance at her forehead and hair. His deep brown eyes returned to her sapphire blue ones with a look of approval.

"You're remarkable."

"I'm. . . ." She chuckled and shook her head, glancing at her lap self-consciously, for this time she thought his compliment sincere. "I'm not remarkable at all. I'm very ordinary and filled with flaws. That's only one of them I just foolishly blurted out."

"Foolishly? I wouldn't call it foolish. I'd call it honest, and a little humble. Not many people assess their motives with that kind of clearheadedness. Is your . . . Paul Hildebrandt as honest as you?"

She met his eyes again, surprised at how she suddenly hated to recall that there was a Paul Hildebrandt while in this man's very enjoyable company. Guilt immediately followed, making her sing Paul's praises perhaps a little too vehemently. "Oh, yes! He's not only honest, he's hardworking, successful and bound to give me an absolutely secure life."

Joseph Duggan studied the clear-eyed blond woman whose first appearance had captivated him thoroughly. Throughout the pleasant meal with her that first impression had only been magnified. She *was* a remarkable woman—pretty, shapely, intelligent, the tiniest bit shy and the tiniest bit bold, honorable to her man and honest about herself.

But dammit, she was spoken for!

# 2

WINNIFRED GARDNER wasn't a morning person. She usually had to claw her way up from sleep like a person brushing thick spiderwebs aside while ducking through an abandoned building. The next morning, however, she came awake as if a light had been turned on directly above her face.

*Joseph Duggan,* she thought, staring straight at the ceiling. *You're going to see him again today! You're going to walk down an aisle with him. You're going to be photographed beside him. You're going to share the head table seated side by side with him. You're going to dance with him.* She smiled, recalling that he'd claimed to be no dancer. She found that hard to believe. He was one smooth mover was Joseph Duggan. In more ways than one, she suspected.

The thought brought her up sharply. Whatever was she doing, lying here at six in the morning, woolgathering about Joseph Duggan when she was engaged to marry Paul Hildebrandt in three months?

Paul. He'd promised to make it to the wedding today, and she was holding him to it! Why couldn't he get it through his flawlessly groomed head she didn't give a tinker's damn whether or not they had a furnished living room by the time they got married? Or even the house he'd insisted was a prerequisite. He was living in it already—so proud of the fact that he'd managed to provide it for her even before the big day. But the house wasn't enough for Paul. He'd taken on contract work to earn extra money for all the worldly goods he told her she deserved, and had installed a computer terminal in one of the three bedrooms, where he often worked Saturdays and evenings, rapping away at the keyboard that produced all the mysterious solutions to problems she could not grasp, in a language she could not understand and in methods that made her feel ignorant when he tried to explain them to her.

But he'd promised: today he'd be with her at the wedding *and* the dance.

With that reassuring thought she got up, concentrating on Paul and the pleasant surprise in store for him when he saw her in *the ultimate dress*. If he complimented her today—and he'd better—she promised herself she'd accept it at face value and not search for ulterior meanings.

The day was clear and sunny, but by ten in the morning the March winds had picked up again. The bridesmaids were all meeting at McLean's Beauty Shop to have their hair done into Gibson Girl hairdos.

When Winnie studied the finished results in the mirror, she knew instinctively Paul would glow with admiration when he saw her. He was as old-fashioned as a man could be when it came to women and femininity, and though it was often a burr under her saddle, preferring as she did casual clothing for her active personality, today Winnie could face him in a hairdo, hat and dress that would please him tremendously.

But—oh—it *was* a flattering hairdo. The style was chosen by Sandy to accommodate wide-brimmed straw hats, thus Winnie's streaked blond hair closely contoured her skull, lifting in the semidroopy Evelyn Nesbit coil that circled her entire head just within the hairline. She touched the puffy doughnut-shaped roll. Inside, a resilient "rat" added fullness. It felt foreign but not altogether alien. The dramatic change in her appearance made her smile at herself in the mirror and feel suddenly very, very impatient for two o'clock to arrive.

Shortly before noon Winnie stepped out of the bathtub, dried her freshly shaved legs, briskly toweled her belly, breasts and arms but stopped dead when she caught the reflection of her hair again in the mirror. She leaned closer, touched the loose tendril coiling upon her temple and decided to go the rest of the route and apply makeup in keeping with the same tradition as the hairdo.

But first she flapped a puffy mitt up one side of her body and down the other, liberally powdering her skin with the scent of Chanel No 5, one of her few daily concessions to femininity. She was wild about the scent! She wondered what Joseph Duggan would think of it, but the sight of her naked puckered nipples made Winnie chide herself for caring *what* he thought. She had no business pondering the man's likes and dislikes, yet he'd been slipping into her mind, unbidden, all day.

Her new underwear—pure white—was again a nostalgic trip into the past, for the merry-widow bra cinched her waist and flared at the cutaway hips with boned stiffness that few modern-day women experience. But the confining strapless support garment was necessary, owing to the styling of the bridesmaids' dresses Sandy had chosen.

Winnie wasn't certain, when she'd finished applying her makeup, whether she'd done the right thing. The plum eyeshadow and darker penciled undershadings duplicated the look of the women pictured on old tin Coca-Cola trays, as did the apple-cheeked look she'd created with bright blush. But it was the lips she studied critically. She'd used cherry red lipstick and an applicator brush, etching the upper lip with exaggerated peaks, then narrowing the corners of her mouth until it took on the Cupid's pucker of Miss Clara Bow. Maybe Paul was right—she ought to dress up more often. It felt marvelous!

She slipped on an everyday dress and then packed up

her gown, dyed-to-match high heels, hat, makeup and hair spray, and glanced out the window to find the wind still bending the leafless treetops at a forty-five-degree angle. With a silk scarf wrapped around her precious hairdo she ran out to the taxi she had called.

Racing up the steps toward the church door ten minutes later, she felt a thrill of anticipation—Joseph Duggan was probably inside already. Would she run into him in the vestibule the moment she stepped inside? Well, if so, at least she didn't smell like gasoline this time! But dammit, she didn't want him to see her with this scarf clutched around her head like a babushka.

But the vestibule was empty except for the florist's delivery man and one of the ushers, still clad in blue jeans and sneakers, his tux in a bag over his arm.

The two dressing rooms were situated just off the vestibule, and when Winnie opened the door to the women's, everything was excitement. Sandy was there already, as well as one of the bridesmaids, Jeanne, and right behind Winnie entered the other, a cousin named Jacqueline. Lighted mirrors reflected long plastic bags, women in half-clothed states and a bride with a bad case of the jitters.

"Oh, Winnie, thank God you're here! I've been higher than a North Dakota kite, worrying that everyone wouldn't get here on time or that the flowers would be late, or the photographer would forget his camera or—"

"All right, Sandra Schaeffer, calm down! None of the aforementioned calamities is going to happen. All of us are here now. The photographer is setting up his equipment inside, and the flowers are already in the vestibule."

As if on cue, there came a tap on the door, and a gray-haired woman poked her head inside. "Anybody in here getting married?" Then she swept in, bearing a broad flat green box, followed by a series of concealing purple bags, and before she left, the excitement had heightened considerably. Mothers and the flower girl soon arrived, adding to the festive nervousness.

The four young women donned their dresses, growing more fluttery and exhilarated with each passing minute.

Sandy was in pristine white, of course, but each of the others wore a different pastel hue: Jeanne's powder blue; Jacqueline's daffodil yellow; and Winnie's that most feminine of colors—pink.

Stepping into the ankle-length gown, Winnie caught the scent of Chanel, drifting up to her nostrils as she lifted first one foot, then the other, and slipped them inside the shimmery taffeta underlining over which the body of the dress was fashioned of organdy. Its skirt was pure vintage 1910, fitting snugly at the waist and hip, then flaring to a bell-shaped hemline that revealed her pink satin pumps with tiny straps across the instep, secured by a miniature pearl button on the outer side of each foot. The bodice of the dress was of simple spaghetti-strap styling, but its elegance was created by the loose transparent lace overbodice that attached in a drooping fashion at the waist, then covered the chest to the throat. In the back it was hooked only once—at the nape—then gaped open in a long slit to the waist. Its sleeves were shaped much like the skirt—belled, loose and slightly slithery. The hat—that crowning touch—was of pink open-weave straw, a wide-brimmed leghorn style not entirely in keeping with the 1910 look, but utterly feminine. It had a pink silk rose nestled where crown met brim, and matching ribbons circling the crown, then streaming behind to the waist. While Sandy went gloveless and carried white gardenias, her attendants wore white gloves and held small wicker baskets of spring flowers whose colors coordinated with their outfits: one of purple iris, another of lemony jonquils, and the last—Winnie's—of blushing pink hyacinth whose fragrance was nothing short of overwhelming.

The two mothers, as well as grandmothers, nieces and flower girl, were all busy pinning on corsages. In the last-minute flurry Winnie caught a lingering glance at her own reflection.

It was crazy, she thought, standing here gawking at herself and wondering what Joseph Duggan would think when he caught sight of her, yet that's exactly what she was doing. The muse made her heart flutter as if *she* were the bride, and when the call came to exit to the nave for group pictures, she placed a hand over her heart, then realized her palm was sweating within her glove.

She picked him out with the surety of a wild bird seeking its life mate within a flock of thousands. Stepping out into the vestibule, she faced a cluster of masculine backs, most of which were garbed in jet black. Even from behind, Joseph Duggan stood out, identifiable by his well-proportioned build and those dark brown curls. He stood with one hand in his trouser pocket, the vented tail of his tuxedo jacket caught on his forearm, tugging it aside to reveal a wedge of taut black fabric stretched across his flat backside. He was speaking to another man, gesturing with his free hand, which was covered halfway to the knuckles by a tier of white ruffles that sprouted from beneath his black cuff. Another band of white showed above his collar, and the relaxed curve of his knee was accentuated by a narrow stripe of black satin that crooked down the side of his trouser leg. His hand clapped the other man on the shoulder, and he laughed. The sound seemed to shimmy its way between Winnie's thighs and her sleek underslip, raising little ripples of pleasure.

Mick approached the pair of men just then, appearing like a snowy swan among crows, dressed totally in white, his tuxedo jacket sporting knee-length tails at the rear. Yet Winnie scarcely afforded him a glance. Her eyes were fixed upon the black-clad figure of Joseph

Duggan as he swung to face the groom, and the two clasped hands, exchanging words too low for her to hear across the murmurous distance between them. Mick drifted away, and Joseph turned in her direction, his eyes slowly scanning the vestibule.

He homed in on her as surely as she had him, his eyes advancing no farther once they found hers. Something tight and restricting gripped her chest. A weightless sense of expectancy buoyed her stomach, and her heart danced hollowly against her ribs. His lips dropped open, and his eyes swept to her feet and up again. The hand came slowly, slowly out of his pocket. Then he smiled, and something sizzling and exciting exploded in her heart. Oh, that smile! That wondrous killing smile! She *hadn't* imagined its brilliance. It was as blinding as ever.

He shouldered his way forward immediately, excusing himself as he rested his hand on a woman's shoulder, gently nudging her aside, all the while holding Winnifred in his gaze.

He approached with both hands extended, palms up. "My God, you look beautiful!"

She gripped the basket in one hand but gave him her other. He pressed it between both of his palms, and she watched in fascination as he bent forward to kiss it. But finding it clothed in the white glove, he kissed instead the back of her wrist, just above the cotton. His lips were warm, his breath moist, and the back of his head a dark mass of ringlets as he bent to her and lingered.

By the time he lifted his eyes and straightened, she was the color of the flowers in her basket.

"Why, thank you, kind sir. And you look—" she braved a hurried sweeping glance "—dashing!" She tried to keep her voice steady, but telltale tremors made it quiver.

"Are you afraid?" he asked and looked down at her hand, working it now between his own. "You're shaking." He galvanized her with his stunning eyes again while squeezing hard on her glove.

She withdrew reluctantly from his warm hold. "Oh, it's just . . . just excitement! Aren't you excited?"

His eyes danced mischievously—around, above, then into hers. "Absolutely," he returned softly. And she was forced to turn away when his dark brown pupils settled upon her bowed red lips and stayed there. He watched her relentlessly—she could feel it—even though he stood at ease, a hand again casually draped inside his trouser pocket. She was conscious of the faint scent of incense and that of candlewicks, and the ever-present aroma rising from the sweet spring flowers resting against her trembling stomach. When she could stand it no longer, she gave in to the irresistible compulsion and turned to study him, though common sense warned her not to.

Whatever Winn had expected him to be wearing, it was not black. Most groomsmen wore baby blue, gray or rich nutmegs these days. Yet she thought she would never again believe black a drab color after seeing it stretched across the muscles and limbs of Joseph Duggan. It set off the froth of snowy ruffles at his chest in an utterly masculine manner. The crisp black bow tie made his sturdy neck look even more manly, and the skintight stretch of black vest was as tempting as a shadowed haunted house, inviting exploration in much the same way as forbidden, yet compelling things are wont to do. Her eyes were drawn to the deep U-curve low upon his midsection, where black abutted white as he again held the left panel of his jacket back, hooked behind his ruffled wrist.

"Did what's-his-name see you dressed like this?" he asked unsmilingly.

Her startled eyes swerved to his. "Paul. His name is Paul. And no, he didn't."

"So I take it he's not here yet." He glanced around,

but his gaze returned to her as if there were no help for it.

"No, of course not. But he'll be here for the service." She fidgeted with the handle of her basket, suddenly wondering if the pancake hostess had made it back last night. "Did what's-her-name see you dressed like that?"

"*Her* name is Lee Ann, and no, she didn't get back yet that I know of. And even if she had, she wouldn't have seen me. We don't live together if that's what you're asking. I live in an old house in Osseo with my two younger brothers."

She felt the heat rising up her chest once again, staining her chin and cheeks. "I wasn't asking that."

"No, I suppose you weren't. But now you know just the same." Was it her imagination, or had his shoulders squared defensively? He had skewered her with a look that demanded she raise her eyes to his, but she took refuge in staring at the basket of hyacinth.

"Are you going to tell me, or not?" he demanded quietly, studying her averted face.

Her eyes flew to his. "Tell you what?"

"If you live with him."

"I don't think it's any of your business." Then why was her heart flailing around like some wounded bird?

"You're absolutely right. But I'm asking, anyway."

She considered lying just to set him in his place, but in the end couldn't. "No, I don't. He lives in the house we'll be living in once we get married, and I live in my own town house on Shingle Creek Parkway."

It hadn't been her imagination: he had straightened his shoulders, for now they relaxed noticeably as he released a pent breath.

"Everybody to the front of the church now, and we'll take the group pictures!" Winnie nearly sighed aloud when the call of the photographer released them from the tension that seemed to dominate both her and Joseph Duggan today.

At the open double doors he touched the holy-water font and crossed himself, just as she did, but he did not offer his elbow. They walked in businesslike fashion up the aisle, just as all the others did, then submitted themselves for juggling, posturing, sucking in and holding breaths, presenting left shoulders to the viewfinder, then right shoulders, then backing off so the bride and groom could be photographed by themselves.

Winnie looked across the way to where the groom's attendants awaited further instruction. Joseph was staring at her as if puzzling something out, and she turned to whisper a trumped-up question in Jeanne's ear just so she wouldn't have to confront his eyes.

The photos at the altar were done, and the photographer herded them back to the women's dressing room where he shot the bride with her mother and father, with the flower girl and quite naturally with her maid of honor. There was the traditional pose of Sandy displaying her ring while Winnie lightly held the bride's palm and admired. But the photographer had asked her to remove her gloves, and she was devastatingly conscious of her own diamond winking up at her reprimandingly. The sequence of shots seemed to go on endlessly, while several of the groomsmen lingered in the doorway, watching. Joseph didn't even bother disguising his obvious fascination with her—he came right in and stood propped against the back wall, watching the session with keen interest.

There followed the old showing-off-the-garter shot, then the photographer bellowed, "Who's the best man and maid of honor?" Winnie's eyes sought Joseph's, and he boosted himself away from the wall. "I'd like a shot of the two of you together. Over here, against this simple background." And they found themselves nudged, pulled and manipulated into positions that pleased the photographer's compositional eye. There was one shot of Joseph bending over to sniff her hyacinths. In the middle of the pose he ruined it by sneezing—and everyone in the room burst out laughing, which managed to relieve some of the tension spinning between Joseph and herself. But it returned in full force when the photographer backed her up against Joseph's chest and asked him to place his hands on her waist.

To Winnie's surprise the man behind her not only spanned her hipbones with his hands but pulled her back flush against his trouser front. She had a flashing forbidden thought that she was nestled against him at a very accommodating height—and yes, he *was* several inches shorter than Paul, and she immediately felt the intimate difference.

The photographer asked her to lift her chin and turn her jaw slightly toward Joseph's. The juxtaposition of their faces brought her into the realm of his after-shave, a totally rich and masculine scent she'd never smelled before. Once, while they stood that way, she heard him swallow.

Then, to her relief the torture was over. The photographer went off to get the flower girl and ring bearer, and Winnie drifted out to the vestibule, trying unsuccessfully to put Joseph Duggan from her mind. But during the relatively short time between then and when they were hustled into hiding so the guests could convene, he remained in her mind's eye, whether within view or not.

The next time they met, the church was filled, the organ was rumbling overhead, and the vestibule was silent of even the most secret whispers. She was vividly aware of how intimately he had pulled her against himself only a few minutes earlier and found it extremely difficult to meet his eyes. She held back, waiting until the last possible moment to join him and take his arm. Finally he came across to her and silently reached for her elbow, a sober expression robbing his eyes of their customary glint.

The organ belted out the opening strains of *Lohengrin*, and he urged her into line behind the lead couples. She felt herself acquiescing with a stiffness that had somehow overcome her since the picture-taking episode. But when he released her elbow and found her hand, then tucked it securely into the folded warmth of his black sleeve, she knew a forbidden delight at the warmth radiating from inside the crisp gabardine.

The flower girl and ring bearer stepped onto the white runner, and she felt Joseph cover her fingers on his arm, then squeeze them as he whispered, "I'm sorry, Winnie. I had no right."

If only he hadn't said that! If only he'd left things as they were! If only she could have walked up the aisle upon his arm with hostility simmering in her veins, everything might have been all right. But instead he had to go and apologize, and make her look up into his unsmiling brown eyes and see how genuinely he meant the apology. And it was at that precise moment it happened. Something fine and compelling and all-encompassing, a certainty that this day was destined to change them both in ways neither wanted nor welcomed.

Yet they were drawn to this place and time by forces beyond their control, with the organ playing a wedding march, and themselves clothed and coiffed in their regal best, stepping onto a white-lined center aisle, each of them trembling just a little and knowing beyond all certainty they should not be.

There is that about a wedding that compels and sweetens and woos like nothing except perhaps the sight of a newborn babe. It is as magnetic as the poles, as undeniable as gravity and as captivating as the quest for love. During the next hour and twenty minutes, while Winnifred Gardner and Joseph Duggan witnessed the marriage of their two dearest friends, murmured the vocal responses and heard the exchange of vows between bride and groom, that magnetic force worked upon them, drawing their thoughts solely to each other, trapped as they were in vulnerable roles.

The priest paused just before asking Sandy and Mick to repeat the vows after him and asked all married couples present to join hands and silently renew their own wedding vows, and reaffirm their own acts of faith.

For Winnifred and Joseph there were no spouses with whom to reaffirm vows. But their eyes locked and held, and bore no smiles, nor twinkles, nor hid the unquestionable fascination each held for the other. It was there. It had been born. And it flamed and burgeoned while the wedding vows were spoken. *To love...to cherish...all the days of my life....*

EVERYTHING WAS DIFFERENT when they reached the vestibule this time. It was joyous, celebratory and spontaneous. The bride and groom received a broadside of kisses from their closest relatives, while attendants, too, became swept up in congratulatory embraces. Winnie was fleetingly aware of being ensconced in Pete Schaeffer's arms and of receiving a tearful kiss on her cheek from Ann, another from Sandy and still another from Mick. But it was the inevitable full-length hug from Joseph she carried away in memory.

In all the confusion she missed Paul somehow, but Joseph's arm contoured her shoulders nearly all the time, and momentarily he squeezed her waist and said, "I'll be right back for you."

Then he disappeared along with the other groomsmen, while the wedding guests spilled through the open double doors onto the sunny steps of the church portal. Then Joseph reappeared at her side, grabbing her hand and pulling her out on the heels of Sandy and Mick, through a spray of rice and smiles and cheers to a waiting line of cars out front.

Joseph ran, towing her along, but Winnie planted her feet and dragged on his arm at the sight that greeted her.

"Wh-what's this?"

Sandy and Mick were already packing her voluminous white skirts into the back seat of a square black automobile with a running board, bug-eye headlights and a rectangular rear window. Behind it there were three others, each at least fifty years old.

"Vintage automobiles. Come on!" Joseph tugged on her hand, and before she could get more than a fleeting glimpse of gleaming maroon paint and a spare tire mounted on the cowl just behind the high curved crown fender, she found herself whisked toward the car. Her foot was directed not to a running board—nothing that modern—but to an individual metal foot plate. Inside, the roof was high, and there was ample space for her wide-brimmed hat, though the car was only a two-seater. As her door was slammed, she turned to find herself confronting a horizontally split windshield, its top half hinged to create a wind deflector when pushed outward.

Joseph jogged around the hood with its distinguished ornament, then clambered up beside her, smiling and reaching to depress a button on the instrument panel, setting the engine to life.

It was difficult to keep from giggling in delight. The steering wheel jutted up at a stern awkward angle, and Joseph looked tall and proper and straight as the engine rumbled beneath the pleated leather seat. Winnie couldn't swing her head around fast enough to take it all in. Her eyes shone with excitement as she turned to her escort.

"Where in the world did you get this?"

"In my grandma's and grandpa's chicken coop."

"It's yours?"

"Since my grandma died, it is. I belong to a classic-car club, and I talked a few of the other members into offering their jitneys for the wedding today, but as you can see, they all agreed with one stipulation: that they drive them themselves."

The cars pulled away from the church, heading toward the main drag of Brooklyn Park, a wide four-lane commercial street named Brooklyn Boulevard. Winnie peered at the lead car. Through its rectangular rear window all she could see was Sandy's and Mick's heads—they were kissing. Craning around, she noted they were being followed by another shining vehicle of estimable age and condition, a stranger at its wheel. With a broad smile and an excited voice Winnie touched the wedge-shaped rear quarter window that gave the car a rakish roadster profile. Out the front she studied the rounded hood, the cowl lights on either side of the windshield and the tips of the side-mounted spare tires. She looked up to find mohair upholstery overhead and reached up to caress it in reaffirmation.

"Oh, this is absolutely beautiful! What is it?"

"A 1923 Haynes Sport Coupelet."

"I adore it! Why, it's perfect! I mean—" she shrugged expressively "—I feel as if we fit right in. I in my Gibson Girl hairdo and you in your elegant tuxedo. Straight out of *The Great Gatsby* or something. Except you really should have your dust coat and goggles."

He laughed—a deep rumble as smooth as the engine beneath them. "Oh, shoot, sugar pie, I forgot them at home. Next time."

"Where are we going?"

"Up and down Brooklyn Boulevard to toot and wave."

"Are we *really*?" Her voice rose excitedly.

"What's a wedding without a noisy procession?"

Just at that moment the lead car sounded a horn. It bleated out a raucous *a-oooga* before Joseph touched something on the dash that added to the blaring announcement of their coming. They passed Park Center

High School, fast-food shops and gas stations and the city bank, while from the parking lots of McDonald's and Burger King teenagers turned from their prized vans and pin-striped Trans Ams to gawk in admiration at the procession of high-riding relics that paraded past.

They made an eye-arresting sight, chugging along with the sun gleaming off their vented side panels and spoke wheels: a 1932 Model B Ford in gleaming black; Joseph's own glistening '23 Haynes-55, whose original color he called "burgundy wine maroon"; a 1936 Plymouth in deep dark blue; a shiny black '22 Essex Coach with turtleback luggage compartment and drum headlights.

Laughter bubbled up in Winnie's throat as she saw heads snap around and mouths drop open all up and down Brooklyn Boulevard. She couldn't resist waving a hand at an awestruck teenager who was pointing a finger at them.

Turning, she beamed at Jo-Jo Duggan. "I suppose this was your idea."

"Mick's and mine. We decided to surprise you all."

"Oh, what fun! I've never ridden in anything like this before."

His eyes left the street for a moment to scan her lacy straw hat that threw dapples across her cheeks. "You look as classic as my car, Winnifred Gardner. Please wave some more to draw attention to the fact that I've drawn the prettiest girl in the wedding party."

It was uncanny, this wellspring of reaction his compliments unearthed. Perhaps it was the festive tenor of the day that made her respond so heartily with gay laughter and a tilt of her hat brim. Perhaps it was a release from the building tension surrounding her own wedding plans. Whatever it was, Winnie felt free and ebullient as they spent the next half hour riding proudly above the mundane modern vehicles going about their Saturday afternoon pursuits, looking too refined, too sleek and too powerful next to the charming '23 Haynes and its three contemporaries.

Winnie found herself totally relaxed as the minutes slipped by. She studied Joseph's profile as he told her stories about his grandfather, who had owned an auto dealership and had accepted this car as a trade-in during his early years but had never really driven it. Instead he had locked it in his chicken coop and allowed it to become his private obsession, coveted and polished, but never used. Only after the death of Joseph's grandmother three years ago had the car come out of mothballs—and then only on very special occasions and certainly never when the winter streets were spread with destructive salt.

The sun had turned warm. The sense of expanding familiarity and burgeoning acquaintanceship spun an ethereal web about the handsome man in his ruffles and tux and the dazzling young woman at his side.

Laughter came readily, and a certain amount of cavalier flirtation was inevitable. She found herself turning to glimpse his strong blunt fingers on the wheel with new interest, his jaw and mouth with forbidden curiosity.

"Isn't it odd that we've never met before?"

He turned, studied her silently, then nonchalantly returned his gaze to the open field beyond the city offices and the library on the outskirts of the suburb where it joined the corn and potato and gladiola fields at the edge of Hennepin County. The procession had broken up now, and the Haynes was purring along on its own.

"Yes, considering how long we've been friends with the bride and groom. I've known Mick since we were in elementary school, but then he went to the U and I went to Vo-Tech."

"And I've known Sandy since high school."

His eyes wandered back to her for a brief glittering

second, then he looked away again. "Well, now that we've met, Winnifred Gardner, there's nothing we can do about it, is there?"

It was a startling question and raised a shiver of apprehension up her arms. Yet she could not be tempted to indulge in spring fancy regarding this man. "I think it's time we headed for the reception. It'll be starting in—do you have a watch?"

He lifted a hand from the wide thick steering wheel and pushed up a ruffled cuff to reveal a winking gold watch. The gesture was at once commonplace, yet captivating. It scared her, her gut reaction to such a simple movement.

"It's nearly four-fifteen."

"We have to be at the reception hall by five, and I've left my street clothes in the changing room at the church."

"We'd better head back, then."

He pulled into a side road and wheeled into the start of a U-turn. She watched his neck as he craned to check the stretch of road behind them. When he turned suddenly and caught her studying him, she shifted her attention to view the rank and file of dried ivory cornstalks marching across an unplowed field to their right.

One car whisked past, then another. It grew silent, and she turned to see what was holding them up. But Joseph was no longer checking behind him for traffic. He was staring at her.

"We've lost the others," she announced unnecessarily.

"Just as well." His hand fell to the shifting lever between their knees, and he nudged it into neutral. "Because there's something I've been wanting to do all afternoon." Her heart and blood sounded the alarm, but with a smooth commanding movement he slipped one arm around her shoulders, the other to her ribs, and pulled her close. He dipped his head to avoid the wide brim of her straw hat, still it all happened so fast she hadn't a thought of resisting until it was over.

He kissed her with a soft exploratory pressure that was rife with inquisitive speculation. His lips were hard, warm, and remained closed for the most part. The compelling contact lasted perhaps ten seconds, and during the last five her hand pressed his lapel more in surprise than resistance. Just before he pulled back, his lips parted to bestow a swift wet stroke of his tongue across her mouth, encountering the seam of her lips and the ivory texture of sleek teeth within. Her lips dropped open, but too late to encourage or to allow the kiss to become more intimate or lengthy.

His dark sparkling eyes were very close. His lashes caught chips of sun and threw them into her eyes. The brim of her hat touched his curls.

"Joseph..." she whispered upon the wings of surprise. "You mustn't do that." She treated him once again to that unconscious one-eyed blink that made him believe her the most charming creature he'd ever laid eyes upon.

"No one ever calls me Joseph. To my friends I'm Jo-Jo. To my brothers, Joey, and to most people, Joe. But I love the way you say it—Joseph."

Inanely she repeated her words of a moment ago, struggling for composure and a return of calm heart. "Joseph, you mustn't...." Pressing his chest, she felt his heart thudding.

"I know. But you mustn't move your lips along with the wedding vows when they're being pronounced and stare at a man with those irresistible blue eyes, either."

"I didn't...." Again she blinked, a slow-motion flutter of a single eyelid that captivated him. But she tipped her head aside slightly as a newborn smile began to play upon her lips. "Did I?"

He dipped out from under the brim of her hat but kept one arm around her shoulders, his other hand gripping her upper arm, keeping her turned partially his way. The shadows from the wide-brimmed bonnet flickered beguilingly across her nose and forehead. A strand of hair rested in a gentle coil against her temple. He inserted his finger into the lazy curl, and it gripped him like the clinging fingers of an infant. "And who were you thinking of as you whispered the words?"

Her lips parted, and the tip of her tongue peeked out to wet the full upper one, but she remained silent, staring up at him.

"Paul Hildegard?" he prompted.

"Hildebrandt," she corrected in a rather dazed breathless voice.

"Hildebrandt, then."

"No, not Paul Hildebrandt."

He touched the end of her nose with a fingertip. "How naughty of you, Miss Gardner, and only three months before your wedding to the man."

She pressed her palm firmly against his lapel and eased away. Though he released her, his shoulder still curved in her direction. "Who?" he insisted quietly.

She dropped her eyes to the flower basket on her lap. "I wasn't thinking of anyone. I was concentrating on the words. They're very beautiful."

His left hand moved. Its forefinger curled, then pressed lightly beneath her chin until she was forced to tip it up. For a moment his eyes danced merrily into hers, then he accused, "Why, you little liar."

"There are times, kind sir, when lying is the wisest choice."

His eyes darkened thoughtfully. He stroked the hollow beneath her lower lip with his thumb—slightly rough on her fine skin—then his hand fell away, and he turned to put the car into gear. The road was clear, and he headed back toward town.

"You're right, of course. So will you lie to him about what just happened?"

"I. . .there'll be no reason. He'd have no reason to ask."

"Was he there this afternoon?"

"Yes."

"And he'll be at the reception?"

"Yes."

"Then I'd better be careful around you, hadn't I?"

She didn't know what to reply or what to make of him. He was utterly direct. She'd never encountered a person as straightforward as he before. It seemed impossible to combat the barrage of reactions he could unleash by such blatant innuendos as his last. Even though such words rolled from his tongue as glibly as quicksilver and sounded like the practiced lines of an actor, he was devastating, this best man with whom she'd been paired for the day. And Winnie knew, she, too, had best watch her step.

"You'll be pleased to know Paul isn't the jealous type."

"What type is he?"

She mused while they cruised southward on Zane Avenue. "He's logical. Computer nuts tend to be that way. If he can't feed the facts into his terminal and come up with a black or white answer—either yes, there's reason to be jealous, or no, there's none—he'll take the logical sensible route and not be."

"God, he sounds like a bore."

"I should resent that, Joseph Duggan."

"And do you?" He turned to chart her expression as she answered.

It rattled Winnifred to realize she'd had to think for a minute before deciding. "Yes. Yes, I do!"

"Wonderful! That's the first sign of a healthy relationship between you and your fiancé that I've seen yet."

"Don't make assumptions. You don't know anything about our relationship since you've never even met him or seen us together."

"But I will on both counts before the day is over, won't I? What do you say we pick up this conversation at the end of it and see where we stand on the subject?"

"I'll be with him at the end of it, so don't wait around for me when the dance is over."

"In that case, remind me to steal a kiss sometime in the middle of the evening when he's not looking. The one I just got wasn't nearly good enough."

Her jaw dropped, and she smacked him on the arm. "Why, you arrogant, assuming. . . rake!"

His head dropped back, and he laughed with full-throated amusement. "*Rake?* God, I haven't heard that word since I saw my last Errol Flynn movie." With characteristic aplomb he captured her left hand and pressed it possessively to his thigh while she tried to yank it free. "Come on, don't get skittish. You look pretty enough for this rake to want to—what's the word—ravish? But I can hardly try it in the middle of a busy four-lane street in broad daylight, so let me console myself with your hand."

"That hand, Mr. Duggan, is wearing another man's engagement ring."

"And I'll turn you over to him as soon as we get to the reception. But in the meantime, quit pulling away."

She stopped resisting and let him hold her gloved hand palm down on his right thigh. His leg was firm and warm, and she knew she should withdraw, but it felt very pleasant, if very naughty, experiencing the flesh of a different man beneath her touch. He was much, much harder than Paul, and his thigh was larger in circumference, yet shorter in length. Realizing she'd been measuring the difference was unsettling. She tried to free her hand, but to no avail. He held it firm.

"Does he dance?" Joseph's eyes never left the road.

"Divinely."

"That won't work."

"What won't work?"

"I was thinking about stopping in there and catching a

quick dancing lesson so I'd be one up on him in that department, anyway." He nodded toward a sign for the Gloria Allen Dance Studio as they passed it, then asked abruptly, "Does he smoke?"

"No."

"Mmm . . . we're even on that score. Is he rich?"

"He will be someday."

"Shot down again!" He eyed her askance. "Just how handsome is he?"

She growled suggestively, and he muttered a curse.

"Is he a good kisser?"

"Mmm . . . the best." She applied a slight pressure to his thigh for good measure.

"And how is he at—" His hand slipped from hers to clasp her thigh.

"Joseph Duggan, you cut that out!" She returned his hand to his own thigh, ignoring the pleasant tingle his teasing touch had brought.

They arrived at the church parking lot then. The other three cars were already there as Joseph pulled to a halt and killed the engine. He hooked an elbow through the steering wheel and turned to her.

"All right, then, a last resort—does he like dogs and cats and babies?"

"Babies, and that's all that matters." She was enjoying herself immensely by this time. They laughed lightheartedly, then Joseph threw a hand at the mohair upholstery overhead and barked in mock self-castigation, "God, is there anything the man hasn't got?"

She simpered, knowing she shouldn't. She gave him a coy pout, knowing she shouldn't. And even as the answer escaped her lips, she knew beyond a shred of doubt that she was shamelessly flirting. She peered up from beneath her darling hat brim and replied, "Yes . . . a 1923 Haynes."

# 3

THE WEDDING RECEPTION was held in a beautiful restored turn-of-the-century house with three stories of corniced gingerbread, wraparound porches, upstairs verandas, cupolas and a grand total of eight bay windows. It was called the Victorian Club, and inside was as evocative of a bygone era as was its immaculate white exterior and latticed backyard gazebo.

Arriving at the Victorian Club where all the wedding guests were waiting, Winnie experienced afresh the phantasmal sensation that for this day she was someone other than Winnifred Gardner, contemporary woman, careered, affianced. Indeed, everything today seemed to tug at Winnie's heartstrings and urge her into a fanciful state of déjà vu, as if she'd been dressed for the part intentionally by some omnipotent force so it could sweep her back to a time she formerly knew.

The four cars pulled to the curb in front of the stunning architectural eye-catcher, and as the wedding party disembarked from the high old-fashioned seats, laughter and gay badinage spilled into the warm afternoon.

Winnie reached for her door handle, but Joseph was right there to stop her with a quick hand on her arm. "Wait!" Immediately he was out his side and around to hers. The foot block was narrow, and as she turned in her seat to search it out with her high heel, Joseph's hands came up, catching her about the waist and swinging her down beside him. His hands were sure and lingered a bit longer than prudent. Was it her imagination, or had he intentionally swung her down too swiftly so her hip collided with his stomach? If so, he took scarcely a moment to savor the contact before turning her by an elbow toward the walk.

Merrymakers had noted their arrival, and a throng of them rushed from the house to encircle and accompany the bride and groom inside beneath a shower of rice, while Winnie and Joseph ran at their heels.

The house was decorated in lush antiques, its oaken floors varnished to a high gloss, and its ceiling-to-floor casement windows topped off by eyebrow sashes and decorated with antique sheer lace curtains that let the daylight stream inside. An elegant staircase curved up from the enormous central entry hall, and wide sliding double doors were rolled back on either side of the generous area, vastly expanding the space where the dancing would be done later. The dining room was at the rear of the house just off the kitchen, which was the only room closed off to guests, for it had been converted to meet modern standards of efficiency for the accommodation of large groups such as today's.

As Winnie stepped inside with Joseph's hand at the small of her back, she caught her breath at the setting. Something here called to her heart, and she turned to Joseph with an appreciative gaze in her eye. "Isn't this place—" she glanced up the thick red runner on the curved stairway "—evocative? I was with Sandy when she first came to see it, and I was so afraid she might not choose it."

"Yes, it's really beautiful." But his eyes made only a cursory swing past the ballroom-width entry and sweeping stair before returning to her as he spoke the words.

"Now, Joseph, you promised."

"I did? What did I promise?" His hand moved caressingly on her back.

"You said you had to watch yourself today, didn't you?"

"Ah, yes, but does that mean I can't admire the scenery?"

She laughed into his glinting eyes, then the two of them turned and ambled toward the rear of the hall, his hand still riding the shallows of her spine. "Do you know what my first impression of you was when I met you last night?" she asked, gazing at the ceiling's domed windows.

"No, what?" He admired the arch of her neck as she looked up.

"That you are a consummate flirt, and that I should take everything you say with a grain of salt."

It was his turn to laugh. "Define the term *consummate*, if you will."

She shrugged, thought about it for a second and made a vague gesture toward the heavens. "Consummate... you know." Again she beamed him a grin. "Perfect."

"The perfect flirt? Is that how you see me?"

"You see? You're doing it again. Perhaps the word I should have chosen is *incorrigible* flirt."

"I think I like consummate better. It sounds sexual, and it's nice to think one woman finds me perfect in some way."

Just then a voice spoke behind them. "Winnifred, dear, there you are."

At the sound of Paul's voice Winnie spun around, pressing a hand to her thumping heart, wondering if he'd heard Jo-Jo's last remark, certain he'd seen Duggan's hand lingering on her waist. It took an effort to keep her voice light and lift her cheek for Paul's kiss while Jo-Jo looked on.

"Oh, hello, Paul. I'm sorry I missed you in the church lobby, but things were so hectic. We were swept outside before I could catch my breath."

Jo-Jo Duggan watched as the tall perfectly groomed man slipped his hands around Winnie's ribs and dipped his head to kiss her briefly on the cheek. "You... look... sensational, darling." As he straightened, his head caught the brim of her hat, and her hand flew up to hold it on.

"Do you like it?" She smiled at the prepossessing man whose blond head towered above hers by a good ten inches.

"Like it!" Hildebrandt backed off and ran his eyes down to her hem and back up again. "I love it. The hair and the hat—" he captured her hands and squeezed them for emphasis "—and the dress." Once more his eyes dropped to assess her more feminine points while she wished Jo-Jo would politely refrain from watching every place Paul touched her and looked at her. "You look ravishing."

From the corner of her eye she saw Jo-Jo grimace, and felt a thrill ripple along her skin. She returned the pressure of Paul's hands and turned him toward her escort. "Paul, I want you to meet the best man, Joseph Duggan. Joseph, this is my fiancé, Paul Hildebrandt."

They shook hands. "Hildebrandt." Joseph nodded.

"Hello," Paul greeted simply.

"So you're the lucky guy, huh?" Jo-Jo transferred his amiable smile from Hildebrandt to the woman on his arm. "She's been talking about you a lot while we were out doing the after-wedding joyride."

"Oh-oh. I'm probably in trouble."

"Not at all. Everything she said was highly complimentary."

Hildebrandt's eyes rested on his betrothed, then made another tour of her appealing hairdo and hat. It suddenly irked Joseph Duggan to watch the man assessing her as if she were a pink-and-white-striped parfait in a stem glass, and he'd just been given a spoon. Hildebrandt surprised Duggan by returning, "Today it looks like you're the lucky man, escorting her when she's dressed like *that*." Then with scarcely a glance at Jo-Jo the suave executive type turned the maid of honor away by her arm. "I'll bring her right back. I have to talk to her for a minute."

Joseph watched the "computer man" commandeer

Winnifred Gardner's elbow and appropriate her. Hildebrandt was dressed in an impeccable three-piece suit of proper navy blue, accompanied by the expected baby blue shirt and striped tie of muted wines and gray blues. His haircut looked like something out of *Gentlemen's Quarterly.*, and his shoes were polished like mirrors. As the pair turned away, Hildebrandt's arm slipped around Winnifred's shoulders, and he pulled her up tightly until she was tipped against his ribs and hip. Her face was raised and wearing a radiant smile as he spoke down at her, then she replied and together they laughed.

The sight of them that way made Duggan want to drive his fist into the wall.

"There's got to be some private corner where we can hide for a minute," Paul was saying.

"To what end, Mr. Hildebrandt?" Winnie teased coquettishly.

He hauled her hip against his, and his hand rode higher up her side, almost to the armpit, fingertips extended toward her breast. "Find me that corner and I'll show you."

She laughed and they rounded a corner, then walked down a broad central hall and eventually came upon what must have been a butler's pantry in its day. Pushing open a swinging door, they found a long narrow room with built-in glass-doored cabinets on their left, bearing wide storage drawers for linens and silverware. There was another swinging door at the far side of the walk-through and to their right a broad window rising from a waist-high counter top to the twelve-foot ceiling. The blue sky beyond was framed by an arching tangle of ivy vines, bare of leaf now, but swollen with buds.

When the door swung closed behind them, Paul confiscated her basket of flowers, set it aside with careful deliberateness, then circled Winnie with both arms, pulling her securely against his body as he dropped his head to kiss her and pressed her hips back against the rounded edge of the ivory-painted cabinet below the window. "Mmm..." he murmured as his tongue slipped seductively into her mouth, which opened willingly. His head moved, and his hand pressed the side of her breast, then kneaded it firmly.

"Mmm..." she echoed into his mouth, smiling beneath his open lips, running her hands over his smooth back.

He lifted his head and backed away only enough to see her but still held her prisoner between himself and the cabinet. "If you look even one-quarter this tantalizing on our wedding day, I'll have a hard time keeping my hands off you in front of the entire congregation."

She ran her fingertips demurely under both of his lapels. "Well, now, wouldn't that be something? The unflappable Paul Hildebrandt, losing control. I think I'd like that."

"I'm far from unflappable where you're concerned, and you know it."

She kissed his chin. "Not in public, you're not. Otherwise you would have kissed me back there in the entry instead of sneaking off into this pantry with me." Was it a subconscious wish to show Jo-Jo Duggan her fiancé desired her that made Winnie voice that comment? She pushed Duggan from her mind and lifted up on tiptoe, seeking Paul's mouth again. But in the middle of the kiss her hat began slipping, and she jerked free, both hands flying up to the long pearl-headed hat pin.

"Oh, shoot. We're not done taking pictures yet, so I have to keep this thing on and make sure my hair doesn't get messed. But I'll be able to get rid of it at the dance tonight, then we can take up where we left off here."

With characteristic seriousness Paul backed away from her and slipped a hand into his trouser pocket. "About the dance, Winnie...."

Already her hands were on her hips—angrily. "Paul Hildebrandt, if you tell me you're not staying for the dance, I'm going to throw a fit right here and now!"

"Winnie, quiet down before somebody finds us in here. It isn't that I won't stay for the dance. I'll just have to leave a little bit earlier than I expected."

She tucked her lips against her teeth and made a pair of tough fists. "So what is it this time? Did the Almighty decree that he needed the lowly Mr. Hildebrandt to process some data before—"

"Winnie, you're being shrewish again."

"Shrewish!" She spun to face the window, presenting her back. "I have a right to be shrewish after you promised." She whirled again to face him. "You *promised*. You said we'd dance until the last dog was hung, and that nothing would make you miss it. So what came up?"

"Must you sound so antagonistic?"

She considered his question seriously. "Yes. Yes, I must, because I'm sick and tired of taking a back seat to your computers and your incessant late hours. It *is* your contract work again, isn't it?"

"They need it by Monday, and this extra money is going to come in so handy when we move into the house."

"Paul, how many times do I have to tell you, I don't care about the house. I can live with a card table and two chairs and a pair of fifteen-dollar bean bags! I don't *need* four thousand dollars' worth of carefully chosen decorator furniture. We'll have the rest of our lives to buy furniture. Now—especially tonight—I wanted to be ours."

"I know." His voice was repentant, and he slipped his hands inside the bell-shaped sleeves of her lace overdress, running them up past her elbows. "I know, Winnie, but I have . . . ideals. Goals. And one of them is seeing that you start with nothing but the best. Everything you deserve. You know I've given my solemn promise to your mother that I'd see to it."

But the subject of her mother was one Winnifred could not quite confront head-on in relationship to Paul

Hildebrandt. If she voiced her true feelings on that score, she feared she'd sound neurotic, or at the very least, petulant. She dropped her head forward, staring at the crisp crease in Paul's trousers as she sighed deeply.

"Yes, I know," she replied wearily. She lifted her head. "I'm sorry I complain about it, but I . . . you . . . ." How was it she always ended up feeling the one in error when this argument erupted between them again and again? His motives seemed very noble on the surface, and her complaints so juvenile, as if she were a spoiled child who demanded more attention after getting her just dole.

She circled his neck loosely with both hands. "Paul, I just wanted today to be special. I feel special, dressed up this way. And I know you'd like to see me dressed up more often than you do. I thought you'd want to be with me."

"I do. And I am." He kissed her nose and looped his hands loosely behind her back. "I can stay for a couple of hours."

"During dinner?"

He brightened and smiled. "Yes, during dinner and for a few dances."

She studied him with a new, disturbing insight, recalling Joseph Duggan's words: "That's the first sign of a healthy relationship between you and your fiancé that I've seen yet." Paul Hildebrandt was all the things a sane woman wanted in a husband. Hadn't her mother reiterated the fact time and again during the past two years?

She sighed again and leaned back against the cabinet edge, pulling him with her. His weight felt secure, pressing against her hips again. She pulled his head down, forgetting about the hat, commanding him to kiss her with a full exchange of tongues that grew into a greedy seeking of body pressure. Her hat fell off. She raised up higher, forcing her curves into his coves, wishing to assure him she would and could be content with a couple of hours with him.

"Paul, I love you," she said ardently against his neck. He smelled of Pierre Cardin cosmetics, as he always did—nothing but the best when it came to image, he always claimed. The clothes make the man. First impressions last longest. He was always clean, flawless and fragrant.

"I love you, too," he said, bracketing her face with his long tapered hands that were ever as immaculate as those of any dentist.

*What's the matter with me tonight,* she wondered. *Why am I assessing him so caustically when he has no outstanding faults? Am I searching for some all of a sudden, after what Jo-Jo Duggan intimated?*

"It's time I got back. They'll be seating the wedding party at the main table soon. I can't hold things up."

"Oh." A shadow crossed his handsome green eyes. "I guess that means I can't sit with you during dinner."

"I'll be seated next to the best man. But we can dance the first dance afterward, all right?"

"I'll mark your name on my program." He grinned, handed her her basket, and turned her toward the swinging door.

The main hall was emptying, but Joseph Duggan was waiting near the archway to the dining room. "Ah, there you are. They're seating the guests first, Hildebrandt, and they've already sent out the call." He noted Winnie's flushed face and that unmistakable swollen look of a woman who's just been well kissed. She'd had a faint sheen to her lips before slipping off with the computer man, but it was all gone now. He noted also a coolness as she told her fiancé, "I'll see you after dinner, Paul."

Hildebrandt left them and disappeared into the dining room. Winnie felt Duggan's eyes assessing her, missing nothing. He wore no grin this time as he advised, "You got a little bit messed in there. There's a hank of hair hanging from under the side of your hat, and you could use a touch of lipstick—for the camera, of course," he finished sardonically.

She felt a surge of color mounting her chest and bathing her chin, and bit back the sharp retort that it was none of his bloody business. "I left a small makeup bag in your car. Would you mind terribly running out to get it for me?"

"Not at all. What does it look like?"

"It's a lavender-flowered zipper bag about so big."

"Be right back." He turned and crossed the entry, but just before the door closed behind him, he paused and looked back with a frown on his face. It made her sizzling mad to feel his skewering eyes were reprimanding her.

When he returned, the crowd in the front hall had thinned even more. He thrust the bag into her hand, and she thrust her flower basket into his. Then he stood behind her shoulder—very, very close—watching her reflection as she faced a long ornate pier glass hanging on a wall to the left of the door.

She fished in the bag for a wand of lipstick, but when she found it, her hand trembled on its way to her lips. Joseph Duggan's brown eyes were relentless as they followed each move she made. She opened her mouth, pouted her lips toward the glass and began carefully outlining them.

"You have very beautiful lips. I like them better when they don't have that red crap on them and are left in their own natural shape."

The wand with its red tip trembled two inches from her mouth. Her eyes met Duggan's in the mirror, and she wanted to ask him please to forgo any further compliments tonight. She just wasn't in the mood anymore.

"Go ahead, princess, put it on, anyway. It'll take away that puffy look that tells what you and Hildegard were doing in the butler's pantry."

"Hildebrandt!" she spit and continued slashing the red hue on her lips.

"I beg your pardon," he returned silkily. "Hildebrandt." He raised his eyes to her hat. "And fix that hair, too. . .for the time being."

Rather than ask the obvious question, she jerked the hat pin free and handed him the hat by swatting it across his belly. He grinned as he added it to his collection of female frippery. It was beyond her why a frilly hat and a basket of pink hyacinth should enhance a man's masculinity as he held them in his wide blunt hands. She dropped her eyes from the reflection, feeling betrayed by two inanimate objects.

She lifted her arms to smooth the single strand of hair that had been jerked from its moorings, tucked it securely into the roll at the base of her neck, found a hidden hairpin and rammed it into place. Throughout the adjustments her chin rested on her chest, and her breasts jutted upward. She secretly peeked up to glimpse Joseph Duggan's eyes on her upturned focal spots, then wander to her bare arms, where the loose sleeves of her dress had slipped down to her shoulders as her elbows lifted to heaven. His gaze moved up and caught her watching him. One corner of his mouth tipped up slowly, and at the proper moment he reached around her with one arm and placed the hat against her stomach. When it touched her, something inside Winnifred Gardner went woozy.

"Thank you," she snapped sarcastically, jerking the hat from his fingers.

"Anytime, ma'am," he drawled. "If the damage is all repaired now, let's go. They're waiting for us, I'm sure."

Luckily the proceedings hadn't been held up, for Sandy had planned a rather unique substitute for the often disliked formal receiving line. Instead of forcing her wedding party to go through the polite ritual of making small talk to total strangers, she'd arranged for all dinner guests to be seated first, after which the members of the wedding party would be formally introduced and would make their entrance through the center aisle of the dining room toward the head table, where all the guests could see them and know exactly who each person was.

As Winnie and Joseph joined the others waiting at the entrance to the dining room, the announcer was calling, "I give you Mr. and Mrs. Michael Malaszewski!"

Joseph burst into applause, then bit his little fingers and shrilled an earsplitting whistle. Winnie clapped her hands over her ears and winced. He grinned, clapped louder and bellowed, "Way to go, Ski!"

The announcer called, "The maid of honor and the best man, Miss Winnifred Gardner and Mr. Joseph Duggan."

He postured a miniature bow, presented his elbow and invited, "Shall we, Miss Gardner?"

She forced a broad smile, laced her hand beneath his sleeve and followed his lead, conscious of Paul's eyes following as she and Joseph made for the head table. When the entire wedding party had been introduced, Joseph stepped behind her chair to pull it out solicitously. As he moved to his chair, she whacked her basket of flowers down between two candles, yanked her gloves off and slapped them down beside her silverware.

As soon as he was seated, he turned his full attention to her. "Well, I detect a bit of frost in the air."

"I'd rather not talk about it while one hundred wedding guests can watch everything that passes between us."

"You're angry with me."

"Yes, among other things."

"Then, I'm sorry. I didn't know you'd be so touchy about things like that. I shouldn't have teased."

"I'm not *touchy*, all right?"

"Then why are you throwing things around and pulling your mouth up like a purse string?"

She inhaled, closed her eyes for a second and forced her facial muscles to relax. "I'm not touchy. And I'm not quite as angry with you as I am with Paul, and I don't want to talk about it, if you don't mind."

"A lovers' quarrel? At a wedding? In a pantry? What could you possibly find to quarrel about when you were only gone five minutes?"

When she refused to answer but turned her head away from him, he searched out Paul Hildebrandt in a far corner of the room. "Mmm . . . your fiancé is looking pretty mellow and happy over there. Apparently *he*'s not mad at *you*."

She snapped her head back toward him. "Mr. Duggan, I said I didn't want to talk about it."

"All right, I'm versatile. What else would you like to talk about?" A white-clad waitress moved before them and offered to fill their stem glasses with champagne. He lifted his own glass and asked Winnie, "Champagne?" At her curt nod he held her glass, too, for filling. "There you are," he said amiably, offering it to her. Their discourse was sidetracked as Joseph declared, "I'd better do my duties as best man. We'll pick this up later."

He arose, raised his hands for silence and turned toward the bride and groom, lifting his glass. "Ladies and gentlemen, I think a toast is in order on this auspicious occasion. It goes without saying that we're all happy for you, Mick and Sandy, and each of us thanks you for inviting us to celebrate your great day along with you. It comes from the heart when I wish you a lifetime of love as rich as the love you're feeling today. May your blessings be many, your hardships be few." He lifted his glass momentarily higher. "To my friends Sandy and Mick Malaszewski." He drank, set his glass down, then moved between the bridal couple. Mick was on his feet, and the two men embraced, their arms wrapped securely around each other's shoulders. Then, as they clasped hands, they exchanged some private words too low for Winnie to catch. But they looked into each other's eyes, and for a moment she thought she saw an emotional glitter in both pairs of eyes. Again Joseph lifted his voice to the crowd. "And, as best man, I believe I'm entitled to what I'm about to take!" The wedding guests applauded as Joseph took Sandy's hand and prompted her to her feet. Then he wrapped her in his arms and planted a long firm kiss on her mouth before backing away and laughing into her rosy face. "Be good to him, you hear? I love that big galoot."

"I will," Sandy answered. "So do I."

Joseph nodded, released her hands and returned to his chair beside Winnie. By the time he refilled his glass and lifted it to hers, there was a warm appreciative glow where her anger had been. He was a man who loved and showed it, and voiced it. Unashamedly. How rare.

"I'd rather not spend the rest of the night with you mad at me, so let's have a toast to peace, okay, Miss Gardner?"

She touched the rim of her glass to his. "Pax," she agreed as the ting of crystal sounded faintly. "And I'm sorry, too. It really was never you I was upset with."

"Good." He drank, but his eyes never left hers as the rim of his glass tipped up, and her gaze remained steadily on his arresting dark eyes until she thought she saw the sparkle of the wine bubbles reflected in their brown irises. A vague nagging ache of tension seemed to disappear from between her shoulder blades now that they were on equable terms again.

Their dinner was served, and while they ate chicken breast and mushroom sauce on a bed of wild rice, they talked about nice safe subjects: his business, the vintage-auto club, her job at the hospital, the bride's and groom's refreshing flouting of tradition in planning this wedding.

"Did you know they're opening their own gifts tomorrow afternoon at Sandy's parents' house?"

"Yes, Mick told me. Will you be there?"

She looked up into his direct gaze. *Lord, but he has*

*devastating eyes*, she thought. *I should answer an unqualified no and stick to it. There's no way I'll get Paul to come along, not when he has work to entice him.*

"Yes, will you?"

"Now I will."

They were playing cat and mouse, and she knew it. Yet she assuaged her immediate guilt feelings by telling herself being with him was "legal." She'd been paired off with him for the duration of the wedding, and wasn't tomorrow part of the ongoing celebration? Suddenly she realized she'd been staring into his eyes for too, too long and dropped hers to her plate, then quickly scanned the room to see if Paul was watching the head table. But he was immersed in conversation with someone else at his own.

"Miss Gardner?" Joseph paused expectantly, and she turned to find those inexcusably beautiful brown eyes still resting upon her. "What does he call you? Winnifred? Winnie?"

"Winnie, most of the time."

"Then would it be okay if I called you Winn?"

Her heart reacted in a way no heart of an engaged woman should react, and she wondered if people noted how often she and Joseph gazed into each other's eyes during the course of the meal.

The server interrupted just then. "Would either of you care for coffee?"

Winnie jumped at the chance to be diverted. "Yes . . . oh, yes, coffee, please." Too late she realized she hated coffee. *Maybe it'll sober me up and make me behave properly.*

"Winn?" The word sent her heart *ka-whumping* more erratically than before, and the tone of his voice compelled her to lift her eyes to his once more. "What did you two fight about?"

"It wasn't a fight exactly, just an ongoing difference between us. And I'm in the wrong about it, and I know it." She glanced at Paul and found him watching her. He raised a hand in silent salute, and she returned the hello, then dropped her eyes to the tablecloth. "You see, Paul is a very dedicated man. He has set goals for himself, for us, actually . . . things he wants us to own, to achieve. Only sometimes when he works overtime, I get. . . ." She stopped, unsure of how to say it.

"You get?"

He touched the knuckle of her index finger where it was threaded through the handle of the coffee cup. At the brief contact she jerked back, sending the liquid sloshing to the rim of the cup. Alarmed, she looked up, striving to put Paul between herself and this very attractive man. "I get a little jealous of the time he spends with his computers. He has a terminal at home in the spare bedroom, and after his regular job he does contract work, programming on an independent basis during evenings and weekends. He does it because we've bought the house, and naturally there are fairly good-sized payments on it, plus he's bound and determined we'll have it totally furnished by the time I move in with him. So I should be grateful I have a man who's got ambition and drive, I know. It's selfish of me to make demands on his time, I guess. But sometimes I. . . ." Again her eyes wandered to Paul, but she left the thought dangling.

"Sometimes you'd rather have his time than the money it can earn," Joseph filled in, leaning forward, resting an elbow on the table and turning his back to the room at large, shielding her from the eyes of her fiancé.

"Yes. I know it sounds absolutely ridiculous that a woman can be jealous of a . . . a panel of silicon chips, but. . . ." Her eyebrows puckered and her lips trembled. "Do you know they even give computers names? He's named his Rita. Rita, for God's sake! I mean, what kind of a man gives a woman's name to a hunk of metal and refers to her as *she* all the time?" Her lips were trembling even more. "And what kind of woman gets jealous of *her*?" She was directly confronted by Jo-Jo Duggan's serious brown eyes, and to her horror she realized her own eyes were floating in tears. "Oh, darn. . . ." She felt utterly ridiculous to have admitted such a thing. She reached up to dash the salt away but had no handkerchief. "I feel like a fool, getting all emotional over a thing like this, but he promised me he'd come to the wedding and dance all night. And I just love to dance, and I thought b-because I'm all d-dressed up and everything. . . ." She stammered to a halt, more self-conscious than ever, after babbling on about such inconsequential and childish wishes.

Into her line of vision came a blurred hand, extending a clean folded handkerchief. "Here, dry your eyes."

She touched their inner corners gingerly and wiped the end of her nose. She lifted her face then, and there was Joseph Duggan only inches before her, unsmiling, watching her too carefully, still shielding her from the rest of the room. "I'm sorry, Joseph. What a stupid thing to do, get all teary eyed because my man wants to work hard so he can buy me a houseful of furniture."

"That's not the reason you're crying, and you know it."

"It's not?"

"Hardly."

"Then tell me why I am."

"Because you're three months away from marrying a man, and all of a sudden you're discovering some very disturbing differences in values between the two of you. Deep differences. You like to dance, and he likes to talk to computers. But is that as deep as it goes?"

"Ye. . . ." She'd been about to say yes but halted to give it some serious reflection. But, thinking, she decided it best not to dwell upon it. "I want to have fun tonight, and this isn't helping. Can we talk about something else?"

"Of course. Are you all dried up now, so I can remove myself from between you and the curious multitude?"

She smiled and chuckled shakily, handed him his handkerchief and sniffed once. "Yes. But I probably am in need of some makeup repair again. If you'll excuse me, I'll sneak back to the foyer and touch up my eyes."

He immediately got to his feet and pulled her chair back. When she stood beside him, he detained her for a second with a hand on her arm. "Winn, if it'll make you feel any better, I'll fill in for old Hildegard on the dance floor, inept as I am. You want to dance all night, you've got it, sweetheart. Two clubfeet and all." He glanced self-deprecatingly at his shoes, then straightened and gave her a teasing grin.

It was like a shot of revivifying sun.

"I think, Joseph Duggan, that you're a very nice man underneath all that flirting and teasing. And I'll hold you to it."

They stood for a breathless moment, transfixed, staring at each other.

"Winn. . . ." His fingers tightened on her arm. But his touch felt too welcome, too good, too exciting. She forced herself to turn and walk away.

# 4

THERE'S AN OLD CUSTOM at Polish weddings that the groomsmen steal the bride sometime during the reception. When Joseph Duggan disappeared an hour later, Winnie missed him immediately. She'd danced with Paul, but now he was gone. She wandered from group to group, visiting with acquaintances, but the zest seemed to have fizzled out of the party once Joseph disappeared. She took her makeup bag to an upstairs bedroom, checked her mascara, refreshed her blush, but wiped all vestiges of the scarlet lipstick from her mouth and applied instead a soft pink, as luminescent as the recesses of a conch shell. She touched Chanel No 5 to her wrists, neck and knees, then went back downstairs to wander around restlessly, listening to the music of the four-piece band that played in the large central hall.

It seemed forever before the front door swept open, and several laughing men crowded through, bearing the bride upon their shoulders. At the sight of Joseph Duggan the night suddenly regained its flavor. He spotted Winnie immediately and was crossing the hall toward her the moment the bride was lowered to the floor.

"I'm sorry I had to abandon you, but duty called." He captured her hand and towed her toward the area set aside for dancing. "But I do keep my promises for better or for worse. Come on, Twinkle Toes, let's make you happy again."

He swooped her into his arms, only to discover her wide hat brim forced them apart. She leaned back from the waist to smile up at him. "I was growing very impatient."

His engaging grin twinkled down at her. "So was I." He tightened his arm and settled her hips to his, but the hat brim still bothered. It nudged the crown of his forehead. He studied it with the look of a police inspector searching for clues, then stopped dancing, raised both hands and reached around her head. He knew where the hat pin was: he'd watched her remove and replace it earlier. When it slid free and the hat along with it, Winnie felt an unwarranted thrill of intimacy—after all, it was only a hat he'd taken off her, nothing more personal. Yet she liked the way he'd done it, without asking, without fumbling.

Unceremoniously he pulled her length back against his, immediately snuggling her close, resting his jaw against her temple while the hat rode lightly against her buttocks as he held it upon the small of her back. The faint brushing movements of the straw brim through her organdy dress brought shivers, and she imagined his blunt-fingered hand and ruffled cuff and how they must look with the hat suspended from them. Then she closed her eyes and simply enjoyed.

He hadn't the smooth expert grace of Paul on the dance floor, but he had superb timing and was content to nestle her against him and circle the floor with small unflamboyant steps. In his arms Winnie felt an immediate shock of difference. Joseph was shorter than Paul. Thus her face was closer to his, touching his; his muscles were firmer, and his hand wider, thicker, harder. His fingers were coarse. He had a workingman's hands, with texture and calluses, in contraposition to the soft warmth of the butt of his palm. He used a different brand of cosmetic than she was accustomed to smelling on a man's neck, for he radiated a pleasant mixture of herb, lime and something resembling cedar. His chin was coarser, and she felt a vague scratching from it against her temple and imagined before the night was over, her hairdo would be disheveled and flattened on that side. She thought again of his hair, but it was beyond her touch, unless she wanted to be so indiscreet as to reach up and feel it above his collar. She'd been wondering what it felt like—all those airy girlish ringlets—ever since she'd first seen it. But she danced in his arms content to know his other textures and scents, realizing they allured far more powerfully than a sensibly engaged woman ought to admit.

"You were gone so long."

He backed away slightly and looked down into her eyes. "Was I?"

Her heart fluttered. "I. . . I was anxious to dance."

"When I left, he was still here. Didn't the two of you dance?"

"Yes, for a little while, but he left shortly after you did."

"Seems we didn't do such a hot job of spiriting the bride away without being noticed."

"Oh, I noticed, all right." *Winnifred Gardner, now you're the one who's flirting.*

His hand moved caressingly on the hollow of her back, but he continued looking down into her eyes. "You were right about him. He's tall, blond, handsome, immaculately groomed, well dressed, and I have to confess, I hung around just long enough to watch you two when the music started. He's a darn good dancer. You both are."

"Well, that darn good dancer is laboring over a computer keyboard right now, so what good does he do me?"

"He may not be doing *you* any good, but I'll have to make it a point to thank old Hildegard for abandoning you the way he did. I couldn't be happier to fill in." Again he brought her up against his body, taking two dramatic swirls, then laughing into her ear when he lost his balance on the second and nearly sent them toppling. She laughed, too, enjoying the feel of her breast flattened to his.

"You were doing just fine before you started getting melodramatic, Joseph Duggan. I don't need Fred Astaire. You'll do very nicely."

The next several songs were fast ones, and Jo-Jo Duggan gamely gyrated his hips and rocked his shoulders, thinking himself rather inept at the sport but enjoying himself immensely nevertheless, just because he was with the prettiest woman in the place.

"Whoever told you you aren't a good dancer?" she queried.

"I can feel it. I don't need to be told."

She glanced at his waist, shadowed within the open panels of his tuxedo jacket, then dropped her eyes a little lower. "Why, look at you. You have exquisite rhythm."

He lifted his chin and laughed at the ceiling, then gave her an open leer that passed from her breasts to her knees and back up again. "So do you, Winn Gardner, so do you."

After that set of fast songs, he removed his tux jacket and left it hanging over the back of a chair. The back of his vest was made of sleek silk, and beneath it his musculature was easily felt. She moved into his arms when the music started again and gently explored his shoulder blades and the hollow between them. Around her waist his arm tightened, and she made a soft throaty sound and nestled more securely into his curves while he dropped his head until his lips rested just beside her right ear.

"Mmm...whatever that is you're wearing smells much better than the gasoline you wore last night."

She laughed. It felt wonderful, laughing against his firm chest, which lifted and fell against hers, while an answering chuckle rumbled deep within him.

"It's Chanel No 5."

"I love it. Does it taste as good as it smells?"

"I don't know. Does yours?"

His fingers moved suggestively on her ribs. "Maybe we should both find out later, huh?"

"Uh-uh," she murmured against his neck. "Can't do that. I'm engaged to another man."

"Oh, that's right. Old Silicon Chip. The guy who left you here with me for safekeeping."

"Why is it I don't feel very safe around you?"

"I have no idea. I'm only filling in for your absentee fiancé. And with fresh reminders every fifteen minutes that you *are* promised to him, and you *do* wear his diamond." His hand left her waist and meandered upward to the small of her back, finding the vertical slit in the overbodice of her dress. His warm palm slipped inside and rode up to her bare shoulder blades, then down over the abbreviated back bodice, remaining inside the lace cover-up.

"What in blazes are you wearing under that dress?"

His point-blank question caught her by surprise, and she answered without thinking of the unsuitability of the subject. "Something old-fashioned and very hard to find these days."

"It feels like you're rigged out with two barrel staves." His hand explored her ribs and side, running down the long plastic stays that held up the foundation garment.

"It's called a merry widow."

Suddenly he lifted his head and met her eyes with his sparkling brown ones. "I wish you were," he whispered.

She cocked her head to one side. "What?"

"A merry widow. I wish you were a merry widow instead of a promised woman."

She came to her senses then, backing away a reasonable distance. But without the length of his warm body, hers felt cold and deprived.

"I think it's time we talked about something nice and safe and . . . neutral."

"You're right. How did you like the dinner?"

"I liked everything but the asparagus. How about you?"

"I liked everything including the asparagus."

That subject was shot. She groped for another, but her thoughts were taken up by him, his nearness, how much she was enjoying being with him. It seemed a long time since she'd laughed this readily or bantered this freely. Paul was so often serious or immersed and out of touch with earth. Winnifred had fleeting thoughts that it was wrong to enjoy another man's company this much. But when Pete Schaeffer asked her to dance, and she returned afterward to Joseph, it felt like home. Already he felt familiar and comfortable.

They danced another fast set, and after it their brows were damp, their breath short. She was fanning her face with an ineffectual hand, and he'd yanked his bow tie loose and stuffed it into his pocket, then rolled up the ruffled cuffs of his white shirt to the elbows.

"This is hot business, your kind of dancing," he chided good-naturedly.

"Whew! I'll say!"

"It's not too bad outside for March. In the fifties. Want to go out for a minute and cool off?"

"We'll probably catch pneumonia."

"We'll only stay a minute, and if you get shivery, we'll come back in. Or better yet, I'll grab my jacket." He retrieved it from the chair, and Winnie found herself crossing toward the great front door without having consciously made the decision to be alone with him.

Outside the moon was at its apex—it was nearly midnight. Stillness surrounded them, for it was too early in the year for frogs, crickets or any of the other night sounds that would bring midnight alive when summer came. They stood on the highest of three white steps, breathing deeply. Joseph slung his tuxedo jacket across his left shoulder, suspending it from two fingers. He scanned the dark star-dappled sky. Winnifred ran a hand up the back of her neck, lifting the tendrils of hair that had come loose. Her nape was damp and the air felt wonderful. Joseph turned, watching the outline of her face as she lifted it, hung her head back and let her eyes sink shut. God, she was lovely. He wondered if she ever had any doubts about her impending marriage; if Hildebrandt was too ignorant to see the dangers of letting a woman like her drift free on a night like this. Around a man like himself.

"Come on. . . ." He slid his hand from the soft inner curve of her left elbow down to her wrist and intertwined his fingers with hers. "Let's walk."

He held her hand loosely, and it would have taken the simplest movement for Winnie to withdraw, but it felt right, ambling down the steps, across the withered pale grass, around the side of the house with her hand innocently in Joseph Duggan's.

The lawn sprawled and rolled in two gentle undulations toward a small creek and a patch of woodland beyond. The Victorian Club had, in its prime, been a property of estate proportions, thus the grounds were measured in spacious acres. Here and there tall oaks lifted their bare branches toward the stars, and a line of evergreens created a black barrier against the slightly lighter hue of the night sky. They sauntered downhill. Winnie felt the heels of her shoes sinking into the grass at times, throwing her slightly off balance. Whenever she lurched, Joseph's fingers gripped hers more tightly.

Ahead of them the white latticed foundation of the gazebo clarified as they approached, its hexagonal rails and roof beckoning as they moved closer and closer. Again Winnie sensed the same queer time-lapse sensation. Déjà vu, perhaps, brought about by the fact that the gazebo, like so many other props today, was a hallmark of another time. In her slim-hipped dress and dated hairdo she felt as if she belonged in the nostalgic enclosure.

She shivered at the strong compulsion of yesteryear.

"Cold?"

She turned to meet his eyes but could make out only that he looked her way, for there were two deep shadows from which he studied her. *What is it about a man with a coat slung over his shoulder that way that's so alluring,* she wondered. The unhurried look of it, perhaps, or the sense that his pose meant he was at ease with her. But just then he pulled the jacket forward and placed it around her shoulders, leaving his arm there, too, to keep her warm. She was surrounded by that lime-cedar scent emanating from the jacket and by a sense of the forbidden, for she knew they were hovering on the brink of something neither of them felt it wisest to begin. They were not dancing now. His arm had no legitimate reason for encircling her.

But the yearning that beckoned to them both was too powerful to fight.

They watched their feet take slower and slower steps, lazy swinging steps in the fashion of idle lovers. They heard the crush of dried grass and within their heads the pounding of their own hearts.

*Dammit, Duggan, don't kiss her. Once you do, you're in for a helluva problem.*

*He told you he had every intention of kissing you again. Will you let him? You must not, Winnifred Gardner. You must not.*

The gazebo was made totally of wood. The steps were wide and echoed as Joseph and Winnie lifted their knees in unison, mounting the risers toward the elevated floor in lazy measured steps. Above them the peak of the hexagonal roof couched secret shadows. She looked up, shivered and held Joseph's jacket closed with one hand. Around them ran a hip-high railing supported by white columns and a half wall of lattices. A wooden bench ran around the five trellised sides of the structure. She began moving toward it, but his hand closed gently around the back of her neck. "You'd better not. It's probably dirty, and you'll soil your dress."

At his touch she inhaled sharply, then held her breath. She shrugged her shoulders, hoping he'd free her from the terrible sweetness of his touch. Instead, he began moving his fingers softly on the skin and hair that were so soft beneath his tough skin. Her neck was cool now as the night sipped up the beads of perspiration generated on the dance floor.

"Joseph...don't," she whispered, terrified of how much she wanted him to ignore her demand.

"In your opinion, does a man dishonor a woman by kissing her if she's already engaged to someone else?"

"Oh..." she groaned and dropped her head backward, intending to shrug his hand away. Instead, the back of her skull touched his knuckles, and as her eyelids slid closed, she found her head moving as if to caress him. His fingers stroked her hairline, then just above—then just inside—the stiff collar of his jacket. She shuddered, and a shaft of liquid fire darted to her loins.

"Joseph, we shouldn't have come out here."

"I know," he agreed huskily.

"Then let's go back in. Quick, before it's too late."

"I'm right behind you. Just lead the way."

Her voice was strained and throaty as she remained where she was. "Joseph Duggan, you don't play fair."

"I'm not playing. I'm as serious as I've ever been in my life when I say something very, very special has happened to me since last night. When I looked up and saw you across the vestibule—"

She spun and covered his lips with her fingers. "Don't!" Her plea was shaken, her breathing harried. "Please, don't."

He jerked his head aside to free his lips but captured her hand and held it to his thudding heart. "Then why did you come out here with me?"

"I was hot."

"That makes two of us."

"Don't misconstrue wh—"

"You came out here for the same reason I did. You feel it, too, but now you're getting cold feet." His heart was ramming his chest walls like a jackhammer.

"You're right. I was wrong. Let's go ba—"

"No! Not yet!" He grabbed the lapels of his tuxedo jacket in both fists, jerked and lifted until she was forced onto tiptoe. But his voice lost its harsh bark and turned into a soft caress as he released the jacket and found her shoulders with his broad palms. "Not yet, Winn. I told you in the car I intended to do this again, and I meant it. But keep that jacket on tight if you know what's good for both of us."

She clung to it, turning the lapels inside, gripping them for dear life, covering her breasts with both arms while Joseph Duggan's hands slid to her shoulder blades and urged her close.

"Joseph, I'm eng—"

His warm mouth smothered the word and drove the fact from her mind. The kiss was gentle, exploratory and totally unhurried. It seemed to say, "Let's see what we think." He slanted his head aside, moving it in gentle circular nudges, licking her closed lips with a come-hither invitation until she could fight the urge no longer and opened her mouth tentatively. His tongue slipped immediately inside, and she hugged her chest tighter. His left arm pressed more firmly around her shoulder, his right moved caressingly until he spanned her lower skull commandingly, making her tip her head sideways to accommodate his wishes. When she refrained from moving her head seductively as he did, he moved it for her, gently gyrating it and forcing her mouth open more fully as the provocative seconds passed.

Within her mouth his tongue was sleek and seeking, circling hers, riding over it, under it, as if the world may as well go its way without them—this must be done and done properly. He delved and stroked, learning her every texture—from rough to smooth. She learned his, too: the wet velvet of his undertongue, the sharp edges of his teeth, the resilient softness of his inner cheeks and the hard ripples upon the roof of his mouth.

They became masters of exploration, overcome with a need to experience all they could of each other's mouths in lieu of taking further liberties.

As Joseph kissed Winn, his nostrils were filled with her flower-sweet scent. The taste of her was a surprise, rather like cinnamon, as if she'd been chewing spiced gum. As he enfolded her in his arms, he forced his kiss to remain gentle, swallowing the sounds of rising amorousness that wanted to murmur from his throat. The smooth cool texture of his own gabardine jacket across her shoulder blades created a desire to jerk it from her and feel her warm skin instead. But she clutched the lapels as ordered, and Joseph thought, thank God. *Thank God.*

He kissed the way he flirted—persuasively, skillfully, beguilingly. He was a head mover and a tongue teaser. A stroker. A talented refined stroker, she could tell already, though it was only her tongue receiving his rapt attention, only her shoulders he caressed. He'd had plenty of practice at this, she was certain. But maybe that's what made him so adept.

The hand on her neck was doing delightful things to the soft hollow up its center, then behind her left ear, and he'd managed to insert his fingers within the lace about her throat. But with its limited space the edge of the opening cut tightly at her Adam's apple, as if someone were tightening a single string about her neck.

She reached up to pull his hand away, for the cinching was making it more difficult than ever to breathe normally. But in the middle of the motion she changed her mind and did what she wanted to do more than anything else in the world at this moment: she flung her arms about his neck and sent the jacket falling to the dusty floor.

Surprised, he lifted his head for a second. His eyes were only two dim circles of shadow, but his breath was warm upon her nose. "Damn that man of yours," he muttered. "Doesn't he know better than to turn you loose on a night like this? Especially around a man like me?"

The reminder of Paul brought common sense rushing in, but before she could withdraw, Joseph embraced her again, tipping his head and meeting her lips with a series of brief plucking kisses, at the end of which he stroked the hollow beneath her lower lip with his tongue. Upon her back his hands wandered freely, inside the slitted lace, up her shoulder blade, under the spindly spaghetti strap, then back down, inside the dress top.

She trembled and tried again to pull away, but his head followed, and his tongue moved along the secret valley just inside her upper lip, tickling the sensitive frenulum, then sliding along her gums. She shuddered harder and raised up on tiptoe, wishing he'd tighten his grip around her waist. But he held her lightly, as if not trusting himself to totally eradicate the narrow space between their hips. She felt his hands shift, then both of them went to the nape of her neck, and he slipped the hook from the eye. Her lace drooped. He eased it forward and lifted both his hands to her elbows, forcing her to drop her arms from around his neck so the bodice could fall free, all the time nibbling and teasing her lips. When she stiffened and began to pull back sharply, he commanded her to stay, clasping the back of her head, pushing the lace overbodice down.

She felt his warm palms slide down the angles of her neck, across her shoulders, easing from them the thin straps that fluttered, then hung loose across her biceps.

She pressed a palm to his ruffles and freed her lips. "Joseph, stop. This is madness."

"Yes, I know. . . ." He kissed the crest of her cheek. He nipped her earlobe. He whispered directly into her ear,

"Winn, you smell like heaven. Forgive me if I can't help wondering what you taste like." The tip of his tongue wet the skin just behind her ear. Goose bumps shimmied up her belly, and she dropped her jaw onto her collarbone to free her neck to his warm lips and tongue.

His fingertips skimmed up her bare arms, jumping over the straps, then finding her warmth again and riding it around the perimeter of her dress top to the back zipper.

"Joseph, please stop," she pleaded.

"In a minute . . . shh."

Her head felt weightless, but her lower extremities suddenly grew as heavy as if she were experiencing labor pains. Everything surged and thrust against the juncture of her legs and left her wanting a corresponding upward pressure to relieve the burdensome weightiness. She felt the liquid musings of her body and heeded their warning, turning aside, backing away, denying herself the pleasure she knew could be found beneath Joseph Duggan's hands.

He clasped her elbow to stop her from running. "You're not married to him yet."

"But I'm promised. And I'm breaking that promise."

"Maybe it should never have been made."

"Don't try to justify this, Joseph. It's wrong."

"I want to touch you."

"I know, but if you do. . . ." She left the thought dangling, but more explicit than if she'd completed it. She gasped faintly. "Oh, Joseph . . . please don't. . . ." But she was adrift in ecstasy, and her voice fell still as her head lolled slightly to one side and back. How could a single finger raise such stirrings of desire?

He slipped it inside the stiff cup of her merry widow and trailed it along, from just under her armpit to the heart-shaped dip at the center of the garment, not quite touching her nipple as he passed.

"You have wonderful skin. Hard, firm, toned—I love

the feel of it. I'd begun to think there was no part of you that was soft, but I've found one soft place." The finger made its return journey but stopped at the nipple and bent the stiff cup downward as he rubbed the erect tip with the backs of his fingers only. "Mmm . . . I spoke too soon."

She was shriveled and goose bumped—it was cold in the March air, and what Joseph Duggan was doing wasn't helping matters at all. She conjured up a picture of Paul's face and backed away, taking Joseph's hand from her breast, folding it between her palms.

"Put my dress back the way you found it. I don't want to walk around with a guilt complex for the next three months."

"Why should you feel guilty? Engagements are meant to give a man and woman time to decide if they've made the right choice. Maybe you're learning here."

"And maybe you're just justifying again."

His warm palms now contoured her ribs. "I'm enormously attracted to you, Winn Gardner. What should a man do about a thing like that? Let it go unexplored? What if—"

"And what if this were just a . . . a passing urge? It's part of the mood of a wedding, wouldn't you say? People get caught up by romance when they see a bride and groom walk down the aisle. They do as Rodgers and Hart put it—'falling in love with love.' And we were more susceptible than most because we walked down that same aisle ourselves."

"Winn, your first impression of me—"

"Shh. Let me finish. You and I are different today than we'd be on a normal day. We're wearing luscious clothes that carry us away from the present and sweep us to the past, just as the ride in your car did. At times today I've even experienced the weird feeling that I'm living in my second life, that I've been reincarnated, and this—" she gestured and looked up "—this gazebo and your Haynes and my Gibson Girl look are all part of the time in which I lived before. That's why it felt so familiar, returning to it again. But, Joseph, that's not true. You and I have to be more careful than most on a day like today. We have to see things for what they truly are." She slipped her spaghetti straps up. "You know what they say about spring and a young man's fancy, don't you?" She turned her jaw aside, not quite glancing back at him. He rested his hands on her hipbones.

"No, I've forgotten. What do they say?"

"You know perfectly well what they say, but I'll repeat it, anyway, since it applies. 'In the spring a young man's fancy lightly turns to thoughts of love.' "

He watched as she inserted her arms into the lace overbodice, dropped her chin to her chest and lifted her arms. Joseph moved to find hook and eye and close them. As he did, her fragrant hair brushed his nose, and it took stern discipline to obey her wishes. But he bent and retrieved his jacket from the floor and draped it across her shoulders again. She clutched it from inside as before, then turned to face him.

"I'm your spring fancy tonight, Joseph Duggan. And before either one of us gets carried away any further, I think we'd both better admit this is more mood than anything else."

He considered her words. She might very well be right. He'd never been affected by a woman quite this suddenly, quite this strongly. He was twenty-seven and had sampled his share of feminine companions, and the one before him now raised his sexual thermometer more rapidly than any he'd met. Was it the occasion? The hat? The hair? The dress? The car? Even his own tuxedo and ruffles and shiny shoes, so different from his usual mode of dress?

Yes, she probably was right. And if so, he had no business upsetting the equilibrium between herself and Hildebrandt.

He drew a deep breath, jammed his hands into his trouser pockets and stepped back.

"So . . ." he said, pulling in a jerky sigh.

Silence hovered between them.

"So," she repeated.

The air seemed detonated by repressed sexuality.

"So, I suppose you don't want to dance with me anymore, either?"

"I always want to dance. Shall we go back and join the others? I think we'll be safe enough inside now. And anyway, there's only about half an hour of music left, then we'll politely say goodbye and exit from each other's lives, as if today and tonight never happened. And in the meantime we'll only talk about nice safe subjects again. Agreed?"

He said nothing for a long time, then finally squared his shoulders and answered, "You're right. That's wisest. Should I apologize for what I just did? I don't want to."

"No, Joseph, no apology is necessary. You see—" she chuckled softly and perhaps a trifle sadly "—you're *my* spring fancy, too."

Then she turned, and her high heels sounded on the hollow floor as she crossed to the steps. He frowned, wishing she hadn't been so sensible. Then he checked his watch to find it was twelve-forty. He had only twenty minutes to come up with a reasonable excuse to keep her with him a little longer after the dance broke up.

# 5

THEY RETURNED to the dance floor, conscious of the fleeting minutes and wishing they had more of them. When the first song ended, Joseph turned from her, and she saw a slash of light gray angling across the back of his jacket.

"Joseph, you're marked."

Quickly he turned to face her. "I'm what?"

"Turn around again. Your jacket is dirty from the floor of the gazebo." He presented his broad back, and as she brushed it free of evidence, she wondered what his shoulders looked like inside the clothing. She was too aware of how hard his muscles were, of how trim his contours, especially down his lower half. He looked back over his shoulder and grinned.

"I could get used to this if you'd let me."

She stopped brushing, hand hanging in midair as he turned slowly to face her again, and she stared at the appendage as if wondering whose hand it was. Then she clutched it to her stomach.

"Safe subjects. . .remember?" she reminded him just as the music began again.

"Pick one," he ordered, reverting to a waltz position with six inches of space dividing their bellies.

She grabbed the first passing thought. "Where did you take the bride?"

"Out to Daytona."

"You mean the Daytona *Club*?"

"Yes."

"Why ever did you pick a place like that?"

"Because I'm a member, and it's a twenty-minute ride, and we had to keep her away an hour, anyway. So we went out there and had a drink."

"You're a member?" she asked, surprised.

"Yes."

"What do you play?"

"Tennis, racket ball, golf. Nearly everything. I like to keep in shape."

Her eyes grew round and glittery. "I do, too!"

"I could tell that from the condition of your muscles. You're as hard and smooth as a watermelon."

"So are you. What's your favorite?"

"Depends on the season. In the summer I like tennis because it's more active than golf. I play baseball, too, with my brothers. In the winter I do some jogging and play quite a bit of racket ball, again with my brothers."

"So do I—oh, not with my brothers, of course. I don't have any brothers. But Sandy and I play racket ball, or we used to, but I suppose that may change now that she's married. She and Mick will probably do that together from now on."

"What about old Hildegard? Doesn't he play with you?"

Was there a sexy glint in his eye, a note of sexual innuendo in the question? If so, she chose to ignore it.

"Occasionally. But he doesn't care for physical things. He likes to be neat and fragrant and unsweaty. He's a brain man. I'm a body woman."

Joseph Duggan's eyes made a tour of her face. He lingered longest upon her lips, then nestled her securely against his sturdy frame. Into her ear he said, "So tell me . . . what else don't you and the computer man have in common besides physical activity and the wonders of silicon chips?"

"Not much else. Only our taste in clothing."

"What?" He backed up and looked down at her breasts, then up at her hair. "What could he possibly not like about your taste in clothing?"

"Oh, I hardly ever dress like this, in all these feminine things. That's his main complaint. I'm active. I like sweat suits and blue jeans and tennis shoes and headbands. He says clothes make the man—or the person, rather. There are times when we get ready to go out, and I know he's disappointed when I show up in jeans and cowboy boots. I'm trying to get used to dressing in cuter things."

"Why should you?"

His question stunned her. It was the first time she'd bothered to probe the issue. She'd always felt it was a shortcoming in her, as a woman, that she preferred boyish clothes. Her mother had never failed to chide her for dressing like a *tomboy*.

"But, even *you* said you liked the way I'm dressed today."

"I love the way you're dressed today. But I'll bet you're sexy as hell in a pair of jogging shorts and running shoes with your ankles bare and your hair bouncing around free." His eyes lifted to it momentarily, then slid down again.

"When you say things like that, it makes me want to jump into my sweats and take a fast sprint around a blacktop track. That's the real me, not the one in this hairdo and merry-widow bra."

"Then let's do it."

"What?"

He dropped his arms from her waist and checked his watch. "It's only five to one. That's early. There's got to be someplace in this city where we can find an empty jogging track that's got at least one streetlight shining on it. Let's go and burn it up. Whaddya say?"

"Are you serious?"

"Dead serious. I've been wracking my brain, trying to come up with some ingenious suggestion for something we can do together. It's almost time to call it a night here, and I find I haven't had my fill of you yet. I want to be with you a little longer. Can you think of anything safer for the two of us to do than jogging?"

She couldn't. A smile touched her lips, then lighted her eyes, and he thought he'd never seen a woman more beautiful. The hair at her right temple was roughened and pulled askew. Once again her lipstick was gone. But she had a beauty that surpassed superficiality. He wondered what she'd look like right after a shower, when all artifice was gone from her face and hair.

"You'd have to stop by my place so I can pick up some sweats."

"And then you'd have to stop by mine so I can pick up some, too."

The night suddenly sparkled with adventure. She didn't have to say goodbye to him yet! "Let's." She smiled impishly.

"You're on!" He grabbed her hand and towed her toward the table to collect her hat, flowers and makeup bag, and two minutes later they were pulling away from the curb in his '23 Haynes Sport Coupelet.

She crossed her left ankle over her right knee, took off the high heel and massaged her foot. "Excuse me, but you have no idea how grossly uncomfortable dyed-to-match satin pumps can be, especially when you buy them for a wedding. You never have a chance to break them in because if you get a mark on them, it's there to stay."

"You mean all this time your feet were aching, yet you kept me dancing without letup?"

"Well, I *do* love to dance." She angled him a cute smirk. "But it's more fun in old shoes."

"So take 'em off. We won't stand on formality around here."

She eased off the other shoe and wriggled her toes. She stretched her legs as best she could on the angular old car seat. "Ohh . . . that feels good."

"Here, give me a foot," he ordered, one hand on the wheel, his eyes on the late-night streets where there was virtually no traffic. "And tell me how to get to your house."

"Take Brooklyn Boulevard to Shingle Creek Parkway and turn right. I live in a town house on the corner." The front seat of the old car was very narrow. She backed up against the door and plunked her heels on the car seat, then pushed her dress down between her up-drawn knees. He captured her left foot and rubbed it firmly, his hand slipping over the silky nylon, sending shivers up her calves.

"Don't lean against that door. These old cars weren't exactly built for safety."

She curled her spine, dropped her head onto her knees and concentrated on the sensual feeling of his thumb massaging the arch of her foot. "Mmm. . .you're very good at that, considering *I*'m the physical therapist." Her voice came muffled from the depths of her lap.

"That's right, I forgot you were. Well, maybe you can give me a rubdown after we run."

She lifted her head and rested her chin on her crossed forearms, which still rested on her knees. "I said I'm a therapist, not a trainer."

He laughed and pressed her foot against his thigh, then left his warm hand covering it. Within five minutes they'd arrived at her house. She rummaged around on the floor of the car for all the trappings she'd dumped there at various times today. There was no interior light in the old flivver, but at last she'd gathered a stack of what she hoped was everything.

"Can I carry something?" he offered.

"Yes, you can bring the plastic clothing bag with my other dress in it." She fished it off the floor, and while transferring the crooks of the hangers into his hand, their fingers touched. For a brief moment neither of them moved. Then she picked up her possessions and hurriedly opened her door. "Come on in and see my house."

There was a For Sale sign in the yard, and he looked back at it while she struggled to fit her key in the lock. "I take it, it's your house that's up for sale."

"Naturally. What would Paul and I do with two houses when he's trying to earn the money to furnish one?"

"No buyers yet?"

"No, the market's been in a slump, the realtors say. But I'm hoping to get more lookers now that spring is here."

Inside she snapped on the entry light, and they faced an ordinary living room decorated in saffron yellow and white. The furniture was nondescript: a striped sofa in shades of brown, two director's chairs in yellow canvas, a table made from an enormous wooden spool—the kind steel telephone cable comes wrapped upon. A wine jug sat on the floor in one corner, sprouting dried bearded wheat and milkweed pods painted in horribly garish purple, red and royal blue. She caught him eyeing the ugly arrangement and offered, "One of my younger patients gave those to me last year, and I haven't had the heart to throw them away. I know they're awful, but I love them in spite of it." She turned, and he watched the slit in the lace along the center of her back shift with each step as she walked away down a hall. Just before she reached what appeared to be her bedroom doorway, both elbows flew in the air, and she reached for the hook and eye at her nape. There followed a soft click as her bedroom door shut, then his long sigh as he ran a hand through his hair. He tried to keep his mind off what she was doing back there. He toured her living room, then the small efficient galley kitchen behind it—a cereal bowl in the sink with three Cheerios stuck to a glutinous puddle of milk, pencils sticking out of a mug that said "Killer" on its side, a tablet on which was written "buy deodorant." He smiled and crossed to a sliding glass door hovering high above the dark yard. He slid it open and stepped out onto a small planked deck. Bracing his hands on the rail, he listened to the soft rush of Shingle Creek chortling in the dark.

She was the kind of woman he'd been searching for for a long time. At least, so far he thought so. Just his luck to find her and learn she was engaged to another man. He hoped Hildebrandt had more than silicon chips in his pants—she seemed like the kind who needed and deserved a mate who was all man, demanding and reciprocating. She had that way about her—the strong sure way she moved, walked, danced. She exuded physicality. And she had the body of an athlete—toned, tensile, firm. Surely a body like that must be agile when it came to loving.

He stepped back inside and closed the sliding door. "Are you decent?" he called.

"Yes."

"Can I come back there?"

A silent pause followed, then she called, "Yes, come ahead."

The doorknob clicked, the door swung open slowly, and Joseph Duggan leaned against the frame, his weight slung on one hip and his hands slipped inside his trouser pockets. His eyes swept her gray sweat pants and hooded shirt, then swerved to the bed where her merry widow lay like a plaster cast of the front half of her body. She snatched it up and stuffed it into a dresser drawer.

"Why aren't you and this computer man living together? Wouldn't it be cheaper?"

"I bought this town house two years ago because he said it'd be the wisest thing to do with my money at the time—an investment, you know? Then when we got engaged, he started looking for a house for both of us right away, and as soon as we found it, I put this one on the market. Unfortunately it hasn't sold, and I'm stuck here until it does."

"Meaning you'd rather be living with him?"

She dropped to the foot of the bed and began pulling

on tasseled white sport footlets and a pair of Adidas. "You're very presumptuous, asking questions like that." Her eyes never left her feet.

"Sorry," he said with not the least hint of pique at her sharp retort. His eyes moved from item to item around the room: the rumpled bed, unmade, but with the spread tossed up, half covering the pillows; her panty hose; one discarded satin pump lying on its side with the tiny pearl against the saffron carpet; photographs stuck into the edge of an old-fashioned dressing-table mirror; a tangle of Ace bandages on a dresser top to his left, lying beside a black perfume bottle, a round white plastic container of body powder, a handful of change, a pair of theater- ticket stubs, a package of Big Red gum and a small plastic case with compartments numbered like days of the month.

He eased his shoulder nonchalantly away from the door frame and ambled over to the dresser, chose the black flask, uncapped it and took a deep sniff. He watched her pull on one tennis shoe while he smelled the perfume and admired the curve of her spine as she bent sharply from her perch on the mattress. Without a comment he placed the Chanel No 5 back where he'd found it, then tinkered around, touching other things atop her dresser, observing that half the compartments in her birth-control pillbox were empty before moving on to the quaint scarred dressing table.

He knew very well she'd observed him inspecting her personal possessions, particularly the pills. And she knew he knew. He admired her for not leaping up and fussing about it in some artificially apologetic way.

"Is this you?"

She looked up to find his palms braced on the top of the dressing table, head cocked to one side as he studied a photo slipped between the mirror and its frame.

"Yours truly," she replied, reaching for her other shoe. He glanced back over his shoulder, still braced on the dresser, and gave her a disarming grin. "You were really cute in the pigtails. But what happened to all those freckles?"

"Luckily I outgrew them."

"Mmm, too bad," he mused, returning his attention to the photo and a string of others. "You played tennis in school?"

"Uh-huh."

"I played basketball and ran in track."

Her shoes were tied. She threw him a defiant look. "You don't seem tall enough to be a basketball player." She stood up, pulled her sweat shirt down at the waist, then reached around him to get a brush from the top of the dresser. He didn't move, only turned his head aside to watch her shoulder and breast brush close to his arm.

"I was one of those quick wily guards. What I lacked in height I made up for in speed."

"I'll bet." She smirked, and he finally straightened, then pulled out a small boudoir chair from under the kneehole of the dated dressing table, slung his leg over it as if he were mounting a bronco and straddled it, facing her.

"I detect a wry note in that comment." He relaxed back, catching both elbows on the table behind him. The two top buttons of his shirt were freed, revealing a V of pale brown hair on his chest. His tuxedo jacket fell aside while the snowy ruffles of his jabot thrust forward, framed by the deep low U-shaped curve of his vest. The pose was unqualifiedly masculine. Unequivocally sexy. And it conjured up in Winnifred's mind the word "hombre." With his knees widespread on either side of the low delicate back of the diminutive chair, he looked more virile and tempting than ever. The black fabric of his trousers stretched taut across his groin.

She raised her eyes to find his had been watching the direction of her study, and she dredged up a comment to put him in his place because she herself was acutely discomfited by what she'd just seen.

"Short and fast, that describes you pretty well, I'd say."

"I'm tall enough to put you where you belong, and I can be as slow as the next man when the occasion merits."

"We *are* talking about basketball, aren't we, Mr. Duggan?"

"Are we?"

She was removing the hairpins from her coil when he answered the last question with one of his own. Her hand stilled in midair, and she treated him to the guileless single-eyed blink that fascinated him so. She did it with her left eye, again in slow motion, and he was certain she wasn't aware of the fact that she possessed this intriguing reflex, or that it showed up whenever she was tense or embarrassed.

Suddenly she seemed to realize she was staring at him, motionless, and began searching her hair once more for hairpins. She pulled out a handful while he watched her every movement, then indolently reached out a palm, waiting. She dropped the pins into his hand, stepped back a safe distance and began brushing her hair while he watched her as carefully as if she were poised prey.

"You have the most fascinating nervous reaction that I'll bet you're not aware of." She kept pulling the brush through her hair but made no reply. "Did you know you sometimes blink only your left eye? In extremely slow motion?"

"I do?" The brush stopped.

"You do. And it makes me want to do things I have no right to think about."

Abruptly, almost angrily, he thrust himself forward, swung his leg over the chair back, stretched to his feet, but turned his back on her. When all was silent for a long minute, he glanced back over his shoulder and ordered harshly, "Keep brushing, for God's sake, and let's get out of here!"

She couldn't help smiling at his smooth black shoulders, wondering if the reason he'd leaped off that chair was the one she thought—because if he hadn't, things were going to start showing any second.

"I'm ready. All I need is a sweatband. Excuse me."

He whirled and jumped out of her way when he discovered her close behind him, waiting to get at a drawer of the dressing table. She stood only a scant foot from him while ducking down to see in the mirror, slipping a braided red headband over her disorderly hair. "I'm a mess, but what the heck. All I'm going to do is run."

Maybe not, he thought, but smiled at her refreshing acceptance of her rather unflattering state. She looked better to him now in her baggy sweat pants than she'd looked in her pink ankle-length dress. She looked approachable, messable and altogether feminine.

AT HIS HOUSE they crept. "Shh!" he warned. "My brothers are sleeping." He snapped on a dim light in an old crowded back entry. Basement stairs led straight ahead, and up one step to the left was a kitchen. It was as vintage as his cars, this house. It was built in the forties most likely and had as much class as a four-buckle overshoe. He'd said it was his grandparents' home, and she could see touches of the grandmother left behind: an ivy in a brass pot hanging by a chain above the kitchen sink; an old black cast-iron Dutch oven with a cover, sitting on a very dirty stove; a kitchen clock shaped like a red plastic teakettle. The floor was covered not in vinyl, but with linoleum—one-foot squares of red and gray straight from 1950. It was worn in front of the stove, and the black sublayer was beginning to show through. Linoleum, for heaven's sake! He left her to go upstairs, and she poked her head into a dark living room and heard the floorboards creaking overhead where Joseph rummaged for his athletic clothes. A bass voice mumbled something, and Joseph's answered—undoubtedly he'd roused one of his brothers. She heard what sounded like an ancient dresser drawer screeching as it resisted closing, then two thumps that might have been Joseph's dress shoes hitting the floor. She switched on a living-room lamp and perused the room: leftovers of grandma's. An overstuffed sofa with a matching chair, both of wear-like-iron nylon frieze; a step table with a bowl of peanut shells on it; an NFL magazine that was six months old and a stack of newspapers not much newer; an embroidered doily that needed washing and starching—or better yet, throwing away; a black-and-red wool lumberman's shirt and a disreputable-looking pair of work boots with leather strings and oily curled-up toes; ancient ecru-lace panel curtains—lace? Stucco walls. But upon them she saw the first touch she knew to be Joseph's: large color photos of vintage cars, framed in stainless steel and fronted with glass. There were five of them in the room, each one classier than the next. She was facing the largest of them when Joseph spoke just behind her shoulder.

"That's my dream. To own one of those babies one day."

She leaned forward and inspected the fancy English round hand at the bottom of the picture. "1932 Duesenberg Model SJ." She turned her head to watch his profile as he studied the picture with a reverence she found enlightening.

"When you get it, will you take me for a ride?"

His hand stole up and squeezed the side of her neck. "Honey, it's a date. I'll find you if you're findable by dry land."

She was suddenly saddened to think that if that day ever came, she couldn't go for the ride with him. She remembered the way he'd kissed her in the Haynes this afternoon, how he'd carefully dipped his head down to miss her hat brim, then had to dip back out again as he retreated. She thought of their encounter in the gazebo.

And suddenly she wished he'd turn her around by the shoulders and kiss her again, without hat or hairdo to be careful of, with nothing more than their soft sweat suits between their two honed bodies. But instead, he only squeezed the side of her neck and spoke about the car before them.

"They say there were less than forty of those made. But they were the most prestigious car ever produced anywhere, and in their day had an exclusive reputation that put Rolls-Royce to shame. They'd deliver three hundred horsepower and perform like no other machine before or since. The SJ could top one hundred miles an hour in second gear! And she could go from a standstill to one hundred miles an hour in seventeen seconds. And you want to know something sad?"

She didn't, but he went on, still gazing at the picture. "The man she was named after was killed in an accident while driving one of these in 1932."

She lifted her face and half turned to look up at him. "In a way that's not as sad as it might have been. He died doing the thing he probably loved doing best in all the world."

His eyes met hers. "You're right, Winn. I never looked at it that way before. And he accomplished a lot in his life that was left for posterity—he and his brother had a lot to do with developing the Indy 500 into what it is today."

"You mean the Duesenberg is an American car?"

"As apple pie."

"It sounds German."

"They were immigrants, the Duesenberg brothers."

Joseph and Winnie stood for a minute longer in the dim light of the farmhouse-style living room with its peanut shells and work boots and its oddly contrasting 1932 Duesenberg.

"Well, good luck, Joseph Duggan," she said at last very quietly, her eyes on his prize, his dream.

He shook himself from his reverie and tugged on her

neck. "Come on, let's go run. I think I know just the place."

THEY RAN around the quarter-mile track of Osseo Senior High School, only a few blocks from his house. They drove over in the Haynes and left it parked in the middle of the deserted parking lot. Silently they crossed the blacktop, made their way inside the chain-link fence surrounding the football field and track and peered at the white-painted lane lines that were barely visible in the deep night.

Then they were running side by side, puffing hard, their breathing coming in long controlled intakes and exhalations. There was only the sound of it and the slap of their rubber soles on the blacktop.

She thought of what a joy it was to run beside a man who enjoyed it as much as she.

He thought of what a damn fool old Hildegard was, to show no interest in sharing this with her.

She thought of what Joseph Duggan's legs must look like inside his navy sweat pants as the muscles flexed and stretched.

He pictured the curve of her buttocks, her flanks, her thighs reaching rhythmically along the track before him—naked.

She wondered if he'd ever get his Duesenberg.

He wondered if she'd really marry a silicon chip.

She wondered if he did this with the Perkins hostess.

He wondered who'd do this with her once she married the wrong man.

She thought she could run like this beside him forever.

He considered asking her to.

They'd circled the four-forty eight times when they approached the place from which they'd started.

"Want to go around again?" he asked without breaking stride.

"No, I've had enough."

They veered off the track, breathing hard, but not hurting. To their right rose a high set of metal bleachers, standing out like white ribs beneath the quarter moon that hung in the southwestern sky. They slowed to a cool-down pace and reverted to walking side by side, blowing and flexing and shaking their limbs. They padded on silent grass in the middle of the oval, heading for the break in the chain-link fence.

The city was silent—it was perhaps three o'clock in the morning. The only sound came from a diesel truck that rolled off down the highway beyond the far side of the football field, than all was still but for their labored breathing. They stopped on the black track—by now their eyes had grown accustomed to the darkness, and its white ribbons of paint stood out like writing on a blackboard.

She flexed forward at the waist, bracing her hands just above her kneecaps, hanging that way. He hung his hands upon his hipbones and leaned backward, blinking, then studying the stars. They both straightened at the same time, facing each other with nothing but three feet of night between them.

He saw her upraised face, bathed in star shine, and the hair upon her temples—damp tendrils clinging down her cheeks below the braided headband that crossed her forehead. Her breasts rose and fell rapidly. He could smell the vestiges of Chanel No 5, brought again to life by her warm sweating body.

"Forgive me for doing this, Winn, but it's got to be done, so I'll know. . . ." His left arm circled her just beneath the ribs, and his right hooked over her opposite shoulder. He pulled her flush against his warm damp body, burying her lips beneath his in a kiss that was wholly different from that shared in the front seat of his Haynes or those exchanged in the gazebo. This was elemental, forceful, like two planets that have been reeling off orbit for several light years and finally collide in a shower of meteorites.

His mouth was open, hot and wet, and his tongue delved into her mouth with ripe demand for response. She gave it, satisfying her own need for this man, telling herself she would satisfy it no further, that this would surely be enough. But she had scarcely thrown her arms around his neck and back before she realized her mistake. This would never be enough—not with this man.

Their sweat suits were damp and scarcely concealed the firmness of the flesh beneath. Hers was equally as toned as his, equally as healthy. Holding her, kissing her with an almost frantic meeting of tongues, he slipped his hand up beneath the ribbed waistband, finding the small of her back damp and inviting. He ran his hand up, up, across the hard flesh just beneath her shoulder blades, collecting the sweet moisture from her skin as he went, moving left to right across the constricting band of her bra where it scarcely depressed her firm muscle.

She, too, slipped one hand beneath his shirt: warmth, dampness and rigid muscle greeted her caress. Their breathing, already labored from the two-mile run, became torturous now as their emotions swelled, and temptation brought their bodies to a fine-tuned peak of readiness.

And, Judas, he felt good. Hard, so hard. Against every surface that touched him, there was nothing less than hard. The soft moldable cotton of their garments conformed to their limbs, leaving little bulk between them to disguise how eagerly they strained toward one another. He stepped forward, placing one leg between hers, and their mutual height made the conformation of their bodies totally complementary. She followed his lead and widened her stance, allowing his hard thigh to press upward against the warm juncture of her legs, and answered the quest for familiarity by exploring him likewise, lifting a knee that was buttressed on either side by his firm thighs. Against the soft hollow beneath her hip, his urgency was transmitted by the thrust of his pelvis.

It brought him undulating rhythmically against her, and she answered, in kind.

Inside her sweat shirt his hand went clear up to her neck, circling it, and threading fingers up into her scalp, which also was warm and damp, and exuded the scent of hair spray, not wholly unpleasant when combined with her own female scent.

Perhaps it was the scents that triggered the violent sexual reaction they both felt. Perhaps it was the sheer exertion of running that prompted them to seek something more that was totally physical. And certainly it was the romantic residuals of the wedding that put them in a frame of mind where each was eager to know and explore the other, after the countless times their eyes had met, their words had enticed, and their looks had conveyed both attraction and curiosity.

He broke away, ending the kiss with his mouth only, for it went on ardently down the remainder of her body while his ragged voice rumbled near her ear.

"I knew it. Oh, God, I knew it."

"What?" Her own voice was slightly gruff and throaty. Her heart was thudding as if she were still pounding around the track at a full sprint.

"That it would be like this when I really kissed you and held you the way I've been wanting to." Suddenly he clasped her head in both hands, compelling her to stoop slightly. "Here. . .feel." Her cheek and ear were pressed against the wall of his chest which rose and fell with torturous speed while, inside, the vibrant force of his heart seemed as if it would crash its way through. He lifted her face, cradling her jaws, and held her that way while he kissed her mouth hard and sure. "That's what you do to me. It's been happening all day, since last night even, at certain times when I'd look at you and allow myself to fantasize."

No matter what she was feeling now, tomorrow, guilt would certainly outweigh any satisfaction she'd realize tonight if she let him continue this sexual foray. She removed his hands from her jaws and stepped back.

"I can't do this to Paul."

"You've never cheated on him?"

"Never. And I won't start now."

He studied her, scowling, then seemed to make a decision. "Good. I'm glad. I might not admire you as much otherwise."

She ran her fingers against her scalp, tipped her head back as if in pain and spun away from him. "Don't say things like that!"

"What? What did I say?"

"You know what you said—one minute loyal, the next untrue. It mixes me up."

"Winn." He pulled her hand down from her head and turned her to face him. "How are things, really, between you and him? If you're mixed up, it isn't because you just met and kissed me. It goes deeper than that."

"Don't probe. I don't like it. And furthermore, it's not healthy at this late date."

"Would it be better two years after you marry him? Or four years afterward, when you have two kids, maybe?"

She stiffened and her facial expression grew hard. "I have to go now. I'm really beat."

She turned toward the car. He watched the outline of her loose sweat suit grow indistinct as she moved away. He considered the countless complications this night might yet bring about for both of them. They'd begun already. She walked with her head down, hands in the warmer pocket across her belly. Her footsteps were tired, despondent. She opened the door of the Haynes and dragged herself up into the seat, then slammed the door.

He looked at the stars, at the blacktop, at the car, at his choices. It seemed there was only one.

When he sat beside her on the high seat, he laced his hands loosely over the steering wheel and stared straight out the two-piece windshield. "I'm sorry I've been ragging you about your relationship with Paul. I had no right. I'm a virtual stranger to you, and I've been drawing conclusions and making judgments ever since I met you. I just want you to know, though, that if you weren't . . . encumbered, I'd be pursuing you full force from this day on, okay?" He turned to find her with a sad expression on her face, staring at the break in the windshield. "You're a dynamite lady, Winn Gardner. I hope he knows that."

She turned, lifted her eyes to his hair and dropped them to his lips. Then she looked him steadily in the eye and said in a very soft voice, "Please don't misconstrue this in any way. But there's been something I've wanted to do ever since I first met you. I want to do it just once to see what it feels like." She lifted a hand to his head, lightly touching the curls above his left ear. "Why, it's soft!" she exclaimed in a winsome voice.

"And what did you expect?"

"I don't know. I've just never known a man with natural curls before."

It took a great effort for Joseph to keep his hands on the wheel; they clenched it now, no longer relaxed as they'd been a minute ago. Her touch was brief, innocent, but terribly sensual, and he thought if she didn't get her hands away, he'd lay her flat on the blacktop parking lot beside the car and see if he couldn't change her mind about cheating on old Silicon Chip.

"Don't!" He pulled back, not jerking, not even forcefully. He simply retreated, and she understood: what she'd done was raising as much havoc with his libido as it was with her own. She tucked her hands between her knees and apologized, "I'm sorry. Let's go."

They remained quiet and solitary all the way back to her house. When they pulled up in her driveway, the car engine remained running, and they looked at each other. Neither of them was willing to call an end to their brief time together yet.

"Would you buy me breakfast?" she asked, feeling foolish and as if she were goading him, when actually it was herself she seemed unable to stop punishing.

"I think I'd do almost near anything for you."

"Then buy me breakfast and afterward wish me goodbye sensibly, without walking me to the door, and if we run into each other at the gift opening tomorrow, don't say more than hello."

"You sure that's how you want it?"

"No. I'm sure that's how it's got to be."

They ate apple pannekoekens at the Pannekoeken Huis, which was only a stone's throw from her town house. As they left the restaurant, the sun split the eastern sky with a bright wink of orange that spread and grew and tinted the rim of the world a brilliant combination of purple, heliotrope and lemon. He pulled up at the curb, and as she opened her door by herself, as she got out, he didn't look at her. When she stood on the street, holding onto the handle of the car door, she still waited.

"Goodbye, Joseph Duggan."

"Goodbye, Winn Gardner."

Both of them felt faintly ill as she watched the car drive up the street. He resolutely refrained from looking at her in the rearview mirror as long as he could stand it. But at last he lifted his eyes to see if she still stood in the street watching him drive away. But then he remembered. The Haynes was built before there were rearview mirrors.

# 6

Winnifred awakened with a violent headache shortly past noon. *The gift opening,* she thought. *I can't face it.* She curled into a tight ball and shut her eyes again, reliving yesterday, feeling guilty for betraying Paul.

She called him five minutes later and came as close to begging as she ever had with him, but he said Sandy and Mick were actually her friends, and he'd prefer to stay home and finish the work he'd begun the day before. Then he added, "But have a good time, darling."

She considered calling Ann Schaeffer and offering her apologies, then going out for a long hard run to work off her frustration but felt it her duty as maid of honor to attend the gathering. She wore faded string-bean blue jeans and a white cotton-knit "Wallace Beery" shirt, the most unglamorous getup she could produce from her closet. She washed the hair spray from her hair and fluffed it with a blow dryer but left it free and uncurled, totally unspecial. She disdained all makeup except a pale application of lip gloss, chiefly because her lips were chapped from Joseph's rough chin, and the lanolin relieved them.

She was fifteen minutes late and expected to confront Joseph as she jogged down the steps to the Schaeffers' lower-level family room. But to her relief he wasn't there. Twenty or more people had arrived, and all the chairs were filled, so she took a seat on the floor near Sandy's feet. Sandy and Mick were just about to begin opening gifts, and Winnie was given the job of recording them in the wedding book.

She had written the eighth name and listed the gift when she looked up to find Joseph had just come in. Her heart went into overdrive, and her mouth watered. He was dressed much as he'd been the night of the rehearsal, in faded Levi's, the same new tennis shoes and same ivory jacket. His thumbs were hooked in his back pockets as he stood for a minute, saying hello, smiling at the group in general as his eyes passed from one person to another. When they came to her, they scarcely paused, and he gave a silent nod, then picked his way through the limited walking space and sat on the floor at the opposite end of the room from Winnie.

He followed her orders of the night before—to the max. He never again looked at her or spoke to her but visited most of the time with a pretty young woman named Connie, near whose chair he sat. There were times when Winnie thought she felt his eyes on her, especially when her attention was given to the book on her lap. But the two times she glanced his way, he was talking and laughing with Connie, who seemed more taken with him as the afternoon progressed.

The two of them walked out of the house together, and Winnifred followed, wondering at the deep sense of abandonment she felt while studying Joseph's back as he walked in front of her beside another woman. He laughed and Winnie's heart lurched. She felt empty and cast aside, wondering what the woman said that had amused him.

The two of them stood on the street beside a strange vehicle, and when Joseph's hand rested on the handle of the door, he looked over the woman's shoulder and saw Winnie, heading for her own car.

"Winn!" he called.

She came up short. Her heart lifted with hope. She hadn't time to ask herself for what.

"I found something of yours in the Haynes. Just a minute." He opened the door to the strange vehicle, and his head disappeared. When he turned, he held one of her pink high heels in his hand, its tiny pearl button winking a reminder in the waning Sunday afternoon. He lifted the shoe above his head and wagged it, walking toward her. They met in the center of the street; Connie remained where he'd left her, waiting.

Up close he looked and smelled wonderful. But he only handed her the shoe and said, "One's not much good, is it?"

"Thank you."

His back was already turning as he said, "It's okay," and waved with a negligent lifting of his knuckles.

He returned to Connie, and that's where he was when Winnie drove away. When she got home, she changed into her running clothes and ran until her body felt tortured.

HER LIFE RETURNED TO NORMAL in the weeks after the wedding. At least, as normal as life can be when you're less than three months away from your own wedding. She kept a list of things that needed checking, ordering or making, and crossed them off one by one: the florist, the organist, the singer, the garter, the pillow for the ring bearer.

She saw Paul several nights a week, usually at his place, and found it necessary to visit her mother once or twice a week concerning various details. At times Joseph Duggan entered her mind in a most distracting way. Then she'd put on her sweats and try to run him out of her system.

But it never seemed to work.

The one place he didn't manage to intrude was at the hospital. She loved her job and the people she worked with, and the patients, each of whom she considered a separate challenge.

The Physical Medicine and Rehabilitation Department of North Memorial Medical Center consisted of four systems: physical therapy; occupational therapy; cardiac rehab; and sports medicine, a relatively new and specialized facet of P.T. that was located in a separate building from the other three systems. But it was with those three housed within the main body of the hospital building that Winnifred worked.

She spent her days gaining the confidence of the patients to whom she was assigned, encouraging them with the often repeated phrase "You can" and making certain they never failed in the problem she assigned them for the day, be it raising a leg one inch higher than the previous day or touching an ear to a shoulder. It was one of the things she loved about being a physical therapist, the constant challenge of gauging each person's abilities and limits, and making certain she never expected more progress than their impaired bodies were ready for.

She worked with both inpatients and outpatients, seeing them once or twice a day until they were either released or had recuperated as much use of the affected body part as possible. Because she came to know each of them personally—their temperaments, personal histories, goals and fears—there was always a grave danger of becoming emotionally involved with them herself. Sympathy was fine and necessary, but when it grew too empathetic, it clouded judgment and affected a therapist's own emotions. Thus, they were taught from the start to beware of sympathetic involvement.

It was a gorgeous day in late April when Winnie was assigned a new patient. She met Meredith Emery shortly before noon, and from the first glance at the burn-scarred ten-year-old, something within Winn's heart trembled.

The child had been standing next to her father when the first match failed as he attempted to light a backyard barbecue. When he went inside for extra matches, he forgot to turn the gas jet down. The resultant explosion burned both of them badly, but the child suffered worse, simply because she was shorter, and the flames caught her at chest and neck level, scarring her face, too.

It was the frightened, lashless, eyebrowless eyes that caught at Winnifred's heartstrings from the very first moment she looked into them. The child's eyes must have been stunning before the accident—enormous, deep brown with large pupils and such wide-open lids. A poppet's eyes.

An orderly rolled Meredith Emery down to P.T. on a gurney, which was topped by a "rack" of canvas stretched onto an aluminum frame, much like an Indian litter. Winnifred met her at the door to the tank room and told the orderly she'd take over from there.

The child had been lightly sedated, but not enough so she wasn't capable of fear at yet another strange face, another strange stainless-steel facility, another new process for her small ravaged body.

"Hello, Meredith, my name is Winnifred. I'm going to be seeing you twice every day for as long as you're here, and together we're going to work on your arms and legs and toes and fingers and everything until you can move just like you did before and be able to run and play and go back to school. How does that sound?"

The wide doubtful eyes only stared.

"Meredith..." Winnie mused, "That's a rather big name for a girl...." Winnifred checked her chart questioningly. "Ten? Are you ten?" She cocked her head closer to the level of the child's.

Meredith answered with an almost imperceptible nod.

"What do your friends call you?"

"Merry." The mouth was misshapen and drawn, and when it formed the words was transformed into a grotesque parody of a child's lips. Steeling herself, Winnifred ignored the pity that gripped her. "May I call you Merry? My name is kind of like yours, too—a little on the fancy side, kind of puts people off sometimes. So I'd like it if you'd call me...Winn." Where had it come from, this form of her name only Joseph Duggan used? She had never before encouraged people to call her by it, but now it soothed her as she looked down upon the unfortunate child.

Winn explained that because Merry's burns had been treated with sulfa and lanolin creams, they must be washed off to prevent infection, then she verbally attempted to prepare Merry for the sight that often terrified younger patients: the Hubbard tank. It was a stainless-steel monstrosity, shaped rather like a nine-foot-long four-leaf clover and equipped with a whirlpool. She explained that Merry could lie just as she was, and she and the orderly would attach four hooks to the corners of the rack, then lift her into the pool, rack and all, as if she were cargo being loaded aboard a ship.

But when the hooks were attached, and the motor began hoisting the child, she screamed and reached pathetically for Winn's hand.

"Nooo! Nooo!"

"Stop!" Winn ordered immediately. The fissure in her heart widened, and she took the small hand, ordering the hoist to be lowered again. The thin hand clung. The lashless eyes cried. And Winn wanted to drop to her knees and cry herself. She soothed the child as best she could, rechecked her chart and made a quick decision.

"Have you been able to sit up yet, Merry?"

"They wouldn't let me."

"Just a minute...I have another idea that you'll like better, but I'll be right back." Several minutes later, after receiving an okay from the child's doctor, Winn took Merry instead into a much smaller, less intimidating tub in which the child could sit instead of lie. Merry was strapped into the swivel chair of a device called a Century lift, and upon it was raised over the edge of the stainless-steel tub, then down inside.

When the ninety-eight-degree water touched her skin,

the tiny body, which had had its chemistry so drastically upset, began to shudder violently. Merry howled and broke into tears, and begged to be taken from the tank, but it was necessary to keep her immersed and agitated by the water for a full five minutes.

They were five of the longest of Winnifred Gardner's life.

When they were up, the child was swathed in dry blankets and laid once more upon her rack and gurney to be returned to her room. But as she left, her eyes clung to Winn's, still filled with tears that made Winn wish to bend low and run a soothing hand over the little girl's hair. Only Merry had no hair. It, too, had been burned in the explosion.

When the gurney rolled away, Winn stood in the silent hall, watching the door through which it had disappeared. She sighed deeply, covered her cheeks with both hands and dug her fingertips into her eyes—they were filled with tears. *This is what they warned us about. I mustn't get emotionally involved. I mustn't.* But how was it possible not to feel anger and pity for a child such as Meredith Emery? Ten years old and already facing a trial more painful and defeating than many must face in a full lifetime.

At that moment Mrs. Christianson, the coordinator of P.T., stepped out of her office and paused beside the doorway.

"Winnifred?"

Winn turned around, her face burdened with pain.

"It's the child, isn't it?"

Winn roughly sieved her fingers through her hair. "Yes, it's the child. I'm not sure I can take this one, Sylvia."

"Of course you can. We all can when we have to. But sometimes it helps to discuss the case. We could go to lunch together."

"I think I'll pass today, if it's all right with you. I need something more than food right now."

Winn spent the next hour in the deserted rehab room, riding the stationary bike until her calves burned, then strapping weights onto her ankles and doing extended leg raises until her stomach and neck screamed for her to stop. Next she strapped the weights to her wrists and held them extended straight out from her sides until her facial muscles quivered and her pectoralis major felt ready to snap!

"What are you doing, Gardner?"

Winn dropped her arms and sank to her knees on the floor, panting, too breathless to answer.

Mrs. Christianson entered the gymnasiumlike room and stopped beside the hunkered figure. "No matter how hard you push yourself, you can't make up for it, you know that" came her sympathetic yet firm admonishment. Winn shook her head, still breathless. Her hair flew and stuck to her sweating forehead and cheeks, and she gripped her knees, trying to make sense out of such useless waste as that suffered by Meredith Emery. "The best I can do is offer to put someone else on the case if it gets to you. Will you let me know if it does?"

Winn nodded blindly. But the image of Merry's slim seeking hand lifting to her in entreaty filled the bleak depths of Winn's mind. She'd stick it out. That was the best thing she could do for the little girl.

That afternoon when Merry came back to P.T., Winn began a program of exercises whereby motion would be maintained—a flexion of the chin, rolling of the head, lifting of the arms—to prevent the child's skin from contracting and losing elasticity. She tried her hardest to instill confidence and optimism in Merry, but for the first time in her own career that sense of optimism was lacking in herself. The ten-year-old burn victim faced not only the enormous task of recovering motor movements and learning to live with a great deal of ongoing pain but would need to accept the horrendous fact that her appearance was defaced, then begin working upon the even more difficult assignment of attempting to regain a positive "body image."

At the end of the session Winn felt drained and depressed. How could anyone expect a ten-year-old to do all that?

The day had been one of the first ever when Winn wished to have any other career than the one she had. When she returned home, she immediately called Paul. She needed him equally as bad as Meredith Emery needed a physical therapist—perhaps worse.

"Paul, could you possibly break free to go to a movie or something tonight?"

"Oh, darling, I wish I could, but I've brought Arv home from the office because he's considering going into contract work, and he wanted to try out Rita and see what he thinks of her."

Rita again! Was that all the man could think of? Anger and jealousy immediately surfaced, but Winn bit back the accusation and asked as calmly as she could, "Then, could you make it an early evening with Arv and come over here afterward?"

"Is something wrong, Winnie?"

"Well. . . yes and no."

"What is it, darling?" To his credit he did sound terribly concerned.

"It's a patient at work."

There followed a long pause. "Oh." She heard his hesitation and understood. He never knew what to say to her when she spoke of the unfortunate, the accident victims, the aged, the diseased. These were repugnant to Paul in some odd indefinable way. They were not perfect, and he found it difficult to deal with imperfection of any kind. Paul Hildebrandt coped best when working within a tidy sphere. "Well, just a minute, I'll ask Arv." Again a silence passed, then his voice came again. "Listen, darling, I should be able to get over there in a couple of hours, okay?"

Disappointment welled. "Okay," she said dejectedly, "see you then."

"And Winnie?" He paused, then added, "I love you."

"I love you, too. See you as soon as you can make it."

During those two hours Winn felt trapped in her own house. She simply did *not* want to be alone right now. She considered going over to her mother's but discarded the idea. Somehow her mother always managed to ruffle instead of soothe. She called Sandy but could sense her friend's impatience to get back to whatever she'd been taken from. Winn suggested they meet one day soon for a game of racket ball, but Sandy offered only a vague, "Yeah, sure, maybe this weekend." At the sound of Sandy's distracted voice Winn wondered if perhaps Mick wasn't waiting in bed for his wife to finish her telephone conversation. At the thought she was chagrined, and felt awkward and excluded—from what, she did not know. Perhaps from the charmed circle of those who shared a part of each day with one special person of the opposite sex. If only Paul were here right now. What she needed most was to be held, petted and perhaps made love to . . . slowly, expertly.

Joseph Duggan's face appeared in her mind's eye, and it brought an inexplicable shaft of longing that momentarily overrode her lingering depression over Meredith Emery.

*I wonder if he ever thinks of me. I wonder how he's getting along with his dim vague Perkins hostess. I wonder if, when she needs him, he answers her beck and call, maybe makes love to her slowly, expertly, then cradles her head against his chest and lets her talk it out while lying in his arms.*

Winn put on her sweats and went for a run that nearly dropped her in her tracks, for she'd worked out so strenuously at noon and had been under so much stress all day she was virtually exhausted.

Paul never came. He called at nine-thirty and apologized, and said Arv had stayed later than expected and would Winnie like to talk about it now over the phone?

No, *Winn* definitely would not like to talk about it over the phone. And anyway, her run, her weariness and the five-hour lag time between the two phone calls had helped her overcome the pressing need she'd carried home from the hospital.

BUT IT WAS BACK AFRESH the following day and each day that week as she worked with Merry during her two scheduled therapy sessions. The child was bright, and it was easy to tell she had been very happy before the accident. She spoke of things like ballet class, gymnastics and ten-speed bikes, all of which she'd have to forgo for a long time. One day she said, "Next summer we're going to go to Disneyland." But the following day when Winn checked the child's chart, she read that Merry had had a very bad night. At 2:00 A.M. her breathing had been interrupted, and oxygen had had to be brought in.

Standing with the clipboard braced against her stomach, Winn felt suddenly nauseous. She reread the charted information, and a premonition lifted the fine hairs along her back.

*She's going to die.*

That night when she called Paul, she didn't ask, she *told* him she was coming right over and needed to talk to him. But when she explained about Merry, he quietly encouraged her not to bring her troubles home from work. It's best if you leave the patients at the hospital, darling, he said. Yet when she walked into the house, she'd once again stolen him away from Rita. Winn closed her eyes and huddled against Paul's chest, cinching her arms around his back, wondering if he was moved at all by human plight. Or was he threatened by it? Was that why he could not let it infiltrate his very analytical mind? It could not be data processed. It could not be broken apart and analyzed on a green screen. Thus, perhaps it was beyond his concern.

He asked her if she'd stay that night, but she declined, dreaming up an excuse about it being somebody's birthday at work tomorrow and how she'd baked a cake that still needed frosting before she went to bed tonight.

Back at home she slumped onto the foot of her bed and fell back, supine, staring at the ceiling. She understood fully for the first time why every instructor she'd ever had in her college medicine courses had adamantly badgered their students about the pitfalls of becoming emotionally involved with their patients.

*Not only will it be painful to you, should they die, but if they don't, you must make sure they never grow dependent upon you. The mark of a good therapist is knowing when to withdraw his or her support and make the patient stand alone.*

Her head hurt. Her neck ached. She wished she were at work so she could stretch out on a table and have one of the other therapists give her a massage. She wished she had said yes to Paul's invitation to spend the night. But she'd felt oddly reluctant to sleep beside him after his failure to understand her need for a sympathetic ear and an understanding heart.

The name "Silicon Chip" came back to niggle.

Had Joseph Duggan been right? Was that all Paul Hildebrandt had for feelings—silicon chips?

She wondered, were she to call Joseph, and tell him she needed him, what would his response be? She somehow sensed he'd have the ready store of human compassion her fiancé seemed to lack.

She rolled to her side and curled up in a ball, blanking out the inviting idea of turning to Jo-Jo Duggan.

THE NEXT DAY Merry's chart showed she'd had another difficult night, and during her hydrotherapy session she had another even worse attack. When the child was returned to her room, Winn sought out Dr. Eldrid Childs, Merry's attending physician. She found him on the fourth floor, making rounds.

"It's about Meredith Emery, doctor," she explained.

"You're her therapist, aren't you?" The intelligent eyes met hers directly.

Winn nodded, then asked softly, "She's going to die, isn't she?"

He studied her silently, tapped the palm of one hand with the fingers of his other, then took her arm and walked her idly along the hall. "Yes, it looks that way. This morning it was more than a lung that failed. It was her kidneys." So often with explosion victims it was not the burns that got them but the resultant damage to vital organs that didn't always show up immediately.

Winn's eyes slid shut, and she struggled to keep from crying. *Next summer we're going to Disneyland.* She gulped at the lump in her throat, but it could not be swallowed away.

"You're involved in this one, huh?"

She nodded, keeping her eyes tightly closed. They were no longer walking.

"Sometimes we're wrong, Gardner. Sometimes they fool us."

She opened her eyes. He seemed to be swimming in a white lake of milk. "Yeah . . ." she grunted thickly. "Yeah, sure."

WHEN HER SHIFT ENDED at 3:00 P.M., she faced her empty town house with the heaviest heart she'd ever borne. The child's eyes seemed to be staring at her from the bouquet of milkweed pods given her in a different time by another patient, but one who'd recovered.

She called Sandy's house, knowing perfectly well her friend was still at work, but thinking just by chance, if she'd stayed home today, the two of them could have a game of racket ball.

God, she needed to pound something, beat something, lash out and get even!

The house haunted. Outside it was spring, the season

of renewed life, with robins nesting, angleworms squiggling and ants building doughnuts of sand. May was here. Trees were bursting with bloom.

Winn needed to be out there where the air was ripe with the promise of summer. She got in the car and drove. Unconsciously. Not caring where she went or whether she held up impatient drivers behind her. She was in an insulated bubble where hurt was temporarily held in abeyance.

She left Brooklyn Park behind and headed into the farm country north of the suburb, where farmers were planting their vast potato fields, and children were riding their bicycles in the driveways in the balmy late afternoon. She turned west off Douglas Drive and headed toward the old-fashioned water tower that lifted into the skyline ahead. Several minutes later she entered the quaint town of Osseo—population 2,906—by one of its lesser-used streets. Winn let her nose lead her, up one avenue and down another, searching for some sign she'd recognize, though she didn't know where it was or even if the business had a sign.

She found it on Second Avenue, two blocks off the main street of town, beside a gravel alley with grass beginning to sprout up its middle. It was a square brick building with old-fashioned double wood doors beside a windowless service door, and the sign said Duggan's Body Shop.

She stepped inside and found herself in a reception area of sorts, if it could be elevated to such a title. There was a desk made of oak, far older than his Haynes, and a nondescript pair of wooden chairs, a file cabinet, telephone and refrigerator, also very ancient, with rounded instead of squared corners. On the far side of the room an open doorway led to the shop beyond, and from it came the *screel* of an electric sander upon metal and the sound of someone whistling along as a country station played a Waylon Jennings song.

She stepped to the open doorway. The body shop had a cavernous ceiling, grease-stained concrete floors and a single line of windows up eight feet off the floor, plus another matching row at eye level across the dated double doors.

A man was leaning over at the waist, running the sander along the flank of an orangy-colored fender on a navy blue car. Two others were bending over another hoodless car, peering at its engine. Above them dangled a set of enormous chains with hooks at the ends, attached to the arm of a monstrosity that looked as if it might drop on their heads at any moment. The man on the left lifted his head, spied Winn and came over immediately, wiping his hands on a stained blue rag.

"Hi." His smile was Joseph's, but his eyes weren't nearly as pretty. "What can I do for you?" The rear end of the man she thought was Joseph was still protruding from the dismantled car.

"Is Joseph here?"

"Sure." He turned and bellowed over his shoulder. "Hey, Jo-Jo, somebody to see ya."

But Waylon was singing louder than Joseph's brother, and the sander was still whining. Brother Duggan crossed toward the bending figure in the washed-out blue jeans and called again, "Hey, Jo-Jo, there's a lady here to see you."

Joseph straightened halfway and looked over his shoulder. Winn's heart seemed to swell and thud while an awful constriction squeezed her chest. He straightened the remainder of the way very, very slowly, reaching blindly for a shop rag without taking his eyes from her. As he crossed the greasy floor, his smile grew broader with each step. Three feet before her, he stopped, wiping his hands. "Well, hello."

She had forgotten the magnetism of his incredible smile. "Hello, Joseph." Her heart was hammering so wildly it was difficult to speak in her customary tone of voice.

"What brings you to the thriving metropolis of Osseo?"

"Am I interrupting something important?"

"No. We're just jerking an engine. One's just like all the rest. It can wait." He shrugged and tossed the shop rag aside. He was dressed in filthy blue jeans and a soiled blue chambray shirt, a pair of boots that might have been those she'd seen in his living room. His hands were black and the nails lined with grease. He looked every bit as inviting as he had in his tux and ruffles.

"I probably should have called first, but I didn't really plan to stop here. I was just out driving and. . . ." She grew terribly self-conscious and gestured vaguely with one hand.

He glanced toward the windows in the double doors. "You got car troubles or something?"

"No. I just wanted to talk to you. I thought maybe you could play a game of racket ball. . . or go out for a cup of coffee or. . . or something," she finished lamely.

He reached for her elbow, glanced at his dirty hand and thought better of it. With a jerk of his head he ordered her to follow. "Hey, John, tell Tommy to turn that sander off. There's somebody I want you to meet."

When she hesitated, Joseph turned, held out a hand as if to take her elbow, but didn't. His brothers came forward, and she saw again the sharp resemblance to Joseph in Tommy's smile. It was there in John's, too, that same contagiousness. "This is the lady I told you about, the one I walked down the aisle with, Winn Gardner." Jo-Jo smiled at her while going on, "And these are my kid brothers, Tommy and John."

She extended her hand, realized too late it was the wrong thing to do, but kept it where it was while Tommy glanced at it, said, "Hi, Winn" and finally with a crooked smile grasped hers in his greasy hold before John did likewise.

"Hey, Jo-Jo, she's all right," Tommy approved.

"Damn right she's all right. But wipe the leer off your face, brother. She's spoken for, as I also told you." Without pause he informed them, "I'm gonna knock off for the day, but you two get that cherry picker on this engine and get 'er hoisted up, then check to find out if those kingpins and bushing are in. If they've got 'em, leave a note on the kitchen table so I can pick 'em up in the morning. I might be late." Then he turned to Winn and said, "Let's go."

It had taken him less than three minutes to give the remainder of the day to her.

Outside he said, "Well, this is a surprise."

"For me, too."

"You and old Hildegard have a fight or something?"

"No, not a fight." She glanced at him askance. "But something."

He glanced at her car, parked at the curb. "I walk to work, since it's only a few blocks. Do you mind driving so we can stop by the house and I can wash up and get my sweats and racket?"

"Get in."

He craned around to check his backside, then grinned at her across the hood of the car. "My front side usually gets dirtier than my back, so I shouldn't get your car seat dirty."

They had just climbed in and slammed their doors when a rotund man came walking down the sidewalk, raised a hand and called, "Hey, Joey!"

Joseph turned, then smiled and hooked an armpit over the window ledge. "Hiya, pa, what's up?"

From her side of the car Winn saw the man bend down, then in the window appeared a smiling face beneath a cap advertising "John Deere." Into Joseph's lap he tossed a knotted plastic bag.

"Your mother says the rhubarb is ripe and sent me over to bring you some. And who's this pretty little thing?" His face was merry as he smiled at Winn, and she understood from whom Joseph inherited his charm.

Joseph awarded her a proud smile, informing his father, "This is Winn Gardner, the lady I met at Mick's wedding. Remember I told you about her?"

"Oh, *she's* the one!" Mr. Duggan doffed his cap. "Well, nice to meet you, Winn. I'm Joey's dad." He thrust his hand across the front seat and shook hers.

"Nice to meet you, too, Mr. Duggan."

"You takin' off for the day?" he asked Joseph.

"Yeah, but the boys are inside."

"Guess I'll go in and say hello and tell 'em ma sent the rhubarb."

When he was gone, Winn's eyes dropped to the bag of pink and green fruit, then lifted to Joseph's face. He smiled and hefted the bag. "Ma thinks we don't eat right since we moved out, and she keeps sending over our favorites."

"They live close to you?"

"Yeah, right here in town. Pa works at the hardware store, ma raises gardens and thinks she's still got to baby her boys." But he chuckled good-naturedly and for a moment Winn envied him his very ordinary, but obviously caring family. There were more questions she wanted to ask about them, but while she drove, Jo-Jo changed the subject. She felt his eyes on her as he commented, "I never thought I'd see you again. At least, not one on one."

"I've had one of those days we'd all like to forget, and I needed something to take my mind off it. I tried calling Sandy, but she's still at work, and Paul was too, and my mother." She clutched the steering wheel and refrained from turning to look at him. "I'm probably out of line, turning to you, but I was just driving and there was Osseo in front of me, and I thought of you and wanted. . .to. . .well. . . ." Words finally failed and, anyway, explanations seemed suddenly phony.

"I'm glad," he said quietly, and pointed to a white

house with red shingles and trim. "That's it." She'd never seen it in daylight before. It was quaint and farm-like, and very much a grandma's house.

Inside, it was just as she remembered, except the kitchen stove had been cursorily cleaned, and the Dutch oven was nowhere in sight. The ivy hung in the west window above the kitchen sink, and the little red plastic clock read three-fifty-five. There was a bag of Taystee bread on the kitchen counter and a cluster of green grapes in the middle of the porcelain-topped table, not even in a bowl, just lying there with half their stems denuded.

The room was ugly. Homey. She loved it. From the red dotted Swiss curtains that had probably been hanging limply since years before his grandmother died, to the worn-off spots in the linoleum where she had undoubtedly stood while preparing hundreds of meals, Winn loved it all.

Jo-Jo uncapped a jar and took up a handful of something that looked like cold cream and began rubbing it into his hands. He turned on the kitchen faucet and scrubbed first his knuckles, then his nails with a small orange brush. She stood behind him, watching his blue shirt stretch tightly over his shoulders as he worked over the old-style double-width sink that had no divider, but a drain board off to one side.

He leaned down, opened a cabinet door and retrieved a square yellow plastic dishpan, then began filling it with water.

Glancing over his shoulder, he invited, "Listen, if you'd rather wait in the living room, make yourself at home. I'm gonna wash up here quick and get rid of most of the grease smell, anyway."

He turned to face the window while one-handedly unbuttoning the dirty blue shirt. He stripped it off and flung it across the cabinet top. Picking up a bar of soap, he bent forward and began scrubbing his face, neck, arms, armpits and stomach. He went at it as if in a great hurry and wasted no time being gentle with his own hide.

She stood in the archway leading to the living room, watching. When he leaned over the dishpan, the white elastic of his shorts peeped from beneath the waistband of his blue jeans. She caught a glimpse of hair under his arms and watched in fascination as the curls at the back of his neck grew wet and changed to a darker color. He turned on the water, cupped his hands and clapped them to his face about five times, snorting into the water to keep it from getting up his nostrils. It was like watching a dog charge out of a river and shake himself. Water flew everywhere, up onto the red curtains, across the faded gray linoleum lining the top of the cabinets and onto his dirty shirt there.

He straightened, groped beside his right hip for a towel that was strung through one of the drawer pulls and stood erect while beginning to dry his face.

When he turned, the towel was still covering his chin and jaws. He stopped dead, staring at her from above the towel. The pause was electric. Two droplets slid off his elbows, then he went on briskly toweling his arms and stomach. "Oh, I didn't know you were still standing there." His eyes followed his hands, and so did hers. She noted the thick brown hair that covered his chest, the hard tough muscles, upper arms that had hourglass dips halfway to the elbow. "I said you could go wait in the living room. I got a new print of a 1920 Essex, but I ran out of room to hang it on the wall. It's leaning beside the davenport. Tell me what you think."

What she thought was that any woman who'd prefer looking at a 1920 Essex to Jo-Jo Duggan washing up would be an utter fool! The scent of Ivory soap was everywhere in the kitchen, and that other curiously lye-like aroma she'd detected about him the first night—she took it to be the solvent with which he washed his mechanic's hands.

It suddenly struck her that she'd run to Jo-Jo Duggan for more than one reason. He had been on her mind ever since she'd met him, and to deny it would be worse folly than marrying a man to whom she was not well suited.

She was studying the Essex when he clattered up the wooden steps that led off the end of the room just beside the kitchen archway. As he took the stairs two at a time, he called back, "Where'd you have in mind to play racket ball?"

"Either my club or yours," she called back, casting her eyes about his living room, noting a tablet with some numbers scrawled on it, two old limp sofa pillows, two empty cans of Schlitz beer, a discarded white T-shirt—bits and pieces of Jo-Jo Duggan's life, the life of a simple workingman.

"Then let's go out to Daytona. I feel in the mood for the ride."

He clattered back down the steps and appeared in the doorway with a navy blue duffel, his racket slipped into a sleeve upon its side. He wore a red jogging suit with a white stripe down each leg and each sleeve, white socks, and had his Adidas in his hand.

Her heart went off like a rocket.

"Let's go." He dazzled her with that high-voltage smile. "I'm all yours."

She had the crazy exhilarating feeling that he was. Or that he could be whenever she said the word.

# 7

DAYTONA WAS a modest golf, tennis and racket-ball club nestled in the hills near a tiny village named Dayton, a scant half-hour ride west of Osseo. Old Highway 52 that led to it was once a major westbound thoroughfare, but since the interstate had been built, it lazed in somnolence, its signs disappearing, its shoulders clothed in woods and grassland, dotted with cows and corncribs.

The afternoon sun lighted the hills to fresh spring green and reflected from the shimmering road surface. The air was fragrant. It was lilac time. Apple trees and wild plums were at their peak of blossom. The fragrant warmth of the spring day rejuvenated Winn's spirit. Bouncing along beside Joseph on the ancient cracked seat of an old pickup truck, she was loath to bring up the subject that had so disturbed her earlier in the day. It was too pleasant, too peaceful riding with Joseph, listening to some old Jim Reeves song—it seemed he was always surrounded by vintage of one sort or another—with the wind blowing in the lowered window, gently lifting the hair on her arm.

Winn sunk low, wedged a knee against the glove-compartment door and let her eyes sink closed. Joseph glanced at her lazy pose but said nothing. She had not brought up whatever it was she wanted to talk about, and that was fine with him. She looked sensational in the mint green jogging suit she'd produced when they detoured to her house. She was slumped low with her nape catching the top of the seat, hair loose and messed, and the breeze from the open window occasionally billowing it. As he studied her, a spirited gust caught a strand and whipped it across her lips. Without opening her eyes she hooked it with the crook of a little finger and pulled it aside. Immediately it blew back and she spit it out, then threaded it behind her ear.

Her eyes opened, and she indolently turned her head to find he'd been watching her. He smiled. She smiled back. Neither spoke as he drove on as before, with a wrist hooked languidly over the wheel, softly whistling "Four Walls" between his teeth.

At that moment Winn discovered something very wonderful: she could comfortably share silence with Joseph Duggan. There were at least a dozen men she knew, including Paul, who'd be chattering away a mile a minute. How pleasing it was to be with one today who was content to smile and whistle softly between his teeth, and let the true mellow voice of Jim Reeves do all the speaking.

Jo-Jo wondered what it was that was bothering her but decided not to probe. She'd get around to it whenever she was good and ready. In the meantime he was doing what he'd wondered if he'd ever have the chance to do again, what had kept him from readily falling asleep many nights since the wedding: he was simply being with her.

They passed Diamond Lake and soon turned the clattery old Chevrolet between two giant boulders, then rolled up the long gravel approach to the clubhouse that sat at the top of a hill. The golf links were verdant. Into the window came the smell of newly cut grass and fresh-turned loam from adjacent farms. On the club land itself were the ancient barn and farmhouse of those who'd owned the land previously.

When Jo-Jo and Winn stepped from the truck and slammed their doors, something fell off underneath it.

"Oops," he said with a slanting grin. "This old heap isn't in quite as good a shape as the Haynes."

"I wasn't going to ask where the Haynes was." Winn came around the truck to find him on one knee, bracing his palms on the gravel and peering underneath the truck's belly.

"This is my everydayer. New cars really don't do it for me. I like the old ones." He reached beneath the truck and withdrew a piece of tail pipe. "They've got character."

As he straightened, he was still grinning. She smiled down at the rusted hunk of metal in his hand. "This one's character is a little loose, wouldn't you say?"

He tossed the piece onto the bed of the truck, clapped a rounded rear fender as if it were the flank of a horse, brushed off his palms and took her elbow. "I love her just the same."

But he was looking into Winn's eyes as he made the comment, and because his crinkle-eyed smile made her so very, very happy, and because his intentional double meaning made her far too giddy, she turned her eyes to the clubhouse as they approached.

Inside they passed a dining room with a field-rock fireplace in its center, and the bar where he'd brought Sandy when the groomsmen had stolen her. After Joseph signed them in at the desk, they parted to go to the locker rooms and check their tote bags.

He was waiting in the hall outside court number two, leaning back with one rubber sole against the wall, repeatedly flipping and catching a can of balls. As she walked toward him, he turned, and the can stopped doing cartwheels. He seemed to have forgotten he held it. His eyes made a quick scan of her length, and he slowly drew his hips away from the wall and smiled.

When she stood close before him, he grinned and said, "Wow" in a soft way that made her blush.

She had a healthy curiosity about his bared limbs, too, but felt it prudent to refrain from ogling. Once inside the racket-ball court, however, with the door closed behind them, there was ample opportunity for more than surreptitious glances without being detected. Assessing each other was almost unavoidable.

The court was a brightly lighted cell with a twenty-foot ceiling, poured-concrete walls, and a twenty-by-forty-foot hardwood floor. It was stark, bare and echoing. Every sound within it became amplified. As Joseph idly bounced the ball, it gave off an audible ping while expanding to its original shape. When he spoke, his voice seemed to reverberate from the walls.

"A little warm-up first?" He tugged on a short white leather glove.

"Yes. I haven't played for a good four weeks. I'll need it."

They looped cord handles around their wrists, spun them to take up the slack and gripped their rackets.

"Why four weeks?" he asked, bouncing a royal blue ball with his racket.

"Nobody to play with lately."

"How about Silicon Chip?"

"He's done it occasionally to please me. But I told you, he doesn't much care for sweat."

Joseph snatched the ball from the air, studied her expressionlessly for a moment, then turned away to face the front wall. Across the center of the court ran two parallel red lines five feet apart: the serving area. They stood just behind it as Joseph sent the ball bouncing off the front wall, giving her a direct easy return. Between them they made a total of eleven good returns before Winn missed.

She retrieved the ball and bounced it to him. As he nonchalantly juggled it above his head, bouncing it off the racket, he said, "You're pretty good, huh?"

"Good enough," she replied honestly. "But I haven't played against many men. You guys usually have the edge on power."

He turned away to the front again. "We'll see."

This time he gave her a more difficult serve, angling it so she had to cross behind him to return it from near the back wall. He didn't have time to turn around and watch her form before the ball sailed over his head and against the right sidewall. Then they concentrated on a volley of shots that lasted longer than the first. This time he missed.

She flicked the rolling ball up with the tip of her racket and gave him an impertinent grin. "You're pretty good, huh?"

"Damn right. And I don't give no quarter to no woman." His brown eyes danced mischievously.

"That's the way I like it."

"Volley?" he suggested.

"You're on."

She won the right to first serve, and as she walked to the red lines, his eyes skimmed down her lanky legs. With each step the muscles hardened and squared, but when she stood at ease, her limbs were shapely and feminine. She wore mint green athletic-style shorts trimmed with white cord around the notched legs. Her tank top was white and showed him the true spareness of the flesh across her ribs, for he'd never seen her in anything conforming before. Her tennis shoes were white with sturdy wedged soles, and as his eyes traveled down to them, he admired the shadows where her ankle tendons dove down into the shoes behind tiny white tassels.

Her first serve came whizzing off to his left, and he missed it completely. As a matter of fact, he moved a full second too late: he'd been engrossed with her shapely ankles.

She turned with a hand on her hip. "Hey, you awake back there?"

"Yeah. Yeah. . .give me another one."

She took three points before he executed a faultless roll-out shot, where the ball hit both floor and front wall at once, then rolled toward them as docilely as if a baby had pushed it with his chubby hands.

Winn swiveled to face Jo-Jo, raised one eyebrow and cooed, "*Whooo-eee.* The man gets serious."

"And the woman loses the serve."

He now stood where she had, and Winn was the curious one. He wore white tennis-style shorts and a disreputable looking T-shirt of navy blue that said Dick's Bar on the back and looked as if it had been relieved of its sleeves and bottom half by somebody's dull hedge trimmer. The crudely slashed fabric curled back on his shoulders, and the armholes sagged halfway down his ribs. Six inches of bare stomach showed between navy shirt and white shorts, and it was remarkably tan for May, as were his sinewy legs above the calf-high socks. She was staring at the socks, one with a gold stripe around its top, the other with a purple, when his serve careered past her head. She completely ignored it and burst out laughing.

"Now who's asleep?"

"No fair, your socks broke me up!" Her laughter resounded from the walls.

He rolled onto his heels, bringing his toes off the floor, and perused his hairy legs. "What's the matter with them?"

"They don't match!" She was still laughing.

"Naw, they never do. Not in a house where three men do their own laundry. *Clean* will do—*matched* we don't need." He grinned up at her. "You ready to get serious now and stop laughing at my laundry?"

"Hit it," she returned.

They threw their total effort into racket ball then, and before the serve had changed twice, they'd quite forgotten to ogle each other. They were immersed in competition, concentrating on the reaching, running, reflexive joy of rivalry. They were well matched, and if physically Joseph had the edge, she was perhaps the more accurate shot. When he gained a point by charging up on a dying pigeon and slamming it off the back wall, she came back with a placement shot so deadly he missed it even after a belly dive. His legs were four inches longer, but hers were quicker. He'd perfected the difficult ceiling shot, and she missed it every time after it caromed from ceiling to front wall to floor, then always beyond her reach. But she had a keen feel for successfully sprinting to meet the ball a mere five feet before the front wall and softly finessing it so it dropped softly, two feet from the wall and fell dead, leaving Joseph no chance to charge forward and save the point.

They reveled in the exhilaration of pushing their bodies to great physical limits. The acoustical room was filled with the high magnified squeaks of their rubber soles on the hardwood floors, the slap of the ball, their grunts—and sometimes groans—and occasionally the clatter of a racket against concrete. They stretched their tensile limbs to their limits. They strained their bodies for the simple reward of beating the ball. They smashed and drove and sometimes watched a shot arcing over their heads, not knowing till the final second whether it would reach the back wall or fall that agonizing three inches from it. Their shirts became soaked and their limbs sheeny. His hair became curlier, and hers stringier. They smiled, teased, cried "I told you so" and sometimes, "Damn you!"

And he took the game 24–23.

They fell to their backs in the middle of the backcourt, panting, heaving, closing their eyes against the white fluorescent glare of caged lights overhead. Star bursts danced before their lids. Their hearts pounded against the cool boards beneath their shoulders. Their legs stuck to the floor. Their weary arms flopped straight out to the side, lifeless. They were in heaven.

He rolled his head to look at her. She was five feet away, but her lax fingers almost touched his.

"Hey, Gardner." She opened one eye and peeked at him. "You're good."

"So're you. But next time I'm gonna whip you, boy."

His laughter bounced off the walls like a well-executed Z-serve.

"My pleasure," he offered, then closed his eyes and rested again. A minute of pure silence passed. Their breathing was less labored. She pulled her shirt up, exposing her stomach, and rested a hand on it. He flexed a knee.

"Oh, God, I needed this." Her quiet admission whispered three times as it came back to them.

He rolled his head to look at her again. "Why?"

Meredith Emery came into her mind's eye. "Oh, Joseph, I've done the worst thing it's possible for a physical therapist to do. I've become empathetically involved with one of my patients."

"Who?" He studied her profile as she stared up at the overhead lights.

"Her name is Meredith Emery, and she's ten years old." He saw her swallow. "And she's the victim of an explosion."

Joseph hadn't guessed physical therapists worked with burn patients, and though he wanted to question her about it, he wisely kept silent.

"She has these enormous brown eyes that . . . that have no eyelashes anymore and no eyebrows, either. And her face has been scarred, and she's bald now. But she showed me her school picture when she had beautiful black hair down past her shoulders." She paused, took a deep gulp of air and went on. "She studied ballet and was a gymnast, too, and now she can't even touch her ear to her shoulder because her skin has lost so much elasticity she has to wear a splint to hold her chin up." A tear formed in Winn's eye and ran from its corner down her temple, disappearing within the droplets of perspiration already there.

Joseph inched nearer and took her outflung hand. She grasped his fingers so tightly his ring cut in almost painfully. Her ragged voice went on. "And next summer her family is all going to Disneyland...and...and...." Suddenly Winn flung a forearm across her eyes and released one gulping sob that echoed from the high bright ceiling.

Joseph rolled to one hip and braced beside her on an elbow. "And?"

"And sh-she won't be g-going along b-because she's going to die." Winn began sobbing unrestrainedly then and attempted to roll away from Joseph, but he clasped her shoulder to keep her on her back.

"Winn...oh, Winn." He lifted her to a sitting position—they were hip to hip, facing each other—and wrapped his arms around her, cradling her against his chest, cupping the back of her damp hair while she clung to him and cried.

"Oh, J-Joseph, sometimes I d-don't understand why."

"I wish I could tell you, but I can't find any reason for the waste, either." He pressed her hair hard, contouring the back of her head. "God...only ten years old." He, too, sounded choked up.

"And she's b-been through such hell already. Pain and scars, and...and sh-she still fights with me when I tell her to—sh-she doesn't know that all the physical therapy is f-for nothing because she'll never l-live to see her limbs m-move as they did on the p-parallel bars." He kissed the side of her skull, then patted her back, feeling the pitiful heaving of her chest against his.

"Do her mother and father know?"

"I don't know. Her kidneys just failed today."

"What are they like? Do they love her a lot?"

"Oh, yes. She adores her mother and...and beams all over wh-when she talks about her father. At least her eyes look like they're beaming, but it's an...an awful sight when they don't have any lashes."

Joseph leaned back, grasped her temples in both hands and repeatedly pushed the hair back from her face, searching her eyes. "Maybe that's what it's all about...love. She had love, and she gave it, so her life wasn't for nothing, was it?"

Winn's eyes swam with tears. The skin beneath them was wet and shiny as he rested his thumbs there. Oh, God, she thought, why couldn't Paul have been this way when I needed him?

"Do you think so, Joseph?" She sat as still as the walls around them. He gazed into her sad wet eyes with their lashes stuck together, then lifted his gaze to her tawny hair and gently brought her forehead to his lips.

Meeting her eyes again, he assured Winn, "Yes, I think so. There's got to be a reason for all of this, and if it's not love, what else could there possibly be? You love her, too, and because you do, you needed to cry and so you came to me. And I think I could very easily fall in love with you. Maybe that's the reason...to bring us together."

"Joseph, you mustn't say that." Her voice was quiet, unchiding, as she probed his dark brown eyes with her troubled blue ones.

"But it's true."

"But there's still Paul."

"Yes...Paul." The pressure on her jaws increased as Joseph held her prisoner with his hands and eyes. "And why aren't you with him right now, crying on *his* shoulder? He's the one who should be comforting you at a time like this."

She pulled away and drew her knees up, looping them with both arms. "Paul has a hard time dealing with the fact of death or even disease. He sees perfection as the ultimate, I guess. The imperfect bodies I work with put him off, and he's uncomfortable talking about them."

"Did he try...this time?"

"He...I...no. I told you, he wasn't home when I

tried to reach him. But when I first got Merry as a patient, I was upset one night and called him then."

"And what did he do?"

"We talked a little bit about it."

"Did he come over?"

She flashed him a warning glance. "Don't judge him, Joseph. He has his own qualities. They may be different from yours or mine, but he has them just the same."

"Such as?"

"Such as his supreme intelligence, his analytical mind, his. . .his tenacity. I mean, when Paul makes up his mind to do something, he does it, if it takes him a month or a year, he does it."

"Such as providing you with a house and furniture?"

"Exactly. I'm the one at fault for wishing he'd—"

"Cut it out, Winn!" he snapped.

"Cut *what* out?" she snapped back.

"Rationalizing about your relationship with him. It stinks and you know it."

"It does not stink! We get along wonderfully!"

"Oh, sure. That's why you came running to me instead of to him today. From what you tell me about him, he must have silicon chips for emotions!"

Her face colored deeply. "You're overstepping, Joseph."

"I'm pointing out what you already know but refuse to admit. The two of you have nothing in common except some goddam house *he*'s living in without you! If you were engaged to me, I wouldn't be letting you flirt around with other men at wedding dances."

"I didn't—" But Joseph forged ahead.

"And your birth-control pills would be sitting in *my* bedroom. And your panty hose would be lying on *my* bedroom floor beside my jockstrap after we ended up every day with a rousing game of racket ball like the one we just played."

She tried jumping to her feet, but he grabbed her wrist and held her where she was.

"Winn, sit still!" he ordered, refusing to release her. "How in blazes did you ever end up with somebody like him in the first place?"

She simmered for a long time while their eyes locked angrily. Her wrist strained against his grip, and at the precise moment she wrenched it free, she spit, "My mother!"

His eyes widened in surprise. "Your *what*?"

"My mother introduced me to him." Winn dropped her eyes, uncomfortable with the admission.

"Go on."

"He was teaching a class on computers that she took, and the two of them discovered this great common interest in COBOL and FORTRAN."

He screwed up his face. "What?"

She waved an impatient hand. "Oh, those are some high-level computer languages. Anyway, she told me she'd met this wonderful man." Winn stopped and shrugged.

"Then why didn't she marry him instead of you?"

Winn stiffened. The corners of her mouth pulled down, and she glared at Joseph. How unflinchingly he hit upon her most vulnerable spot. How many times had she submerged the very thought, believing it too touchy to allow herself to think, much less voice!

"I don't think that's funny, Joseph."

"Why? Did I hit a nerve?"

"The nerve here is yours, and you're displaying plenty of it."

"It's nothing to be ashamed of. You wouldn't be the first woman who agreed to marry somebody because he was her parents' choice."

"That's not why I'm marrying him," she claimed, perhaps a little too emphatically.

"Then why are you? Did he sweep you off your feet—sexually?" Her mouth puckered tighter. He drove on, "Well, it's sure obvious you didn't fall for him because he shared your interests. Or your goals or your tastes! You've already told me enough about him to know you're like steam and he's like ice. They may both be made of the same element, but that doesn't mean they're anything alike, Winn, and you know it."

She crossed her forearms on her knees and dropped her forehead onto them. "I didn't come here so you could make me feel worse than I already did, but somehow you're managing it."

"I'm sorry, Winn." He rested a hand on her slumped shoulder, but she shrugged it away. "I didn't mean to make you upset, but so far the only thing I can name that the two of you do well together is dance, and he leaves you behind to do that with me? I should think you'd be the one picking out these gaping holes in your relationship, not me."

She raised her head wearily. "Don't you understand? Our wedding is only six weeks away."

His eyes pierced through her. "Yeah. Scary, isn't it?"

Winn did leap to her feet then and leaned over angrily to scoop the blue ball off the floor. She began bouncing it vehemently with the racket while presenting her rigid back. "Do you want to play another game or not?"

He glared at her shapely back, her erect shoulders and the irritation she displayed as she whapped the ball. He grew more than irritated. He was frustrated and angry that she refused to explore the mistake she was making in her choice of men just because of a few social commitments.

"You bet I do. And we'll see who whips who." She was standing in the serving lane when his answer bit the air just behind her shoulder. Then he went on, "I won the first match, Gardner. The serve is mine."

She felt properly chastised and not a little embarrassed. There were men who extended the courtesy of always letting ladies serve first. It had always peeved Winn. She'd win on her own merits or not at all. How dare Joseph Duggan imply that she was trying to grab an unearned advantage!

Wordlessly she retreated to the backcourt, leaving the serving lane to him. When the first ball came, it whistled off three surfaces before she reached it just in the nick of time. The volley was long and exhausting, and he took the point. Her ego was definitely stung, for she'd tried her hardest to take the initial point after their argument. As he bounced the ball preparatory to serving, she held her racket in a position that definitely stated, "Attack," leaning forward from the waist, rocking her hips from side to side, intensity written on every muscle of her face and stance.

The longer the game went, the better they both played. They were neck and neck at fifteen, and her lungs felt ready to explode. She felt a slight cramp in her right foot but shook it off, promising herself Joseph Duggan would lose this game, come hell or high water.

He slammed a power shot off the back wall, and she missed it.

She executed a beautiful pass shot and left him standing on the opposite side of the court from where the ball rebounded.

At nineteen all, the sweat was running down their legs, backs and bellies. Her bra was soaked, and the band of her shorts stuck to her skin. His shirt—what there was of it—was so dark with sweat she wondered why he bothered to pull at its shoulder to swab his forehead.

She served a deadly one that struck with the speed of a copperhead and took point twenty to tie him.

On his next attack he reached and leaped at a scorcher skimming no farther than a quarter inch away from the wall. But in his intensity he grew careless, leaped too hard and hit the concrete, then bounced off and landed with a thick thud, flat on his back.

He winced, bared his teeth, grabbed his right knee and rolled back and forth, sucking air.

She dropped her racket and ran, falling to her knees beside him. "Joseph, I'm sorry. Oh, Judas, what is it? Is it your knee? Here, let me see."

He rolled and winced all the more.

"Joseph, let go. See if you can straighten it."

He felt her fingers on his arm and forced himself to lie back, releasing the knee and leaving it flexed while his foot rested on the floor. Her hands grasped the backside of his calf, then one of them eased over his shinbone, forcing him to straighten his leg. He gasped and arched his chest higher. She laid the leg on the cool floor, touched it exploringly here, there, there, there. She made him work it back and forth, gently probing the muscles, the kneecap.

His initial shot of pain eased slightly. "Well, what do you think, doc?" he asked.

"I think we'd better get some ice on it right away and, depending on how it feels within the next hour, have it X-rayed."

She stood up, reached a hand down to help him. "Can you use it?" He could, but he limped. She wrapped his arm around her shoulder and together they hobbled back to the dressing rooms.

"If you shower, use cool water, not hot, and I'll meet you back here as quick as you can make it." He'd already pushed open the locker-room door. "And Joseph?" He stepped and looked back over his shoulder. "I really am sorry."

"It's not your fault, Winn. I was playing stupidly, with all body and no brains. I deserved it."

She thought it best if he didn't drive the truck because it had a floor shift, and until they found out how serious his injury was, the leg definitely shouldn't be strained. She stalled the old rattletrap three times before she'd even managed to back it out of its parking space. It chortled and chugged and nearly snapped their necks when she shifted from first to second.

But it made Joseph laugh. And when she heard him laugh, she was so relieved, she laughed, too. She talked him into letting her take him to North Memorial Medical Center, even though he said he didn't want to check into any emergency ward.

"All right, then I have another plan. But we'll have to sneak to do it."

"Sneak?"

"Into P.T.—it should be deserted at this time of night—and we'll put an ice pack on your knee and wait to see if you think you need the X ray."

"Why should you have to sneak when you work there?"

"Because I could get fired if we get caught. The hospital is liable if you're using their facilities, and unless you're officially admitted, they have no legal recourse if something happens to you on our equipment. But it won't. I'll see to it."

"But what if you get caught?"

She angled him a devilish corner-of-the-lip grin. "You'll be indebted to me for life."

A SHORT TIME LATER they pulled up before the Abbott Street entrance, a back door used for patient pickup, which was deserted now at 7:00 P.M. and also was the closest route to Physical Medicine.

Just before Winn got out of the truck, Joseph reached out to lay his palm on the seat beside her. "Winn?"

She stopped and turned to him.

"I'm sorry. You were right. I overstepped."

Judas, but the man had eyes she couldn't get enough of. "We'll see," she answered cryptically, then the truck door slammed behind her.

It was quiet and dark in the rehabilitation room, and he stood in the doorway, interested in its every fixture simply because it belonged to her world, and he wanted to know as much about it and her as possible.

The room was like a narrow gymnasium with ceiling-to-floor windows at one end. Along the walls were various pieces of exercise equipment lined up: two sets of portable wooden stairs with handrails, two stationary bicycles, a refrigerator-freezer, low tables topped with blue mats, more mats on the floor and various ordinary wooden chairs.

She led the way to the far left end of the room. "Sit here," she ordered, "on the table." It was scarcely knee height and easy to fall back upon. She stood beside him and ordered him to stretch out on his back. He clasped his head as if about to do sit-ups and looked along his trunk to watch her untie and remove his tennis shoe, then the clean sock he'd put on only a half hour ago. He wore the red jogging suit again. He had six-inch zippers up each ankle. She slid the right one up, then pushed the pant leg past his knee until it drew tight around his thick thigh and stayed there.

Whatever he'd done, he'd done to the muscles just below his knee, and as she surrounded them with competent hands, she gently probed and tested.

"Relax," she ordered, "You're all tensed up with your head raised like that. I'm not going to hurt you."

He fell back flat and answered all her questions, telling her what each touch felt like. Her fingers were gentle and her palms soft as she explored the muscles below the knee, then the knee itself, and finally worked her way up his thigh, probing. He tried to concentrate on the discomfort, because her hand felt so good, and because he was having difficulty disassociating the therapist from the woman. Her hands skimmed over the hair-roughened surface of his leg all the way to the top of his thigh.

At last, when he thought he was in mortal danger from the wonderful feeling of her hands upon him, she dropped them. "It's not a hamstring, and it's not a knee. I think it's your triceps surae."

"My what?"

"Triceps surae, the muscles found in the lower leg. You may have pulled one or more when you fell after hitting the wall."

"How can you tell?"

"Three things. Pain, heat—it's hot right here. . . ." She touched a sensitive spot lightly. "And swelling. You've got all three." She crossed to the refrigerator while he lay thinking about another swelling that she'd come awfully close to promoting. She returned with a flat pack that looked like a miniature inflated mattress and carefully wrapped it around his leg just below the knee and secured the Velcro patches.

"For the first forty-eight to seventy-two hours ice is best, then if it's still bothering you, we'll switch to heat."

"We? Does that mean I'll see you again in the next couple days?"

She withdrew her hands from his leg immediately, then realized what she'd done and let her hands drop to her sides while sitting down on the edge of the table beside him, crossing her knees.

"If your leg is giving you pain, of course I'd be happy to help you work with it and save you the cost of outpatient care. But if it's not. . . ."

He reached to take one of her hands and twisted their fingers together.

"And if it's not?"

She studied him silently, and from nowhere came the appealing one-eyed blink that he could read so well by now.

"Joseph, you're an extremely attractive man." She rubbed the back of his hand with her thumb. "But how many times in a woman's life does she meet an attractive man whom she must resist? Once I'm married, I'm not expecting never again to be face to face with men who raise my temperature a notch or two. It's bound to happen, but it's how I react to it that's important. I'm not denying I've. . .reacted to you. You're a very persuasive man, Joseph, and sexy to boot. But I'm involved in wedding plans that are so mind boggling I wouldn't even care to list all the people and dollars involved. My mother—" again her thumb brushed his hand softly "—well, my mother is a very frugal woman and always concerned about security—investing, saving, planning for the future. But this time she's throwing caution aside and going whole hog. Nothing's too good or too expensive for Pau—" She caught herself in time and finished, "For us."

But Joseph heard her slip. "Just make sure you aren't making a mistake, Winn."

She dropped his hand, placed hers on her thighs and pushed herself up to her feet. "There's no such thing as a sure bet, but I know mother will be ecstatic when I marry Paul, and he'll be terribly good to me, and I'll have all the security she always wanted for me."

"All the security she never had?" Joseph questioned.

Winn pondered silently, then answered, "Yes. It's not hard to see through her. Security is her biggest hang-up."

"Because of your father?" She had never mentioned her father.

"Yes."

"Did he leave her?"

"It wasn't a question of his leaving. He never stayed long enough to leave. He got her pregnant while they were dating, then disappeared, and she never heard from him or saw him again. She's had a rough time making something of herself with me to raise and nobody else to rely upon. But she's a scrapper. She made it through business school and became a superb private secretary, and she didn't stop there. When things changed, when computers came along, she didn't rest on her laurels or make up her mind *she* wasn't going to go along with such upstart ideas. Instead she went to learn how to use them. And of course, that's when Paul became her teacher."

They fell silent again. But it was not a comfortable silence this time. Joseph wanted to tell her she was being a fool. She wanted to tell him to mind his own business.

At length, she picked a neutral subject. "How does your leg feel?"

"Numb."

"Good. Let's see it now."

She removed the ice pack and examined the leg again, had him flex it, stand on it, and judged it to have pulled muscles, not broken bones.

"I don't think you'll need an X ray. How does it feel when you walk?"

"Better since the ice."

"Good. Would you like to see the tank room where I work with Merry?"

"I'd love to."

She showed him around the rest of the Physical Medicine Department, but much of the time Joseph was thinking of other things than the Hubbard tank, traction units and treadmills. He wondered how she could be so sensitive to the needs of others, yet so ignorant of her own.

When they got back to his house, he tried to kiss her, but she pressed a hand to his chest and turned away.

"No, Joseph. My mind is made up."

"Can I call you?"

"No."

"I think you're making a mistake. I think you and I would be—"

"Don't say it."

"You think it's just spring fancy, but I don't."

"Goodbye, Joseph, I hope your leg gets better." She turned to her own car and practically ran the few steps to it before slamming herself inside its sanctuary, as if a mere enclosure of metal and glass could insulate her from the powerful force that compelled the two of them together.

He watched her back up and took a step toward the car as he thought he saw her start to cry. But before he could advance, she stepped on the gas and roared down the street.

# 8

THE SHELL PINK INVITATIONS had been in Winn's possession for three weeks already. Proper bridal etiquette demanded they be mailed four to six weeks in advance. She had lists of addresses from both her side and Paul's, but it seemed there was always some other detail cropping up, some interruption just as she sat down to the task of doing the addressing.

*Am I delaying because I think Joseph is right?* But even the suggestion made her quail. Attempting to stop the tidal wave of fevered planning that advanced with deadly intent would be like trying to hold back a natural disaster. The plans gained momentum, force and inevitability as they rolled along. The planning of a wedding, Winn learned—much to her dismay—involved so many petty details they managed to detract from the main event, which was the marriage of a man and a woman.

Fern Gardner, for all her being totally inexperienced in such folderol, proved herself as capable and structured as a drill sergeant. Not an iota went unconsidered. She'd made a calendar listing the specific days by which each particular must be checked upon, each decision made, each person telephoned, each piece of frippery purchased. And Winn *did* consider much of it frippery. Had it been left entirely up to her, Winn would have elected a quiet wedding with a few close friends and relatives invited to her mother's house or anyplace simple and left all the grandstanding for those women much more suited to it.

Yes, she'd enjoyed dressing up and celebrating the day of Sandy's wedding, but for herself she preferred things much simpler. She was an artless woman of ordinary tastes and would have been much, much happier if all the silly special effects could have been sidestepped.

But Fern Gardner, self-made success, abandoned by her lover at age nineteen, mother of an illegitimate daughter, needed the reassurance and illusion of security attendant with a large flashy wedding. She had only one daughter and that one lucky enough to have attracted a man whom Fern had virtually handpicked. She wasn't about to stint on this most auspicious day of Winnifred's life.

Within the week following Winn's confrontation with Joseph Duggan, her mother called at least eleven times, always for some mindless non-cruciality that made Winn grit her teeth while answering. The realtor called twice asking her to leave the house so he could show it in the evenings. At the hospital Meredith Emery brought brochures of Disneyland and asked how soon her hair would grow back. The furniture store called to say the new living-room sofa, chairs and tables had arrived, and Paul called to ask if they shouldn't take one evening to go out and choose lamps, pictures and also to buy one particular item he'd spied while out browsing on one of his lunch hours: a table-style chess set with inlaid two-toned wood top—perfect for a living-room accent piece.

"A chess set?" Winn echoed, dismayed.

"Not just a chess set. A very special chess set."

"But why?"

"I told you I'd give you another lesson when we had more time. I know you can get the hang of it."

"But, Paul, you know I'm no good at chess."

"You'll learn, darling. I have every confidence in you." He laughed lightly.

Suddenly she experienced a jagged flash of irritation. Unconsciously her back stiffened, and she coiled the telephone cord six times around her finger until it cut off the circulation.

"I'll make you a deal, Paul," she announced with a hard edge to her voice. "I'll come and look at your chess set if you'll agree that for every hour we spend playing it, we'll spend equal time playing racket ball."

A long silence followed, then his chuckle, more patronizing than humored. "Now, Winnifred, you know I'm all feet on the racket-ball court. I've never been a jock and never pretended to be. I'll leave the physical workouts to you."

She yanked the phone cord off her finger and rammed a kitchen chair with her foot till it slammed under the table with a resounding clatter. "Fine! Great! Then what do you say if one or two nights a week we each find somebody else to play our games with? You can find someone with an analytical mind to pore over your chess table with you, and I'll find somebody who likes to rap a ball around a racket-ball court." Naturally the picture of Joseph popped up, dressed in white shorts with his bare belly showing below a whacked-off T-shirt. "Paul, are you there, Paul? What do you say?" she hissed. "Maybe old Rita will oblige you, huh?"

"Winnifred, you're being unreasonable."

"Oh, am I? And what are you being?"

If there was one thing Paul Hildebrandt prided himself upon it was his ability to reason. The electric silence told Winn her words stung.

"It was just an idea, that's all. Naturally, if you're opposed to the chess table, we don't have to go look at it."

Suddenly the back of Winn's nostrils burned. She felt like dropping to her knees and bawling. He thought the issue here was a chess table! Judas priest! For a brilliant man he could be utterly dense.

"Well, what about going out to choose the lamps and other small items?" he was asking.

She opened her mouth wide, drew an enormous calming breath, ran four agitated fingers through her hair and said to the floor, "I don't care. I'd like to do it . . . whenever you want." But once the words were out, she realized one of the two statements had to be untrue. Which was true? Either she wanted to do it, or she didn't care.

"Day after tomorrow, then? I'll come and pick you up around seven."

"Fine," she answered despondently. "Seven."

"Good night, love. Get some good rest now. You seem a little high-strung lately, and it's probably all the last-minute details piling up."

It was not the details and Winn knew it. The details were being handled with parliamentary punctiliousness by Fern Gardner, who only checked with her daughter as a matter of principle, not because Winn's approval was either sought or necessary. No, Winn's problem had nothing to do with details. It had to do with a curly-haired Irishman whose sexy eyes she could not forget, who played a wicked game of racket ball, drove rusty pickups and kissed like Prince Charming.

WITHIN A HALF HOUR of Winn's hanging up after her conversation with Paul, Sandy called.

"Hi, kiddo, how're the wedding plans coming?"

Winn had to force herself not to vent her wrath upon her unsuspecting friend—after all, Sandy had no idea of the turmoil within Winn lately. "Pretty well, considering mother's handling all the last-minute glitches with her usual steel-trap deadliness."

"Oh-oh! Something's up."

Winn sank onto the chair she'd earlier kicked so hard. "No, nothing's up. It's just that I have other things on my mind besides wedding, wedding, wedding. But neither mother nor Paul seems concerned."

"The little girl at the hospital?"

"Yes, among other things. She's dying and I—" Winn drew a deep breath and battled the almost irresistible urge to tell Sandy everything, including her feelings for Jo-Jo Duggan, to be honest and open and ask her friend's opinion about the whole matter. But before she could broach the subjects, Sandy went on.

"Well, I have just the thing to take your mind off your troubles and put you in a happy frame of mind. I guess you know what it is. We've talked about it long enough."

Winn covered her eyes and braced an elbow on the table. *Oh, no, not the shower.*

"It's the shower. I've just been waiting to hear from you until I put the date on the invitations. And it's getting awfully close. I think we'd better have it maybe week after next, or the week following that. Do you have your calendar handy?"

It was staring at Winn from a nail on the wall beside the telephone, and as she looked up at it, it suddenly became blurred by tears. Sandy was waiting for an answer, and here she sat, recalling how Paul had once walked up to that nail and said, "I hope you don't plan to drive nails into the walls of our new house this way." If she wanted to drive a four-inch railroad spike into her wall, by God she'd drive it! On the ugly stucco walls of Jo-Jo Duggan's kitchen there hung a calendar with a picture of a tin lizzie, and a header advertising Duggan's Body Shop. Next time she was there, Winn promised herself to check and see what he'd hung it up with.

Apparently Winn took longer to mull over the shower than she'd realized, for Sandy's voice came across the wire once again. "Winn, have you sent out your wedding invitations yet?"

"No, I've been working on them."

"Well, the shower invitations shouldn't really go out until after people get the ones for the wedding. Don't you think you should get going?"

Fern had called four days in a row to issue the same reprimand. Winn felt pressured and antagonized. "Yes, I'll make sure I have them out by the weekend if I have to stay home from work one day to finish addressing them." But at work Merry needed her, and she'd no more have deserted the child for a single precious day of her remaining life than Winn would have jumped at the chance to own a chess table of inlaid wood.

They chose two weeks from Saturday for the shower and agreed that Sandy would delay sending her invitations until midway through the following week, giving Winn enough time to get her own out first.

When Winn hung up the phone, she resolutely dragged out the box of pink envelopes and notes, the lists of addresses, her own phone book and a pen. She had addressed five when the phone rang again.

"Hello, Winn, this is mother."

What would it be this time? Had the apricot-rose crop failed in Florida? Winn bit back the sharp response and answered, "Hello, mother."

"Have you got the invitations in the mail yet?"

"No, but they're almost done," she lied.

"Winn, have you taken a look at the calendar lately? Those invitations should have been in the mail no later than last Saturday."

"I know, mother, I know."

"And now something else has come up. Perry Smith has just received word that he's being transferred to Los Angeles."

For a moment Winn was disoriented. She couldn't figure out what Perry Smith's transfer had to do with anything concerning her. Evidently her mother expected some moan of dismay that was not forthcoming, for her voice crackled with indignation. "Well, for heaven's sake, I should think there'd be some reaction from you. After all, there's not much time to find someone else to do the singing."

Oh, yes—Ramona Smith, Perry's wife, had agreed to do the music at the wedding and had already discussed the choice of songs with Winn.

"It's not the end of the world, mother. I'd be happy with just the organ, anyway. Mrs. Collingswood might be twittery, but she's wonderful when she touches a keyboard."

"Oh, Winnifred, don't be ridiculous. Whoever heard of a church wedding without vocal music? The songs are all chosen, and they've been planned into the entire service. Don't tell me you have no intention of asking someone else."

"I don't know any other singers, mother. I didn't even know this one. You found her."

"Well, it's imperative that we move fast on this."

Winn's temper snapped. "*You* move fast on it if you want to, mother. I've made all the fast moves I can stand for a while!"

Her mother's voice softened, but with an effort. "Darling, you're not yourself these days. Why, I swear you sound as if you really don't care about these decisions one way or another."

"Frankly, mother, I don't. If you want a different singer, get one. Tell him he can sing 'Betty Lou's Gettin' Out Tonight' for all I care. And hire a sequined chorus line to dance along with it!"

She could see her mother's stunned face and feel her hurt surprise at the rebuff. "Oh, mother, I'm sorry. Please just do whatever you want and let me know, all right?"

THIRTY MINUTES LATER Paul called again. "Your mother and I just had a long talk, Winnifred, and she tells me you just snapped at her and hurt her feelings, and have washed your hands of making decisions about the singer. Winnie, you really shouldn't treat your mother so. . .so. . . ." He ended with a sigh.

"So what?"

"You know. You're short with her all the time and find fault with everything she does when she's really bending over backward to facilitate matters and help us plan a very high-class wedding here."

"Maybe I didn't want a high-class wedding, Paul. Maybe I just wanted you to pay mother a few glass beads, open a vein, exchange blood with you and slip away to a tepee in the woods." Where had this caustic person come from? Winn was being unfair to Paul, and she knew it but couldn't seem to curb these cutting remarks. She felt him tightly controlling his anger.

"I understand, you're under a lot of pressure right now, so I'll excuse you for getting short with me, but I think you owe your mother an apology."

Dear God—it struck Winn—he's marrying me as much for the mother-in-law he'll inherit as he is for the bride he'll get. Still, she softened her tone. "Paul, do me a favor, will you? Call mother back, and you two discuss the singer and pick one. Will you do that for me, please?"

There followed a moment's pause while he decided how to handle this suddenly unreasonable fiancée of his. "Yes, I'll be happy to. My mother might have a name for us, too. I'll take care of it, darling."

"Thank you, Paul."

After hanging up, she addressed twenty-five more invitations, then dropped her head onto the tabletop and bawled as she'd been wanting to for days.

Her back ached. Her eyelids burned, and she felt like driving an entire box of nails into the kitchen wall, making a regular design of them all around the frame of the sliding glass door and maybe starting across the wall that abutted it. Instead, she left the invitations strewn all over the table, shucked off her clothes and dropped into bed. She was just dozing off when the phone rang—again!

She flung back the covers and stomped out to the kitchen, angry at being awakened and made to get out of bed.

"Hullo!" she growled.

"Hello," came the masculine voice she'd been trying her hardest to forget. Tears burned her eyes again. Her heart slammed against her chest. She covered her eyes with one hand and leaned her forehead against the cool glass of the sliding door in the dark.

"Are you alone?" he asked.

"What do you want, Joseph?"

"You."

The line hummed with a taut silence. Winn's feminine parts surged to life—nipples, stomach, inner reaches all pressing for contact with him.

"Don't," she begged in a voice very close to tears.

"I'm sorry, Winn. I complicate things for you, don't I?"

"Yes, oh, God, yes."

She heard him sigh as if close to defeat, yet unwilling to accept it quite yet. "Are the wedding plans progressing without a hitch?"

"Yes. I'm addressing the invitations."

"Oh." Again there followed a poignant silence. "Will you do me a favor, Winn? Will you send me one?"

"Jo-Jo," she sighed.

"Oh, I won't come. I'd just like one to keep."

"J—Joseph, you are b-being exceedingly unkind."

"Winn, are you crying?" He sounded anxious, as if he'd clutched the phone closer to his mouth.

"Yes, d-damn you, I'm crying."

"Why?"

"B-because! He wants to buy a chess table for the l-living room, and some w-woman I don't even know is m-moving to Los Angeles. . . and b-because Sandy wants to give me a sh-shower . . . oh, God, I don't know, Joseph. I only know I'm supposed to be happy, and I'm miserable."

"How's the little girl?"

"Oh, thank you for asking, darl—Joseph. Nobody else really cares how I feel about her around here. Sandy asked, but when I answered, she hurried on as if to avoid the subject, too."

Winn paused for breath, and his soft voice fell upon her ear. "Back up a minute, Winn. Start at the beginning of that."

"I. . .you don't make sense, Joseph Duggan." But he made perfect sense and she knew it.

"You were about to call me darling."

"No, I wasn't."

"Try it anyway and see how it feels." *Joseph Duggan, consummate flirt,* she thought. But she knew him to be far more than that now. His voice was odd as he asked, "Is that what you call Paul?" It was one of the only times she recalled Joseph referring to her fiancé by his correct name.

"No. He calls me darling. I call him Paul."

"We've got sidetracked. Tell me about the little girl, Winn."

Why did the name Winn sound more like an endearment from Joseph's lips than the term darling from Paul's?

She told him about Merry's lack of progress, about the brochures from Disneyland. She told him about the singer whose husband was being transferred to Los Angeles, about the argument with her mother, about the shower and the gift registration she was supposed to decide upon at a local department store, where she was expected to choose a china pattern she didn't give a damn about and crystal glasses she'd be uncomfortable drinking from. She told him she'd just made the final payment on Paul's wedding ring, and that her mother was harping about buying something called a unity candle that was to be used in the wedding service, though she herself didn't understand why it was necessary. And she ended by telling him Fern had now come up with the idea of providing limousine service on the day of the wedding.

"Limousine service!" she cried, exasperated. "Of all the phony things."

"Your mother sounds as if she loves you very much."

"My mother is putting on a show she wished for and never had herself. She's playing fairy godmother."

"Then if you have to go through with it anyway, let her. Why do you agree with her one day and buck her the next? You're the one in the wrong, not her."

"But she's railroaded me into all this...this circus stuff I never wanted."

"Then why didn't you tell her a year ago when you should have instead of letting her believe it was what you wanted? Or is it really your mother you're upset about at all?"

"Joseph, I'm tired and I want to go to sleep."

"And I'm frustrated and I want to see you again. Will you drive up to Bemidji with me this Saturday?"

She couldn't believe the man! Five weeks until her wedding, and he suggests she flit away with him like a carefree sprite. "Bemidji! You want me to take off with you just like that and drive up to Bemidji?"

"Yes, to an auction sale."

She was flabbergasted. "An auction sale. Jo-Jo Duggan, you're crazy. I'm addressing my wedding invitations, and you invite me to an auction sale."

"Yes. There's a '41 Ford on the billboard, and there'll be a swap meet, and I might be able to pick up a piece for my '54 Cadillac pickup I haven't been able to find. I thought we might drive it up there."

"And what about Paul? Should I invite him to come along with us?"

"Sure. We'll put him in a coffin, and he can ride in the back."

She gave a nasal snort of laughter before she could stop herself, then covered her nose with a hand. "That's awful, Joseph!" she scolded.

"With a comfortable pillow and blanket, of course," he added, "not a satin lining. And a thermos of iced tea to keep him company for the long ride."

She resisted the gravity of his teasing and became serious once again. "Joseph, I have to go now."

"My leg could use some of that attention you promised."

"Goodbye, Joseph."

"And I've signed up for dancing classes."

"Goodbye, Joseph."

"And I can't find anybody who's half as good as you on the racket-ball court, or who kiss—"

She forced herself to hang up gently. But she dreamed of his curls and crinkly eyes that night.

THE PRENUPTIAL CRAZINESS continued the next day when Fern reminded Winn to send the caterers their time schedule and be sure not to forget to put return postage on the R.S.V.P. notes, and to tell her she'd found the perfect stem glasses for the toasting ceremony of the bride and groom. Winn shook her head as if she'd just been landed a right uppercut. They had to *buy* special glasses for *that*?

At eight that evening Winn sat at the kitchen table pouring on the steam to her addressing operation. A knock sounded, and Paul came in without waiting for her to answer.

"Winnie, darling, the most wonderful thing has come up!" He swept into the kitchen and stepped behind her chair, grasping her shoulders while bending low to kiss her neck. "I've been asked to go out to California for a week. The company is sending me on a tour of The Valley! Imagine that—*The Valley*!" She knew by now there was only one "valley" in Paul's vocabulary. He referred to "Silicon Valley," the world's foremost computer-manufacturing area.

"When?"

"I leave tomorrow for a week. There'll be tours of all the major computer-manufacturing plants and opportunities to learn about all the latest technological advances." The entire country knew that the area just south of San Jose had been in the vanguard of computer technology and was populated with brilliant young men and women whose genius in the field would see many of them millionaires in their thirties. Their expertise was so valued in the industry that the term "The Valley" was now recognized worldwide. Innovations came from The Valley so fast and radically that a computer was often obsolete almost before it rolled off the assembly line, bettered by its successor. Winn understood how the opportunity must excite Paul.

He urged her up from her chair. He kissed her ardently, then asked, "Can you get along without me, darling? I know there's a lot going on, and I know I shouldn't be leaving you at this time, but it's the chance of a lifetime, Winnie." Seldom did his eyes dance like this. She looked into them and tried to conjure up even a quarter of the electric response generated by the mere sound of Joseph Duggan's voice crossing a telephone wire.

"Of course, I can get along without you for a week. All I really need to get done right now is the invitations, and you can't help me with them."

"Oh, thank you, darling." He cupped the back of her head and lifted her toward his kiss—an excited, searching kiss—then wrapped her in both arms and pressed her body close to his. She clung and kissed him back with an almost violent twisting of her body against his, pressing and writhing against him. But it didn't work. She was forcing the issue, and when her body failed to respond as fully as she'd hoped, Winn realized Paul was stimulated as much by excitement over the trip to Silicon Valley as he was by his bride-to-be.

"Winnie," he groaned in her ear. "Let's go to bed. God, it's so good to have you like this again. Something's been wrong for the last few weeks, and I haven't been able to put my finger on it. But tonight you're like you used to be."

She kissed his jaw as she answered, "No, Paul, not tonight."

He drew back, hurt. "But I'll be gone for a whole week."

"I have my period." It was a lie, and she suffered the weight of guilt for it while he encircled her in his arms again, slipped his hands beneath her shirt and caressed her breasts while groaning into her ear.

"Damn!" he murmured at last, forcing himself to release her.

She offered him a consolation that hardly eased her conscience. "When you get back, we'll go out shopping for the lamps and buy you the chess table, too."

"I love you," he declared gently.

His eyes were filled with admiration and gratitude, but he was as eager to leave as she was to have him go when he left a short while later.

After he was gone, she returned to her wedding invitations and attacked them almost frenziedly. She worked that night until midnight and the following night till ten-thirty when she became drowsy and got up to make a pot of coffee to help keep herself awake. She finished the last pink envelope around 1:30 A.M. and licked two hundred and twenty-five stamps before going to bed. She wondered if it was the taste of the glue that made her feel slightly nauseous.

ON FRIDAY MORNING—precisely four weeks and one day before the big event—she dropped the two hundred and twenty-five shell pink envelopes in the big drop box at the post office and breathed a shaky sigh of relief. Tonight when Paul called from California, she'd tell him. *Then* she'd feel excited.

At work she wrapped patients' limbs in hot packs, then put them through their various rehab exercises. She determined the resistance levels of those who rode the stationary bikes and decided how much weight to strap to those limbs needing strengthening. She gave massages, had a consultation with a doctor regarding a new patient to whom she was being assigned, went to lunch with two co-workers and told them she'd finally mailed her wedding invitations.

And at one o'clock that afternoon, Mrs. Christianson called Winn to her office and quietly announced that Meredith Emery had died.

Winnifred tried valiantly to control her tears.

"But she's due for her therapy at two o'clock," she said inanely, as if the reminder would bring the child back to life to meet the schedule.

Mrs. Christianson took Winn's hand, led her to the exercise room and forced her to sit on the edge of a table, then sat down behind her and started massaging Winn's shoulders and neck.

"You've got very close to this one, I know, Winnifred. And it's hard when you get close. Take the rest of the day off, then go out this weekend and do something wild and crazy to take your mind off it."

The woman's hands were superbly trained and exceedingly adept. She gently kneaded without pinching. But the pain couldn't be massaged away. It went too deep. Winn bent forward, braced her elbows to her knees and dug the heels of her hands into her eye sockets.

"Go home, Winnifred. Go home and take a run, then soak in a hot tub and call that man of yours and celebrate life with him instead of dwelling on death."

But Mrs. Christianson didn't know that man of hers was two thousand miles away, paying homage to a bloodless nerveless entity called "the computer."

Still, Winn followed her supervisor's advice. She put

on her green shorts and sweat shirt and ran. She felt the overwhelming need to be outside where blossoms and fresh-cut grass gave testimony to the green resurrection of the world. She sucked in the fecund late May air and counted the number of people who were out planting their backyard gardens, and watched a pair of kites sailing far above her head, realizing two hearty and hale people held the other ends of the strings. She lifted a hand in greeting to every toddler on every tricycle she passed. She cut through a park where pet owners were out walking their dogs and through the parking lot of a small neighborhood grocery store where husbands were stopping to buy cartons of milk on their way home for suppers with wives and children. She steeped herself in life, clinging to each piece of evidence that it thrived, carrying those pictures with her while her legs pumped and stretched and passed the point of easy endurance. She ran on, feeling the heat build in her muscles, welcoming it as a reminder that she lived, panted, burned and ached.

Back at home she draped herself across the kitchen counter, pressing her hot cheek to its cool Formica surface, hardly able to stand for several minutes while her breath beat against her upthrown arm. When her heart had calmed and her breathing slowed, she stood beneath the pummeling hot shower before eating the most calorie-filled foods she had in the house—all starches and sugars and the forbidden junk she rarely put into the body she kept at its peak as a defense against all those she encountered daily who were not as lucky as she.

Paul called. She told him about Meredith Emery in as unemotional a voice as she could manage. He listened and offered a token response of sympathy before reminding her that it was best not to bring her worries home at the end of the workday, especially with a job like hers.

Rage grew within Winn that he, who spent night after night locked away from her, clattering the keyboard of a computer named Rita, should tell her not to bring her career-oriented concerns home at the end of the day!

In bed she tossed and flailed, and studied the black square of window and tried to cry but failed.

At 11:00 P.M. she gave in and called Joseph Duggan.

One of his brothers answered, then Joseph came on the line and grunted sleepily, "Yeah?"

"Joseph, it's Winn."

In the tiny house in Osseo, Joseph Duggan stood in his jockey shorts beside his grandmother's kitchen sink, which was piled high with dirty cups and plates, and pictured the woman whose voice now spoke in his ear. He pictured her as she'd looked the day he turned and found her watching him scrubbing up after work.

"Winn," he repeated, as if the name released a flock of white doves.

"Joseph, I need somebody tonight. I can't...oh, please, Joseph, can you meet me?"

"Anywhere. Anytime."

"Will I sound ridiculous if I ask you to play a game of racket ball at this hour of the night?"

"I'm already tying my Adidas."

"My club is open till midnight. It's closer than yours. I'll meet you there. Ask at the desk which court, and I'll tell them you're my guest."

"Let me go, so I can hurry."

He ran through the house searching frantically for anything to throw on, grabbing the first thing he found—a pair of sawed-off blue jeans and giving up when he couldn't find a shirt fast enough, so heading out without one, only his shoes in his hand, and his racket.

At the club he careered to a halt before the sleepy night-desk attendant and impatiently whacked a palm down beside the registration book. "What court is Winn Gardner in?"

"Number six."

He jogged down the long corridor and panted to a halt before the only court in which the lights were burning.

She was waiting in the middle of the floor, huddled, arms to knees and forehead to arms, facing the front wall. He stepped down onto the wooden floor and paused.

"Winn?"

Her head snapped up, and she spun around on her buttocks.

"Oh, Joseph, thank you for coming."

He crossed the distance between them with a strong muscular stride. "Don't you dare thank me for coming, Winn. Not me."

She swallowed hard and had an awful, belligerent set to her jaw as she rolled to her knees and looked up at him, standing above her. "Work me hard tonight, Joseph," she demanded sternly. "Don't give me no quarter. Promise?"

Their eyes clashed, and he wondered what this was all about but let her carry it to whatever end she desired without enlightening him in the meantime.

"I promise."

She leaped up and stripped her sweat shirt off almost angrily, flung it out into the hall and slammed the door. He watched, frowning as she strode to the center of the backcourt, dressed in a white T-shirt and green shorts.

"Serve!" she ordered, disdaining warm-ups, staring at the front wall almost as if she'd forgotten Joseph was there except as an instrument to do her bidding.

He strode to the serving lane and gave her what she wanted. He worked her like a slave driver, giving her everything he had. She smashed the ball with a vehemence that was awesome. She drove it and backhanded it, and all the time her teeth were clenched and her jaw bulging. She rushed forward to meet each oncoming ball as if her life depended upon meeting it in time. She was vicious and at times almost ugly in her grim fanaticism. But in that ugliness lurked a true beauty, that of the athlete who pushes her body to its physical limits. She arched her back to a torturous angle as she reached for high shots behind her head. She lunged with a pure surge of might and sometimes climbed two steps up the concrete walls in her frantic effort to wreak whatever vengeance she must upon a dumb blue sphere of rubber.

The sweat flowed freely. She swung at a shot and missed, then when the next serve came, cracked it dead center while gritting for emphasis, "God*damn* you!"

They played at the torturous pace for thirty minutes, then Joseph had to know. He stood at the serving line with his back to her and stubbornly refused to turn around while asking, "Did you send out the wedding invitations?"

"Yes!" she barked, "Serve, dammit!"

Joseph felt as if she'd stabbed him in the back with a broken blade.

They played fifteen minutes more, but now he was attacking each shot as recklessly, as angrily as she. Tonight it mattered not in the least who won or lost. It only mattered that they slammed the ball against the concrete walls and got even with the world's injustices and demands.

*"Why?"* he growled as his racket punished the innocent ball.

"Because I couldn't *stop* it!" She, too, performed an injustice to the game of racket ball with her next return.

"Is that why you're doing this?"

The whistling return he'd expected to fly past his ear never materialized. Instead, behind him all was silent. He whirled, white lipped now with fury. Dammit, he loved this woman! They stared each other down—she was poised as if to turn her racket on him while he gripped his own racket with a fist so tight it made veins bulge like blue rivers up his arms.

"Is that why?" he demanded angrily.

"No!" she bleated. Then, without warning, Winn Gardner collapsed to her knees, hugged her head and broke into a torrent of sobbing.

Jo-Jo's racket clattered to the floor. He was bending to her in less than a second, knee to knee, grasping her arms in a painful grip. "Winn, please tell me what this is all about."

Her hair was strewn and wild, for it had not been pampered after its last washing. It prodded the air around her face while her mouth yawned in anguish and tears streamed from her tormented eyes. Her fingers plucked at Joseph's chest as if searching for a shirt to grasp.

"Oh, God, Joseph, she died."

And then he understood.

"Winn. . . Winn. . . ." Gently he embraced her, kissing her temple, wanting to slip her inside his very body to protect her from further pain. "I'm sorry, darling. I'm sorry."

Her body jerked. Her arms clung. The salt of sweat and tears intermingled upon his neck as she buried her face there and wept. Incoherently she babbled out her sorrow while he quietly held her, understanding the meaning if not the words. Joseph and Winn were bound together wherever their bare skins touched by the sweat they'd forced from each other's bodies during the grueling combat of the past half hour. He ran his hands as far around her as he could and drew her in as if his arms were attached to a winch, and only she could release its catch. Their knees were widespread now, their stomachs and breasts molded flat together. Her hurt became his. And because she cried, his eyes misted, too.

When her sobbing grew terrifying, he plowed his hands through her hair and forced her head back, covering her mouth with his in a blessed surcease of solitariness. Their tongues, like the ball they had just battered, drove and smashed and volleyed, continuing to fight the fight of the living against the invincibility of death. Their heads moved as if they were fighting each other with their open mouths, when there was truly no fight at all, only enormous relief from tensions both emotional and sexual.

He pushed her back and fell with her onto the middle of the vast empty floor, covering her hard-muscled body with his own. His elbows struck the floor, then her head was cradled in his arms in a half awkward, half meshing embrace while their well-matched bodies fused. His hips shifted to one side, and a knee nudged hers open. She complied with profound defiance of everyone and everything save Joseph Duggan, placing her soles on the floor, widening her straddle until he was couched securely within her thighs, and she could freely and angrily thrust up against him.

At first their breaths were ragged, hers still shredded by the last vestiges of weeping. But soon they became conscious of the faint hum of the overhead lights in the otherwise still room. Neither their lips nor hips had separated when the writhing and lashing out stopped.

Their kiss grew tender, the movements of their heads mellowed into those of lovers exploring something wondrous. Her knees were still flexed, but they relaxed now, and one of them slipped down to lie flat against the floor while the other caressed his hip.

Combat became caress.

Grip became greeting.

Anger became accolade.

They moved as a wave moves upon the shore, one upon the other, slipping up to explore, cover, then receding to await the next nudge of nature.

His body was hard. He used it to encourage, to invite, but not to assault or punish. She lifted rhythmically in acceptance, and he backed away the shortest distance possible, only enough to see her wide blue eyes, filled with acceptance of the inevitable, and with something else, trembling, breathless loving.

"Joseph, what have I done?" She spoke of the invitations, of course.

But he wouldn't have her asking of them now. "You've made me fall in love with you. I love you, Winn. Take me home with you."

"For the night, Joseph?" she asked uncertainly.

"Yes, for the night, for only tonight if it's all I can have."

"Yes, Joseph, oh, yes, darling. I think it's time I find out if you're right about a lot of things."

He pushed himself from her, sat back on his haunches with one of his knees on either side of one of hers. Their eyes were polarized now, unable to break apart. He caught her hand and rolled to the balls of his feet, pulling her up with him.

# 9

SHE STOOD IN THE SHOWER, listening to the spray echo through the ceramic enclosure of the deserted locker room. Her eyes were closed, her face uplifted, slick palms working the bar of soap. She supposed the guilt would come later, but now there was nothing except sweet anticipation and a painful ache in the center of her chest from sexual suppression. How many weeks had it been since she'd met Joseph Duggan and recognized the vibrant carnality trembling between them? Only eight, yet as each of those weeks had passed, it'd left her more and more certain that her body pined for his.

She opened her eyes, stared at the nozzle of the shower, backed away from the warm liquid needles and ran the bar of soap around her neck and both breasts, down her belly, across her hips and down her legs. She disdained the cloth, using her own hands instead to cleanse her skin and feel the quivering nerve endings just beneath its surface. Her breasts felt engorged with eagerness, the nipples hard and pitted like steel thimbles.

*Oh, I want him. When was the last time I felt this way? This ready?* She had repressed all her bodily urgings for Joseph Duggan until, now, after the stimulus of lying beneath him, they retaliated. Tonight there would be no denial. Tonight. . .she gasped. And bent quickly to wash her legs and feet instead. Hurrying now. Hurrying.

Her shampoo smelled faintly of lily of the valley. She wrapped a towel turban fashion around her head and secured the loose end at her nape, then dressed in a pair of red nylon knit shorts and a simple white U-neck pull-over, slipping these over panties only, no bra. She stuffed her shoes and socks into her tote bag and padded out barefoot to meet Joseph.

He was waiting outside the door to the locker room, barefoot, too, wearing nothing but the pair of faded cut-off denim shorts he'd worn on the court. Her eyes fell to them, then to his right hand in which he held a wad of something cotton and white—his underwear?

"I took off in such a hurry I didn't think about clean clothes," he explained. Oh, God—it *was* his underwear! Her dastardly eyes dropped to the fringe of the faded blue jeans. They were slightly stretched, untidy with drooping threads, and cut off so high that the tip of one white pocket peeped out at the leg line. His hard leg protruded from the soft blue cloth, creating an arresting contrast in textures and filling her imagination with what he must look and feel like naked inside the cutoffs.

The surge of sensuousness she'd experienced in the shower magnified a hundredfold. She raised her eyes and found him studying her breasts, obviously unbound within the scoop-neck shirt, and even as he looked, they started puckering. He swallowed and raised his eyes to the towel wrapped around her head.

When Winn spoke, her voice sounded as if she had strep throat. "I forgot my brush, so I'll leave this on till I get home." But neither of them made a move toward the stairs leading up and out. Then, when they finally did, they jerked as if they'd got a load of buckshot in the tail.

Walking up the steps just ahead of him, she felt his eyes on her back, and the sensation was almost as palpable as a physical touch. In the lobby he slipped a hand along the bar of steel that crossed the heavy plate-glass door at waist level. She saw nothing but his bare arm as he pushed the door wide and let her pass before him. His rusty pickup was parked next to her car in the deserted parking lot. Overhead a bluish light buzzed, and insects sent up a humming around it. Instinctively she headed for her own car, and just as she reached it, his hands clasped hers.

"Winn, if you'd like, I can leave my truck here so it won't have to sit in your driveway all night."

His offer brought back reality: they had made one conscious choice, and one only. To become lovers for the night. Beyond that, nothing had been decided. If she told him to leave the pickup, their liaison took on overtones of sordidness and dishonesty. And though she didn't want to consider her relationship with Joseph Duggan in that light, there couldn't be another pickup like his old junker in the whole metro area. She was forced to make a choice.

"Yes, you can ride with me. I'll drive you back over here in the morning."

He dropped her hand, turned away and picked his barefooted way carefully around the tail of her car. He opened the back door, threw his racket and shoes inside, then slipped into the front seat beside her.

She lived only two miles from the club, and it took little time to drive that far along deserted Seventy-seventh Avenue. But when they reached the intersection at Highway 52, the light was red. As they sat, waiting for it to change, he studied her face, lighted to pink by the reflected glow, her eyes refracting a pair of red dots from the overhead traffic light. He sensed guilt coming to give her second thoughts and slid across the seat, put an arm around her shoulders and turned her face to him with the pressure of a single finger on her jaw.

"Winn, I won't be a hypocrite and tell you not to think of him. But when you do, and I know you will more than just once during the night, will you think of me, too, and remember that I love you?"

The light turned green in her eyes. She clutched the

wheel and left her foot on the brake. *I love you, too, Joseph,* she thought but could not say it. To do so would be unfair to both of them. Instead she lifted her lips to his, touching his jaw with her fingertips— it was rough in contrast to the sleek satin of his mouth as his lips parted and the tip of his tongue greeted hers.

When the kiss ended, Winn said softly, "And I won't be a hypocrite and say I'm going to put him from my mind because he's there right now, and you know it."

"Then I'll do my best to get him out of it temporarily if you'll just drive on through this green light, Winn Gardner, and take us to someplace a little less public than the intersection of Highway 52 and Seventy-seventh Avenue."

But the light had turned red again, and they had a full three minutes more to blandish each other with lips and tongues.

At the town house the For Sale sign was still perched on the boulevard. The lights illuminated it momentarily, then arced around and a moment later died with the engine. Joseph turned to study Winn, but now that the moment was here, she was nervous. She opened her door, leaving him to do likewise and follow her up the sidewalk and the three steps leading to her front door.

There, he didn't reach to take the keys from her hand, but took her tote bag instead, leaving her with both hands free. Still she felt inept, and it seemed forever before she found the hole in the lock.

Finally the dead bolt clicked back, and she led the way inside into the dark recesses of her tiny front foyer and the living room, listening to the soft thunk of the door closing behind him, then the almost imperceptible *shush* of his bare feet on the carpet. She reached blindly and found his hand. He followed, recognizing the direction in which she led him, turning right along the short hall leading past the bathroom to her bedroom. Another right turn and he knew he was standing at the foot of her bed with the high dresser to his left and the old-fashioned dressing table to his right. Her fingers clutched his rather frantically now, and he felt her trembling.

Did she expect him to drop her on the bed in the dark, and afterward creep out like a clandestine debaucher? Did she think that if it happened under cover of darkness, it would be easier to forget later?

He slipped from her fingers and found the wall switch in the dark. A pair of matched boudoir lamps flashed on, reflecting themselves from the mirror of the ancient dressing table.

Winn's face was in shadow as she whirled to face Joseph. His hand was still on the light switch. "If I'm going to have only one night with you, I certainly don't intend to have it in the dark. I want some memories to take away with me...of how you looked when you made love."

She dropped her eyes to the floor, and he dropped his hand from the light switch. He leaned to set her bag on the floor, then paused expectantly, waiting for her to make some sign of invitation. Instead, she studied the carpet beneath her bare toes.

"I'm very nervous," she admitted. Her voice wasn't its usual calm self. It was high and pinched.

"So am I. Agreeing to go to bed together, then putting it off for the better part of an hour is a little nerve-racking, isn't it?"

She glanced up shyly—he was grinning warmly—and laughed nervously.

"I...I'm sorry this room is in such a mess. I'm afraid I'm not the best housekeeper. Other things always seem to come first."

"At home my bed is made up only on the days when I change the sheets." He glanced at the tousled bed. Her sheets were white, the blanket army green and the spread a burnt orange—not exactly the boudoir of a vamp, yet it suited her.

With three unhurried steps he moved to stand before her, but when he reached to touch, she ducked aside and avoided him. Before the dressing table she reached up to remove the towel from her head. He took up a hipshot stance, hooked his thumbs in the back waistband of his shorts and watched as she bent forward at the waist, then rubbed her hair briskly. His eyes slid down the curve of her spine to the red knit shorts that magically rode up and down at the same time: up at the hem, revealing the gentle half-moon of skin where her white underwear stretched up to reveal a sliver of derriere, and dipping down at the waist as the elastic curved, revealing two knobs of her vertebrae thrown into shadowed relief.

Silently he moved up behind her and placed his hands on her waist. She jerked erect and met his eyes in the mirror, her own framed by a shock of wet wild hair. He heard the catch in her breath, then they both held motionless. When she realized how unsightly her hair looked, one hand came up to drive it back from her forehead.

*Why, she's hiding. Of course. She felt vulnerable with her hair wet and tangled. No woman dreams of making love with a man for the first time looking less than perfect.* Yet her fresh wet state seemed totally perfect for Winn Gardner.

He captured her hand and lowered it to her side.

"Sit down," he ordered softly. "Let me."

Her knees quivered as she stood transfixed by his stunning brown eyes in the mirror. Blindly she stepped around the tiny boudoir chair and lowered herself to it, feeling first with her hand to check her aim.

His eyes swerved away. "Which brush? This one?" A dark hand came into her range of vision, and she watched it select a brush from the three that lay on the vanity top.

"Yes."

It was a coarse plastic brush with a knob on the end of each bristle. As he lifted his hand, and the bristles bit into the hair at the top of her forehead, the knobs caught and forced her head back against his chest. Immediately his left hand came to press warmly against her forehead. "Tell me if I'm being too rough," he ordered, his eyes now on the top of her head while hers followed his every movement, mesmerized. Through her cold damp hair, his chest burned warm, then he backed away and completed the stroke, ending between her shoulder blades. He brushed slowly, lazily, and with each stroke her shirt grew wetter. An involuntary shiver shook her, and goose bumps skittered up her arms. Immediately he glanced up.

"Are you cold?"

"Yes."

He ran his hands down her arms, pulling her back against his stomach while his eyes locked with hers in the mirror.

"Your shirt is wet."

She swallowed, the ache of anticipation intensifying across her chest.

"Give me the towel again."

She handed it up, and he transferred his attention once more to her hair, folding it between two layers of terry cloth and drawing the remaining moisture from it before tossing the towel onto the floor, then giving her hair a final smoothing. She closed her eyes and lolled in the sensuous delight of the brush massaging her scalp, then tickling its way down her back.

"Put your arms up, Winn."

At his soft command her eyes fled to his, and she realized he was deliberately taking this one slow step at a time to give them longer to get used to each other. There was no hiding the fact that her breasts peaked up into two hard points, nor the fact that they were rising and falling with torturous rapidity as she obediently raised her arms above her head. He grasped the hem of her shirt, inverted it, peeling it up and over her elbows, leaving her torso naked, lighted by the lamps and exposed to his adoring eyes.

"You're beautiful, Winn," he breathed, "just as I pictured you." Her shoulders pressed firmly against his midsection, and she felt his hardness against the center of her back. His right hand still held the brush, but he seemed to have forgotten it. He slid both palms down around her neck, her collarbone, then outward to the top curves of both breasts, around their outer perimeter and finally to their soft lower swells, carefully avoiding the nipples, which stood out like twin rubies set in identical mounts. His eyes coveted them, but still he touched only the skin surrounding them. Her breasts were small, firm, conical, and she wondered how much space they would take up in his palms.

His hands continued to tantalize. She felt the smooth handle of the brush circle her skin, so much smoother than the rough fingertips that rode the paired curves, too, then slipped beneath them like mirrored images before lifting both breasts sharply, pointing her nipples more directly at their reflected faces high in the mirror.

"When I first met you, I wanted to do this. I told myself that someday I would, and that when I felt your flesh for the first time, it would be as hard and firm as mine is." He allowed her breasts to fall free, then ran one hand down to her ribs while stretching to set the brush on the tabletop. Then both hands were spanning her ribs, sliding down into the hollow above her navel as he dipped his head low and kissed her naked shoulder. "Your skin is perfect, not soft like most women's. Whoever said soft skin was sexy?" His thumbs circled and dug into the backside of her ribs as his hands rode back up and sheltered in the hollow just beneath both overhanging breasts again.

*Will he never touch my nipples,* she thought, wondering how long she could endure the agony of expectation. But still he didn't. He bit her shoulder tendon, and his tongue tickled it, making her give a one-shouldered shrug, followed by an involuntary shudder.

Against her skin he said, "You smell too much like me from the soap at the club. All these weeks while I imagined you, I thought you'd smell the way you did the night of the wedding."

Every word he said fueled her libido. He straightened. His palms cupped the lower halves of her breasts, his thumbs within a quarter inch of their crests now. "Are you self-conscious, having me look at you this way?" *Let her say no. Let her be proud of her well-cared-for body.*

"No," she whispered.

"Are you self-conscious looking at yourself this way?"

"No." She covered the backs of his hands with her own. "Only impatient."Then she guided them up, up, until her distended nipples seemed to drill into his palms like diamond bits. She gently moved from left to right, her eyes sliding closed. Her shoulders shifted back and forth, too, and behind her she felt him moving in complementary motions.

"Oh, Joseph, Joseph, you make me so impatient."

"I've been impatient for a good eight weeks. What's a few more minutes?"

Her eyelids lifted, and she met his gaze in the mirror. "Have you? Have you really?"

His palms contoured the outer rims of her breasts while he gently twisted the nipples between thumb and forefinger, sending currents of tension zigging downward to meet the fire between her legs that seemed to connect the two disparate parts of her body.

"Right from the start. I wanted you that first night, I think, but after you talked me out of pressing the issue in the gazebo, I decided you just might be right. It might have been spring fancy and nothing more. . . what with you in your finery and me in mine, and everything setting the stage for romance. But even though I backed off, I didn't stop thinking about you, wanting to do what I'm doing right now, wondering how to go about wooing a woman with another man's ring on her finger."

"Are you wooing me, Joseph?"

His one-sided smile brought the devil's sparkle to his eyes. "What does it feel like to you?" He bent to probe her ear with the warm wet point of his tongue.

"I thought we were having a one-night affair because I was in need of comfort."

His hands flattened her milky white orbs with their tips pinched against the edges of his hands. "Be honest with yourself, Winn. Yes, you needed me, but this has nothing to do with comfort. This is something we saw coming from the first time we laid eyes on each other, isn't it?"

She gasped slightly and arched her back against him. "You're hurting me, Joseph." Her hands pulled at his.

Immediately his hold lightened. "I'm sorry," he whispered gruffly. His head dropped down, and he kissed her shoulder again, then her jaw and the tip of her ear, caressing her breasts now with the consideration of a penitent. She tipped her head back until it rested on his bare shoulder and covered his hands again with her own, following his explorations with her fingers, which lined his and learned the texture of hard knuckles, hair and blunt nails.

Into her neck he murmured, "Ah, Winn, I love you. This isn't just some crazy spring fever, this is the most terrible thing I've ever gone through in my life."

Her heart seemed to swell and her blood raced. She wanted to confess her love, too, but in lieu of the words she was not allowed to say, she could only offer, "I know, Joseph, I know. I've been going through the same misery."

He forced her face to turn and lift, and kissed her with an ardency that fired her blood anew. His tongue tempted with provocative ministrations, circling, probing, riding along her teeth and within the most intimate confines where cheek met lip. He suckled her tongue the way she longed for him to suckle her breast, raising a deep yearning that beat against the inner walls of her femininity and made her arch back in delight and quest. She had to have more or die, it seemed. Unable to tolerate the constraint any longer, she swung up off the chair, then surprised both herself and him by ordering, "Now you sit." She grabbed up the brush. "What's good for the goose is good for the gander."

Caught off guard by her sudden reversal of roles, just when he'd been about to make his move, he stood with his shoulders and chest heaving while the awesome power of his breath beat between them. His fists were clenched. The shadow in his navel became rhythmically wide, then narrow, wide, then narrow again.

Muscle by muscle he forced himself to relax, then with his dark eyes boring into hers, he swung onto the chair. But instead of facing the mirror, he faced her, straddling the small stool as he'd done once before, running his hands up the backs of her thighs, cupping her buttocks and pulling her up close. He pressed his face into the warm pillows of her breasts, but immediately she pushed his shoulders back, gaining her freedom.

"Not yet. I feel feminine and powerful when I make you wait, just as you made me wait. Let me hang onto it for a little while. Relax . . . close your eyes . . . please."

He did. And stopped trying to claim her, resting his wrists on the low wire back of the chair, letting his relaxed fingers trail toward the floor. His shoulders slumped a little. His head relaxed and his lips parted slightly. Though his breathing was still pressured, the rest of him waited in apparent repose.

She adulated his hair with her eyes before doing what

she'd thought of doing countless times. She lifted her fingers and threaded them through his curls. But his locks had coiled tightly as they'd dried, and only at the crown of his head was his hair still damp. So she brushed it, running the bristles back from his forehead to the base of his neck, then from his temples to the same spot. When she drove the brush through the curls, his chin lifted and his head was tugged backward. But his eyes stayed closed.

"The two things I loved first about you were your hair and your eyes. Even that first night I had the terrible urge to touch your curls, to smell them." She leaned forward and buried her nose in the soft strands, kissed his warm skull—his hair was the finest texture of any she'd ever felt, and as she sniffed its clean scent, his moist breath dampened the fullest part of her right breast. Still he remained docile, not grasping or nuzzling. Pleased, she returned to her delightful chore. She'd been brushing for a full minute when she felt his fingers behind her right knee. They brushed upward until they encountered her red knit shorts. Her breathing shattered, and she glanced down sharply only to find his eyelids still closed. His fingers glided slowly down to her knee again, then made the same titillating journey up and down her opposite leg. The brush continued drawing through his hair, but slower . . . slower . . . slower. . . .

His knuckles caressed her inner thigh and trailed upward to tease the tender flesh at the top of her leg. Then he treated the opposite limb to the sensual harbinger of things to come.

Her hand now lay still upon his head, the brush caught in his curls while the backs of his fingers brushed upward again and slipped within the elastic of her panties. But instead of retreating, his fingers continued moving up to her hip where they explored the hollow before making the leisurely journey back down again.

When they touched flattened hair, his fingers paused, and both Joseph and Winn opened their eyes. His head was thrown back, hers dropped forward. Neither of them saw a visible movement on the other.

He slipped his fingers fully within the white tricot garment and sent rivers within Winn's body flooding their banks. Her left eye blinked slowly. Her wrists fell limply across his shoulders, and her tongue stole out to wet her lips. His free hand found her back and drew her closer until she took a single step, and her knees came up against the back of the chair.

His warm wet tongue touched the bare skin of her stomach just above her waistband, and then his teeth grasped the elastic of her red shorts and worried it suggestively before he fell back again, gazing up at her blue aroused eyes.

He turned his exploring fingers over so the pads rested against her flesh, but still they encountered little, for Joseph reached from an awkward angle, sitting below her, straddling the chair as he did.

"Kneel down," he ordered in an odd, thick voice.

His hands pressed her hipbones, and without hesitation she dropped to her knees. His right hand splayed upon her back while his left slipped down inside the elasticized waists of both garments, searching for the object of his desire.

Then the brush dropped to the floor with a muffled thud as an agonized sound came from her throat.

His lips found hers, and she gripped his shoulders while his explorations took on a rhythm upon which she rode as if posting with the canter of a horse. A deep groan vibrated in his throat, and she slid one hand down his hard chest with its sleek covering of hair, passing a tiny nipple, then continuing down the wedge of hair that led to the brief strip of fabric covering his loins. When she caressed and measured him through the cutoffs, it was with zipper and placket adding to the fullness of his flesh.

His widespread legs gave her full access to him. She followed his example, slipping her fingertips up inside a frayed leg, encountering first the resilient texture of a soft masculine orb that was flattened by his shorts. He groaned and stretched backward, removing his lips from hers. But still, she couldn't reach. He moved sinuously, lifting his hips from the tiny chair, bracing against the dressing table on an elbow.

She reached for his waistband, and at the touch of her warm fingers on his stomach, he jerked in a breath and held it, creating slack between his flesh and the garment. The muscles of his stomach were like sculpted teak as she touched them with her knuckles while working the heavy metal button from its hole.

She thought about the white cotton he'd earlier clenched in his hands. She reached for the zipper and eased it down with agonizing slowness.

He jerked again as she touched him deliberately for the first time, but tentatively, almost shyly, with fingertips only, then he settled his hips back against the chair and waited. He lunged forward now in the chair, whispering harshly in her ear, "Winn . . . Winn . . . I've wanted you to touch me for so long."

She'd always thought it was women who voiced such yearnings, but his heavy breathing and words of encouragement made her realize he was different from most men. He was unashamed of admitting his vulnerability, and this pleased and excited Winn.

When her hand closed around him for the first time, he groaned and rammed one hand inside her back waistline, the other in the front, bracketing her like a saddle made of warm flesh, until his fingers met and nestled within her warm folds.

"Oh, Joseph, you're so good at this. I knew you'd be.

I use to lie awake at night and imagine the different ways you'd touch me . . . oh!" She gasped and arched backward, and his tongue slipped into her mouth with a rhythmic imitation of the stimulation he was bestowing.

The upward pressure increased, taking her with it until she realized he had stood and bowed his legs around the tiny chair, then kicked it behind him, pulling her to her feet in front of him.

With a swift flexing of one knee, he took her shorts and panties down to the floor. When he raised up again her hands were waiting to skim down his ribs and shimmy his cutoffs over his hipbones. They hit the floor with a soft jingle of change from one pocket, and he stepped from them and swept both arms around her, as they'd been before, one along her center front, the other center back, resuming the sweet insinuation of which she'd not yet had her fill. Their mouths met with a voluptuous exchange of tongues while her hand stroked, caressed, explored.

"Easy, lady," he whispered gruffly into her mouth. "I'm about at my limit."

"So am I."

He lifted his head and smiled. "So soon?"

"Too soon?" she inquired diffidently.

"Mmm. . . ." His eyes caressed. "Not at all. Come here. . . ." His hair-spattered legs nudged her smooth ones until she came up against the foot of the bed and fell backward.

He dropped to his knees on the floor, parting her legs with his chest as he fell forward, spreading his hands wide across her ribs while kissing the soft valley at her waist. He pushed himself higher, driving his chest hard against the bony feminine structure that lifted to greet his flesh as it pressed.

Then at last—oh, sweet last—he kissed her breasts, taking turns, a kiss on the left, a kiss on the right. A lick across the left nipple, which lifted in frustration, and then across her right. She clutched the back of his head and would not allow him to move away, directing his mouth to the puckered tip that strained willingly against his tongue, which at last closed over it. Wide, wet, wonderful taking of what she offered, what he'd put off encountering until he, too, had known intense desire for it. He stroked the nipples with his pursed lips as if they had length, much as a clarinet player softens and plies the reed of his instrument before trying to force perfect notes from it.

But the perfect notes were forced from Winn's throat as ecstasy found voice. They were wordless notes of praise and heightened desire. She writhed beneath him and lifted her hips in invitation. But he pressed her flat, taking his time, leaving her breasts with the outward drawing and dampening strokes until the need for more was actual pain down the center of her body.

His warmth disappeared from her breast, and she opened her eyes to look down at him. He was studying her without smile, his eyes slightly somber in the mellow light from the dresser lamps. "If I'm going to get you for only one night of my life, I want to have all of you. I don't want to look back and wish I'd done what I wanted to do."

She braced up on both elbows, her blue eyes immersed in his intense brown ones. His pose announced his intentions, and her heart thrummed crazily as she wondered if she were adventurous enough for him. Yet she felt so right with him, her inhibitions waned before the power of his eyes. They were both exceedingly physical people—she should have guessed that in the love act he would be as physical as he was on a racket-ball court. She sensed him waiting for her approval and lifted a hand to caress the hair above his ear. He turned to bite her little finger and spoke with it still between his teeth.

"You still smell too much like me, and I want you to smell the way I remember you smelling. So, lay back, Winn, and indulge me, please, pretty lady."

She paused uncertainly, then fell back, watching cautiously as he rose to his feet and crossed to her chest of drawers. From its top he took a round white plastic container upon which lay a white fuzzy puff. He slipped the cover off, then turned back toward the bed. Her eyes followed as he came to sit beside her, his knees hooked over the foot of the bed while he twisted at one hip, then fell back onto one elbow. He set the body power on her far side, dipped the puff and said, "Lift your chin for me."

She did, letting her eyes drift closed as the scent of Chanel No 5 filled her nostrils. He fluffed it upon both of her breasts, her ribs. "Lift your arms." She threw them lazily over her head and let erotic images drift across her mind, powered by the evocative scent. He dusted her armpits, then the arms themselves, replenished his supply and leisurely began an excursion down one leg, pushing himself to a sitting position, finally lifting her foot from the floor, bending forward to reach its instep. Her other leg and foot received the same attention before he bent her leg forward and kissed it lightly, then let it drop.

Once more he dipped the puff, applied a white cloud to her abdomen, and the soft hollow of her inner thighs. He leaned, gave her belly a lingering kiss, then ordered, "Roll over."

With hands still thrown above her head, she rolled. The soft tickle of the powder puff touched each inch of tensile skin as she turned her cheek into the rumpled bedding and relaxed. When he brushed the hollow behind one knee, she flinched and rubbed it with the opposite foot.

"Ticklish?"

"Mmm-hmm," she murmured into the bedspread.

"Mmm . . . interesting." He trailed only the finest tips of the puff along her hollows again, and she writhed and reached back to slap his hand away. He chuckled deep in his throat, then the mattress shifted, and she heard a light thump on the floor, the touch of plastic to plastic, and a moment of silence before his knees cracked.

His cool rough hands surrounded her left foot and bent it at the knee. Something warm—his nose—touched it, running from big toe to heel before he kissed and wet the arch, then lowered the foot again and ran a string of moist kisses up her calf, pausing longer at the hollow behind her knee before continuing along her firm thigh, over one buttock, which he bit lightly, then up its rise to her vertebrae. When he reached her neck, his knee was pressed between hers, and a palm rested on either side of her head.

"Winn, my beautiful Winn. If I do something you don't like, just stop me."

But she couldn't imagine putting a stop to heaven. He knew the female libido as he knew the angles of a racket-ball shot, anticipated Winn's every response, much as he could anticipate the caroms of a ball off walls, ceiling and floor.

He played her with an expertise she found at once appalling for all the practice it must have taken him to become so facile at it, and debilitating for how accurate he was about her most vulnerable spots.

He smoothed his hands over her shoulders, lowered his naked length upon her back and writhed his hips while slipping his hands beneath her to caress her flattened breasts. And all the while his tongue searched and teased her neck, her earlobe, her nape, the tendons below her arms, her waist, her buttocks, then down her legs until he knelt on the floor again.

With gentle but relentless hands he turned her over onto her back again. He kissed the insides of her knees, her thighs, bringing responses singing to the surface of her skin, plunging her into a new realm of wantonness where nothing mattered except that he bring ease to the awesome throbbing within her body.

When he touched her, she was unprepared for the fiery heat of it, and her hips leaped convulsively . . . once. Then her fingers took great fistfuls of the bedspread and twisted. And twisted. It was like nothing she'd ever experienced before, not only in its power to stimulate, but in its far greater meaning, the total giving over of one's self to another for that burning space of time. It was the epitome of vulnerability. The epitome of trust.

As she lifted to him, she heard his murmured wordless protestations of love. The pleasure was terrifying. And so intense at times she whimpered, hearing her throat creating sounds it had never made before.

She would realize much later that at one point while he stroked her ever closer to the brink of climax, her mind pictured a line of black powder with the sparkles of fire sizzling along at a steady relentless pace, burning its way closer and closer to the detonator, then reaching it at last and sending the earth into the sky.

"Jooooo-seffff . . ." she growled in two elongated vowels of ecstasy as her body quivered and pulsated.

Then her hips collapsed. There were beads of perspiration on her face and along the center of her chest. Her throat hurt from the rasping cries he'd forced from it. She was lethargic, limp. She was sliding down the bed, drawn by strong hands that curled beneath her knees and tugged. When her hips reached the end of the mattress, Joseph's face appeared above her.

"Winn Gardner, I love you." His elbows trembled as he braced a palm on either side of her head, then his warm swollen lips pressed to hers. And she tasted of the sweet fragrance with which he'd earlier powdered her.

His rigid body hovered at the entrance to hers, and she reached to guide it within, offering her deepest self as his heart's ease. She learned a new wonder about this act of love: how magnificent it is to experience it in an already sated state. For while Joseph thrust above her, she was replete and aware, taking exploratory interest in each of his tensed muscles as they rippled along her ribs, corded at his inner elbow and bulged across his chest. Her palms hovered lightly on his buttocks, feeling them grow hollow, then round, with each driving stroke of man into woman. She contoured his hips and felt the smooth movements of meshing in his superbly toned body. His back—ah, his back, how warm and strong and tough it was as he undulated. She came to know its texture beneath her palms, then beneath her heels, beneath her calves. And once she reached the backs of her fingers to the soft masculine orbs that swayed against her as he rocked into her flesh, her light touch an accolade to the act they shared.

He was an exquisite male animal, a sensitive human being. He was more than her sexual nemesis. He was her love.

When he climaxed, he drove her a foot up the bed with the force of his final thrusts, and a magnificent animal sound escaped his gritted teeth.

Then he fell, exhausted, almost knocking the breath from her.

# 10

"WINN, what are we going to do?" The sheen had dried from his shoulders. He lay on his side, his troubled brown eyes probing hers.

"I don't know."

"You can't marry him. You just can't."

She closed her eyes and the lids trembled. She opened them, and he saw the turmoil she faced. A terrible hurt grabbed his heart like a giant fist, wringing.

"Could you really do this with me, then go back to him?"

"What other choice do I have?"

He lay with an elbow folded beneath an ear. With his free hand he caressed the side of her face, his fingertips delving the messed hair at her temple.

"I want to say, marry me, Winn, and I think that's what I want. But it's happened awfully fast. I need some time alone with you, more time than we've had. We both need it so we can explore the possibility. I'm twenty-seven. I've waited a long time to find the right woman, and I don't intend to make it a temporary commitment when I get married."

"Neither do I."

His thumb had been stroking her cheekbone but fell still. Their somber gazes grew too intense, and she closed her eyes to shut out his compelling face.

"Look at me!" His hand pressed hard in emphasis. She opened her eyes again. "I love you, Winn Gardner. But I don't want you to do the thing that's wrong for you. I've spent a lot of time sending out little digs about him and you, hinting that he's not right for you, not good enough for you. Is he?"

Her lips opened and she wet them. Her nostrils flared, and the hint of tears sparkled in the downward corners of her eyes. But she didn't know how to answer. How could Joseph think Paul had to measure up to *her* when she was the one who'd betrayed him? The strong hand left her cheek and brushed the hair back beside her ear, then fell to rest on the narrow space between their chins. "Tell me what he does to make you happy." She tried desperately to think of one single thing but could come up with no answers. "What about in bed?" Joseph pressed. "Has he ever done what I just did to you?"

Her eyelids became half-shuttered as she dropped her gaze. His knuckles pressed up on her chin, forcing her blue eyes and blushing cheeks to confront his direct gaze. "Has he?"

"No," she whispered.

"Has anyone?"

Her blush deepened. "No."

"The first time..." he mused wondrously. His forefinger measured the width of her lower lip, then slipped inside and touched her teeth. "Why with me?"

She tried to turn onto her back and shift her gaze to the ceiling, but he wouldn't let her. "Why did you let me?"

"Just because...because you...you tried it, and it...it felt right."

"You mean nobody else has ever tried it with you before?"

"There haven't been that many, Joseph."

"How many?"

"Four. You're my fifth."

"And who are the others?"

"My high-school steady and two others during college before I met Paul. And now you."

"And now me...." At close range he saw that her

eyes had startling aquamarine depths scattered within the surface blues. That unconscious single-lidded blink came at what—by now—he considered quite the appropriate time. "On the day you dropped your wedding invitations into the mail, you allow me liberties you've never allowed even the man you're going to marry. Why?"

"Because I feel free and open with you, and at the moment it happened I felt committed. I wanted...it seemed...." She tried to cover her face with one hand, but he grasped the wrist and prevented it.

"Don't be ashamed before me...not ever, Winn. There's absolutely no reason to be. It seemed what?"

"I've read about it before and seen pictures, but it always seemed...perverted. And then with you it became...." She picked at the bedspread between their chins and finally lifted her eyes to his. Such eyes he had. She loved his eyes. "Exalted," she finished quietly.

His intense eyes studied her somberly. He sighed—a wholesome sound—and kissed the bridge of her nose, between her eyes, then lay back, studying her again.

"And after that you could still marry him?"

Angrily now, she sat up, slipped from the end of the bed and crossed the hall to the bathroom, from where she informed him, "You don't realize what all is involved, Joseph! You're not the one whose mother has hired caterers and cake decorators and florists and laid down big chunks of money as deposits for every service about to be rendered!"

He rolled to his back, cupped the back of his head in both hands and snorted at the ceiling. "So it's the money?"

He heard the rush of water, then what sounded like the slam of a drawer. Her voice grew louder and closer as she reappeared and came to stand at the foot of the bed, still naked. "Joseph, you don't quite understand about my mother. I'm a bastard she had to raise without a penny of help from anyone. She went through a pregnancy without a man and had me with no father to sign the birth certificate, and she's lived the twenty-five years since as frugally as it's possible to live. Security—that's always been her hang-up. And to her, money was the only security she could obtain, because she had no man for emotional security. So money came to mean a lot to her, and she slowly earned more and more of it but hoarded it very jealously.

"Until now. When I became engaged to Paul, she loosened the purse strings for the first time. She's giving me the kind of wedding she thinks is most socially acceptable. Can you imagine her chagrin if I were to go to her now, after the invitations have been sent, after the announcement has been put in the paper, after showers have been planned, and announce that I changed my mind?"

His eyes held none of their devilish twinkle now. They bored into her while he lay with his armpits exposed, his belly hollow. Unexpectedly he snapped up, stretching out a hand to her. "Come here. Could we please continue this conversation tucked cozily under the sheets together instead of like cold angry strangers?"

Immense relief flooded her as she leaned to place her hand in his. He gave one hard tug, and she fell half on top of him. He held her upper arms tightly and informed her, "I don't like arguing about it any more than you do, but we both knew it'd happen once we made love, didn't we?"

"Yes, I suppose we did."

Their troubled eyes clung, and hers were on the verge of tears when he released her and ordered, "Get in. I'm shivering."

She crawled on hands and knees to the top of the bed, and he slipped in beside her, snuggling under the blankets and wrapping both arms around her, settling the top of her head just beneath his chin. She rolled on her side and circled his ribs with one clinging arm.

"Is it because I haven't asked you to marry me that you won't call it off with him?" he asked.

"No, Joseph. It's the thought of canceling all the social obligations, all the commitments that scares me to death. I'd look like a fool, and that I could handle, but so would my mother and Paul, and they don't deserve that."

"What other social commitments?"

She sighed and rolled away from him slightly. He wouldn't have it and pulled her back where she'd been. "Tell me," he ordered.

She told him succinctly, listing everything she could think of: invitations, postage, caterers, personalized napkins, champagne, limousine, unity candle, photographer, jeweler, tuxedo rental, bridesmaids' dresses, bridal gown, registration book, ring bearer's pillow, garter, gifts for her attendants, organist, the singer and even the special stem glasses for the nuptial toasts. When she finished almost breathlessly, the hand that had been squeezing her shoulder fell limp onto the mattress.

"Oh, my God," he muttered.

She laughed, and it was such a relief. "See, I told you."

"You mean everybody goes through all that when they get married?"

"No. Only the stupid ones."

"You mean you don't want any of it at all?"

"I always thought the perfect wedding would be to get married with only my favorite relatives and my best friends present, maybe in some pretty garden or field someplace when the lilacs are in bloom. Then maybe a quick dinner at my mother's house and slip away to the North Woods and sleep in a tent in two zipped-together sleeping bags for one solid week, with nothing but bears and raccoons and porcupines for company."

His arm came around her again, caressing her naked back, her spine. "Mmm . . ." he murmured against her hair. "Sounds perfect. Let's do it."

"Jo-Jo, be serious!"

"I think I'm getting more serious by the minute. You and I find more in common the longer we know each other." He yawned all of a sudden.

She closed her eyes, wholly content, curled up against his warm naked limbs. "Jo-Jo, I can't marry you," she said lazily. "Besides, you said you haven't decided yet."

"Did I?" he murmured disinterestedly.

"Mmm-hmm."

Her hand fell still in the midst of fanning across his chest. Beneath her fingers the rise and fall of his breathing became long and measured. The lights still burned. But neither cared. Their limbs grew liquid and their eyelids twitched. A gentle snore sounded through the room, and Winn's eyes flickered open. At the sight of his relaxed lips and face she smiled sleepily and curled up tighter into her pillow, her fists beneath her chin and her forearms pressed against his warm ribs.

His snoring grew a little louder, and she nudged him. "Roll over, Joseph."

"Wh—" His eyes flew open, disoriented.

"Roll over."

He rolled onto his right side, and she right behind him, circling his belly with an arm and pressed her body securely against his naked backside. There was no spot on earth she would rather be.

IN THE MORNING they awakened almost simultaneously and smiled at each other with the unaccustomed joy of greeting the face of the one each loved first thing in the day.

"I like sleeping with you." He lifted both arms above

his head and posed like Charles Atlas, everything bulging and quivering from chin to waist.

"That's because I don't snore."

"Did I?"

"Just a little."

His arms hauled her close. "Mmm . . . I'll have to make up for it some way, won't I?"

"And also for the extra charge on my light bill."

He glanced back over his shoulder. "Oh, did we leave it on?"

"Mmm-hmm."

"You just wanted to check and make sure it was me with you if you woke up in the middle of the night with your hand on anything important."

"Yup!" she agreed, and they both laughed as he rolled her beneath him and braced up on both elbows.

"Come with me today," he urged.

"Where we goin'?"

"To the auction in Bemidji."

"Ohh, the auction. I'd forgotten."

He smiled into her eyes. "Will you come?"

She twisted one of his curls around her finger and smiled up at him very naughtily, then purred, "Try me, big boy."

"Oh, for shame!" he teased.

She looped her arms around his neck. "Well, you can't blame a girl for getting to like it, can you?"

"Winnifred Gardner, I'm shocked."

"Yeah, I can feel the shock absolutely *growing* on you."

"Oh, that. Well, you can't blame a boy for responding to the off-color innuendo of a fiery little sexpot who—"

"Fiery little sexpot!"

"Fiery little sexpot who keeps a cup in her kitchen with the nickname Killer on it."

"You take that back, Jo-Jo Duggan, or I'll make you sorry!" She yanked the curl.

"*Ow!* Watch it, Killer, you're askin' for it!" He got her by both wrists and showed her who was master here.

"Yes, Mr. Duggan, I am," she simpered.

He kissed her finally with a mock show of uncontrolled passion, writhing around as if he were swimming on top of her. She was laughing beneath his mouth, and her words came out muffled.

"Are you going to ravish me?"

"You bet, and you're going to love it."

"Am I supposed to fight you or cooperate?"

He mellowed. His squirming turned to undulation. He was assaulting her mouth, chin, throat, then breasts with breathtaking tenderness. "I never did care much for unwilling females."

"Have you had many . . . unwilling ones?"

His stubbled jaw was like a steel brush against her tender breast, and she loved it. "None."

"And what about the other kind? How many of them?"

He reared up, meeting her eyes. "My share. Does it bother you?"

She had a flippant remark on the tip of her tongue, but instead she cupped his face in both hands and spoke earnestly. "Oh, yes, Joseph Duggan, I hate every one of them for having you before I did. And I have no right."

"You have every right. After last night."

Tears sprang into her eyes, and her soft lips parted on a quick indrawn breath, not quite a sob, not quite a sigh. It had to be said. Feelings this strong simply must be voiced.

"God help me, Joseph, I love you."

"Then God help both of us, not just you."

This time when his body slipped inside hers, it was with great tenderness. Their coupling was totally different from the first time. It was rich with slowness, unfrenzied, almost studious. They watched each other, both faces and bodies, and loved with eyes, as well as the physical parts that joined. They neither spoke nor called out, for their union was not meant to ease, but to blend their spirits. And so it did. Only Joseph reached a climax, but it mattered little to Winn. This she could give, yet be the grateful one when it was over.

And this physical union, for all its simpleness—wholesomeness almost—was shattering.

"I love you," he vowed when it ended.

"And I love you," she answered. Then she cried.

THEY MADE A PACT AFTERWARD that those would be the last tears of the day, that they'd be carefree, happy, and speak of no other people but themselves.

They spent the day going to Bemidji in Joseph's 1954 Cadillac pickup, a funereal gray monstrosity twenty-two feet long, with all its coffin rollers intact and sporting four doors, velour upholstery sumptuous enough to be used in any coffin and a roomy three feet of space behind the seat, from which the name "flower car" had been derived: the space for carrying the funeral flowers.

But the vehicle was luxurious to a fault. During much of the five-hour ride, Winn lay sprawled across the seat with the soles of her feet hanging out the window and her head snuggled in Joseph's lap.

Five miles outside of Bemidji they followed directions on the auction-sale billboard and parked the Caddy beside the narrow gravel road lined with cars on both sides for a quarter mile in either direction. They spent the day meandering the farmyard amid farmers wearing bib overalls and wives with their pin curls tied up in blue handkerchiefs knotted above their foreheads.

Joseph and Winn kept their promise. They forgot about all the outside forces working against them and enjoyed only each other, holding hands, laughing, occasionally dipping behind a large piece of machinery to exchange kisses. The '41 Ford was a rusted, wheelless heap that wasn't worth bidding on in Joseph's estimation, but they loved listening to the silver-tongued auctioneer calling the sale with mercurial glibness.

"Heep-hayy-o-what-am-I-bid-for-this-little-beauty-of-an-automobile-do-I-hear-five-hundred-to-start-five-hundred-five-hundred-do-I-hear-five-hundred-hayy-oo-take-the-safety-pins-off-your-pockets-folks-do-I-hear-four-fifty-she's-a-racy-little-number-just-needs-a-little-dip-in-penetrating-oil-do-I-hear-four-fifty-they-don't-make-'em-like-this-anymore-four-fifty-four-fifty-do-I-hear-four-fifty-to-start-all-right-we'll-do-this-the-hard-way-do-I-hear-four-hundred-to-start-four-hundred-what-am-I-bid-fooooour-fooooour. . . ."

Jo-Jo laughed. Winn joined him. It was utterly refreshing, holding hands in the sunshine, listening to the red-faced potbellied auctioneer plying his trade. Dogs and children scampered through the crowd, while housewives from neighboring farms poked and prodded amid the housewares on display, gleaning bits of the personal lives of those holding the sale from the oddments strewn across the yard: chairs, books, tables, potbellied stoves, doilies, pickling pots, carpet sweepers, bales of twine, dishes, hog feeders, treadle sewing machines, hay balers, scrolls of music from a roller piano and a claw-footed swivel organ stool with four amber marbles clutched in its feet.

"Imagine what we'll have strewn all over our yard when we're seventy years old and having an auction sale," Winn mused.

She and Joseph sauntered along between a line of blossoming honeysuckle bushes and a set of eight oak spoke chairs. He swung their hands between them. "Are we going to be seventy years old and having an auction sale?" He grinned down at her and kicked his feet out idly with each step.

"I said *imagine*."

"Oh. . .imagine. Okay, let's see. There'll be a whole truckload of old beat-up tennis shoes and an even bigger one of rackets, and ragbags full of grungy sweat pants and sweat shirts with the arms cut off."

"And the bellies," she put in.

"And the bellies," he seconded. "And what else?"

"And a yard full of your vintage cars, Joseph, all in mint condition, and we'll get rich, rich, rich from them and spend our eighties cruising oceans in the height of luxury."

"And there'll be a shed full of white plastic containers and white fluffy powder puffs."

"Oh, almost forgot them." She squinted an eye at the sun while peering up at him. "But why a whole shed full?"

"Because I'll have used up a lot of Chanel No 5, powdering you every night for fifty years."

"*Every* night?"

"Every night."

"But, Joseph, you'll be seventy years old!"

He grinned luridly. "Imagine how good I'll be at it by then." He leaned down and bit her nose.

"We *are* talking about powdering, aren't we?"

"That, too."

"Quit talking dirty, old man, and tell me what else there'll be."

"Oh, the cribs and high chairs from when our kids were babies."

She jammed her hands into her hip pockets and confronted him belligerently. "Joseph, we are *not* selling our children's furniture, so just put the idea out of your head!"

"But why, my little flower?"

She sauntered on saucily. "Because we have our grandchildren coming to visit, silly. We'll have to leave the crib set up for them."

"Oh, of course, you're right, Killer. But can I sell that set of china with your nickname on it?"

"What set of china? It's only one cup."

"Well, I'm growing tired of the queer looks people give me when they see it sitting on the kitchen cabinet beside our liniment and Geritol. I always wonder if they think it belongs to *me*!"

They eyed each other, snickered, then snorted, then broke into gales of laughter while he tossed both arms around her and held her loosely, rocking back and forth at the sheer joy of enjoyment. Then he tugged her hand and sat down on one of the honorable-looking old kitchen chairs. "Come here." He pulled her down onto the chair next to his. Its seat was toasty warm from the sun beating down on it all afternoon. Around the honeysuckle hedge before them, bees buzzed and gathered nectar. Down the yard the auctioneer still called, his voice lifting to them faintly through the mellow butter yellow afternoon.

Joseph still held Winn's hand, sitting beside her on the heated wooden chair with an ankle draped casually across a knee.

"What?" she asked, mystified by his sudden shift of mood.

His rich brown eyes were partially hidden behind half-closed lids, their long lashes creating needlelike shadows upon his cheeks as he smiled at her and brushed a thumb lightly over the back of her hand.

"I just want to sit here a while and soak it in. And look at you."

And that's what they did. . .for a full thirty minutes. They sat in the sun on hard rung-backed chairs, facing a row of fragrant bushes, and looked at each other. Holding hands. Rubbing thumbs. Remembering. Wishing.

*When did I last study any person this well,* Winn thought. *When did I feel this rapport with another? When did it feel this right, just sharing the same sun with someone? What a stunning and good thing to do. How wise of Joseph to know the value of minutes like these.*

She partook to her heart's content.

*I love this man's face, hair, form. I love his gaiety and earthiness, his lack of artifice. I love the sound of his laughter, the turn of his brow, the line of his jaw. I love the common ground we find. The time I spend with him has a quality none other holds for me. We relate, Joseph and I. With him would life be this good, always?*

Only Joseph's unsmiling lips moved as he spoke. "You feel it, don't you?"

"Yes." There was no need to clarify.

"We could have it, you and I, I think."

"I think so, too, Joseph."

"But we made a pact, didn't we?"

"Yes, we did."

So he removed his eyes from her precious face and—still holding her hand—bent forward to rest his elbows on his knees. She had promised no more tears. She lifted her face to the sun, hoping it might sip away the faint dampness that had gathered on her lashes. Joseph's callused thumb rubbed her knuckles, and she wanted to sit like this with him forever, wishing, until maybe the auctioneer might come by and ask, "What am I bid for this man, this Joseph Duggan."

And Winn would say, "All that I have." And it would be that simple.

"It's a long drive home," he said quietly. "Time we start back."

SHE DIDN'T LIE with her head in his lap on their return trip, and he didn't claim to be sleepy. She sat most of the time close against his shoulder, her bare heels hooked over the edge of the seat, and her wrists looped around her ankles.

The ride was quiet. And long. And introspective. It screamed with unsaid things. Supper at a roadside restaurant was a failure, for neither was hungry, though they both ordered, then picked desultorily.

It was 11:00 P.M. when they pulled up in Winn's driveway. Joseph killed the engine, but neither of them moved. He stared at her front door.

At last he asked, "Can I come in?"

"No, not tonight."

He didn't ask why. He knew. Sighing, he slumped low in the seat and began kneading the bridge of his nose with his eyes shut.

"Joseph . . . I . . . thank you for—"

"Dammit!" he growled angrily, interrupting, turning his face away from her, staring out the side window while holding his lower lip with thumb and forefinger.

She paused uncertainly, reached for the door handle, but at its first click his hand lashed out and grabbed her arm. "What are you going to do?"

Her teary eyes met his across the broad seat. "Think . . . long and hard."

"And?"

"And I need time, Joseph. Promise me you won't call or try to see me until I contact you."

"*Sit?* You expect me to sit doing nothing while you go back to him and make wedding plans?"

"Joseph, don't! You promised!"

"Yeah, well that's easier said than done."

"Please don't ruin the end of a perfectly wonderful day."

"It isn't over yet. I said I want to come in."

"Joseph, this isn't—"

"All right, then!" he snarled. "I won't come in!" In a flash he was across the seat, grabbing her roughly into his arms. "There's plenty of room to do what we both want right here." His lips slammed onto hers, but halfway through the kiss she was gripping him violently and pulling him heavily against her breasts. She was both appalled and aroused by his anger, for she'd felt the wild frustration mounting within her body, just as he had, all the way home. It erupted now in a spate of pure animalism for both Winn and Joseph. Instead of fighting, she succumbed, clinging to his shoulders only momentarily before squirming down accommodatingly while he arranged his limbs upon hers with little gentleness or patience. His mouth was as hard as his arousal as he ground them simultaneously against her, gnashing her flesh with his lips and hips in an effort to quell the seething within. The punishing kiss lasted less than a minute before Joseph reared back, breath heaving harshly, and began jerking his shirt open. He yanked it out of his waistband while kneeling above her, one leg on the floor, the other angled across her body. Their eyes pierced, shameless in their intent while she, too, roughly unsnapped and unzipped her jeans, then together they stripped them down her right leg only, for they were too greedy to remove them entirely.

His clothing hadn't cleared his ankles before he threw his body down on hers. As he fell, he caught her behind a knee and forced the leg wide. Her foot caught the window ledge, and she used it for leverage, thrusting up to greet and welcome him, fully aroused now, both.

And so they sought restitution, he driving deep, she surging up to meet his oncoming force with an elemental need to settle the conflict between them that both knew could not be settled this way.

But it felt good. Fruitless as it was, it relieved. They pummeled each other, fingers gripping hips and buttocks almost painfully as he growled and she sobbed, and in the end, together, they cried out. An anguished, replete, wonderful, pitiable wail of gratification.

Her climax was devastating. His, awesome. And when their spent bodies lay tangled and sated, they understood perfectly what they had accomplished. And what they had not.

His voice, when at last he spoke, was thick with contrition, muffled in the collar of her blouse, which hung half on, half off her body.

"Oh, God, Winn, I'm sorry."

"I am, too."

"Why did I do that when I love you?"

"Why did I? I'm just as guilty as you are."

"I'll never do it again, I swear, not in anger."

Was he crying? My God, was he crying? "Shh!" she soothed. His skull was damp as she wove her fingertips into his hair. "Shh." His arms tightened about her proprietarily. He lifted his head and spoke in a racked whisper.

"Did I hurt you, Winn?"

"No. I'm fine. A little messed, but fine." He rolled his shoulders back and groaned softly, squeezing his eyes shut and catching a hand in his hair.

She attempted to lighten his burden and make him smile. "Did I hurt you?"

He gave a single mirthless huff of laughter and slowly eased himself off her, tugged up his jeans, lifted her legs across his lap and sat behind the wheel again. He crossed his arms on it, then lowered his head.

She withdrew her feet from his lap, arranged her clothing and threaded the fingers of both hands through her hair with an enormous sigh. He sat slumped over without moving.

"Joseph, I have to go in now."

His head lifted slowly. His eyes looked tormented.

"I'll call you if and when I get myself freed from other commitments."

He sat silent and unmoving as black water. She leaned across the seat and placed her lips lightly on his, touched his chin and begged, "Don't blame yourself. It was both of us."

He swallowed. The sound was loud in the bleak silence.

"Goodbye, Joseph."

When she slipped away, he lurched, as if coming awake from a dream to find her truly escaping.

"Winn, wait!"

But the door slammed, and he watched her run to the house as fast as she could.

DURING THE FOLLOWING THREE DAYS Winn learned things about crying she'd never known before. By Tuesday night she thought it might very well be possible to cry oneself to death. Sunday was spent alternately sobbing and drying up, running for the Kleenex box, then for ice cubes to soothe her stinging eyes. To make matters worse, Paul called, asking, "Where *were* you all day yesterday and last night?" And Winn was forced to make up a lie. To make matters additionally worse, Joseph called, too, ignoring her order to stay out of touch. His message was that he loved her and was despicably miserable and wanted to see her again. Though she managed to stave him off, she was deluged with fresh tears after she hung up.

Monday, with Merry gone from the hospital, Winn's gloom continued, camouflaged behind the cheeriness she forced for the benefit of the other patients. Monday night Paul called to say he missed her and would be home Wednesday at 4:00 P.M., and could she pick him up at the airport. She almost expected the ring that came just after nine. This time Joseph cursed at her, then apologized profusely, then called her Killer in the most heart-wrenchingly sweet voice she'd ever heard. "Hey, Killer. . .I love you, you know." Once more she cried herself to sleep.

At six-thirty the next morning Joseph called again. "Dammit, I didn't sleep a wink again last night! You *are* going to kill me yet, woman! Please tell me you aren't going to marry him."

Judas priest, what a wonderful way to start the day—crying again! She made it through eight hours at the hospital and returned to her town house exhausted, but had barely flopped to her back in the middle of the living-room floor when the phone pealed, and it was her realtor, asking if she could leave the house around seven so he could show it. To a couple who'd seen it before—a hopeful sign, he finished. With a sigh she told the realtor where she could be reached, but just as she was leaving the house, Joseph called again.

"Joseph, I can't talk. I've got to get out of the house so the realtor can show it. And this is a good prospect, too, 'cause it's the second time this party is looking at it."

He sounded desperate. "Winn, don't you dare sell that house!"

She squeezed her forehead in an effort to stop the tears that immediately began stinging. "Joseph, I have to go."

"Winn, please, I love y—" he was barking into the phone when she tenderly hung it up. She drove to her mother's house because she couldn't think of anywhere else to go where the realtor could reach her.

Before she was two steps inside her mother's kitchen, Fern Gardner demanded, "What in the world is wrong with you?"

"Nothing."

"With eyes like those. . .who are you trying to fool?" Fern took a grip on her daughter's chin and inspected at close range. "You look awful, dear."

"Thank you, mother," Winn replied sarcastically.

A knowing glint came into Fern's eyes. "Ah, you miss Paul, is that it?"

It was all Winn could do to keep from ruefully laughing. During the following hour, while Fern rambled on about how smoothly all the wedding preparations were going, Winn gritted her teeth and clamped her jaw. There were times when she wanted to scream at her mother to shut up. Finally she escaped to the bathroom, just to get away from the constant wedding prattle for a few minutes. There, locked in, she stared at herself in the mirror. *Tell her, you coward, tell her!* But the prospect of walking out there and dashing all her mother's bright hopes was daunting, to say the least. *What are you waiting for, Gardner? Your R.S.V.P.'s?* Winn's stomach hurt. At times she felt light-headed, and often her palms sweated. It struck her that this horrendous misery bore all the same symptoms as love.

Out in the living room the phone rang. "Winn, it's for you!" Fern called.

To Winn's dismay it was the realtor. He'd just received a firm offer on her house.

*Winn, don't you dare sell that house! Winn, goddammit, I love you!* Panic welled, and all of Winn's symptoms grew spontaneously worse. Stalling for time, she told the realtor she'd have to think about the offer and would get back to him either tonight or tomorrow. "It's a good offer," he reminded her. "I wouldn't wait too long to accept it." Winn hung up and stared at the wall.

"Did someone make an offer?"

"Yes."

Fern threw her hands in the air. "Hallelujah! It's as if fate stepped in just in the nick of time. Darling, I'm so happy for you and Paul."

That did it. The tears burst forth like a geyser, and Winn fell back into an upholstered armchair, covering her face with both hands, sobbing uncontrollably.

Fern couldn't have been more amazed. "Why, Winn, dear, what is it?" She bent to one knee and soothed the back of her daughter's head while the sobs shook Winn's shoulders.

"Oh, m-mother, it's the w-worst thing in the wo-world. It's so awf-awful that when I t-tell you, you're g-going to want to d-die."

Fern's dread billowed. "Are you sick? Is it some health problem or . . . or—"

Winn shook her head so hard the hair slashed Fern's face. Into her palms she sobbed, "It's wo-worse!"

"What could be worse?"

Winn lifted her streaming eyes and ran the back of one hand under her nose. "I c-can't m-marry Paul, mother. I d-don't love h-him."

Fern looked stricken. She turned as gray as Jo-Jo's funeral truck. Her mouth slacked, and she fell back as if landed a blow in the chest. She pressed a hand to her heart and spoke in a strained reedy voice. "You can't mean that!"

"I do. I mean every word of it." Winn tore out of her chair, heading for the kitchen Kleenex, then turned to find her mother still on her knees on the floor, stunned. "I don't love him, mother. I l-love somebody else." Now that it was out, Winn felt almost exultant.

"Somebody else!" Fern's face hardened, and she lurched to her feet angrily. "How dare you come to me three weeks before your wedding and tell me such a thing!"

"I don't know how I dare. It scared me all week, just thinking about it, but I decided it was either you or me, mother, and in the end I picked me."

"And what does that mean—you or me?" Fern spit.

"Either I can make you happy or I can make me happy. Mother, can't you see it's really you who admires Paul, not me?"

Two high spots of color appeared in Fern's outraged cheeks. "How dare you speak to me like that!"

Winn sighed and slumped. "Mother, sit down, please. There are so many things we should have talked about during the last year that we never did. About Paul, and me . . . and you . . . and even Rita."

Fern's chin snapped up. "Rita? You mean his computer?"

"Yes, his computer. Sit down, mother, please." At last Fern perched on the edge of the chair that matched Winn's. She crossed her knees stiffly and looked as if she'd just eaten a worm. "Mother, Paul and I have only one thing in common that I can think of. Dancing. And he'd rather stay home and punch his computer keys than do that with me. It's *you* who has things in common with him, not me. I should have realized that when you first introduced him to me. Now I do, and I can't go through with this marriage and take him as surrogate husband to make up for the one you never had."

Fern's lips pursed, but she refused to meet her daughter's eyes. "Are you intimating that I chose Paul for you because I couldn't have him for myself?"

"In a way, yes, but—" Fern spit out a pent breath and rocketed from her chair, presenting her back. "Not in a romantic way, mother, please understand. He's everything you ever wanted for me because he represents stability, security, all the things you had to fight for because you never had a husband. But those things aren't enough for me. I need someone who enjoys having fun, who laughs, who's physical, who . . . who. . . ." Winn thought of Joseph, and it was as if a beam of sunshine shot into her head.

"I assume you think you've found him in this other man."

"Maybe."

Fern tossed a disdainful glance over her shoulder. "And while you're deciding, what shall I do with all the guests who've been invited to your and Paul's wedding? What should I do with the gifts that have already started arriving here at the house? And the caterers and the flowers and the photographer and the gown?" With each succeeding word Fern's voice grew sharper and higher until she was nearly shrieking. "Do you know how much money this extravaganza has cost me!"

"Not exactly," Winn answered meekly, "but I can imagine."

Fern swung on her daughter, closing in. "You don't get deposits back for those things, sweetheart!" she declared with a sting in each word.

"I know, mother. But I'll pay you back, I promise."

It was silent for a moment, then Fern snorted and turned away. "You'll pay me back." She chuckled coldly. "And you'll pay me back for the embarrassment I'll suffer every time I meet a friend on the street?"

"Mother, this isn't easy for me, either!"

"And what about Paul? Have you told him yet?"

"No." For the first time Winn's voice softened. "I'll tell him tomorrow. I'm picking him up at the airport."

"What a wonderful welcome home for him," Fern jeered.

Suddenly Winn felt sorry for her mother. "Did losing my father turn you so hard and cynical that you can't be happy for me that I've at least made the discovery in time? Would you rather have had me marry Paul first and then find out it wouldn't work?"

Fern's shoulders seemed to wilt a little. She propped one hand across her stomach, dropped her face into the other. Wordlessly she shook her head.

"And you haven't asked me anything about Joseph, mother," Winn added softly.

"What does . . .*Joseph* do for a living?" her mother obliged coldly.

"He runs a body shop."

Fern raised one eyebrow, snorted softly and left the room.

But the worst was over. Winn had little doubt that telling Paul wasn't going to be nearly as hard as telling her mother. Oddly enough, it seemed Paul was less emotionally involved than Fern Gardner.

HE CAME OFF THE PLANE, beaming, with a clothing carrier slung over one shoulder. "Winn, I've missed you." He gave her a kiss while they walked, and launched into a joyous recitation of the wonders of Silicon Valley.

"Do we have time for a cup of coffee?" Winn asked before they headed for the luggage pickup.

"Sure. Anyway, there's so much I want to tell you."

Odd, he didn't notice Winn's uncustomary distractedness while they sat over coffee in The Garden restaurant at Twin Cities International. He was carried away with exuberance. Winn felt extra guilty to have to prick his balloon, but by now all she wanted was to have it out in the open so she could start making restitution and get her life back on track.

After nearly thirty minutes Paul asked, "How is everything back here?" Only then did he notice the shadows in her expression. "Something's wrong, isn't it?"

"Yes, Paul, something's very wrong. You aren't going to like it when I tell you, but I promised myself I would, immediately. It's bad news for us, and it's going to hurt you, I'm afraid. For that I'm sorry."

He leaned forward and took her hands in his, studying her with a look of deep concern. "What's wrong, Winn?"

She'd rehearsed it dozens of times. She took a deep breath, gripped his fingers and said straightforwardly, "I want to call our wedding off."

He blanched and went speechless for several seconds. "Temporarily?" he asked.

"No. . . permanently," she answered quietly, releasing his hands.

To Paul's great credit he reacted with poise in spite of the fact that his face went from bleached white to peony pink in a matter of five seconds. "Oh. . . I see." When Winn remained silent, he amended, "No, I don't see! I thought everything was so great between us."

"Paul, answer me honestly. Which brings you greater—" she searched for the proper term "—*ongoing* joy—me or your work?" He considered for a moment and turned a brighter red than before. "See?" she insisted, leaning forward. "I'm not criticizing you for it. I'm telling you something we both should have recognized long ago. We joined forces because of mother, because you and she had so much in common that when she met you, she thought she just had to have you for me. But, Paul. . .I. . .I don't think I love you. I admire you. I respect you. But I don't love you." She paused, then asked, "Will you be very, very honest and tell me if you really love me. Or did we fall together because it worked so smoothly, having the support of our parents as we did? And consider if you wouldn't enjoy me much, much more if I played chess and loved to tinker with computers myself, and enjoyed talking about them with you like mother does. Paul, that's the kind of woman you need. Somebody with an analytical mind that's as inquisitive as yours."

"I can tell you've been thinking about this for a long time."

"It's been. . .coming on for a few weeks, yes. But I was caught up in the crazy whirlwind preparations for the wedding and couldn't face telling the world—not to mention my mother—that I was canceling everything."

"Can you really do that at this late date? What about all the invitations you sent out already?"

"I'll handle everything, Paul. And I'll make it clear whose fault it was."

His eyebrows took on a frosty expression. "Is there someone else, Winnie?"

This was the most difficult question of all, for Paul didn't deserve to be hurt. "Yes, Paul, there is."

He inhaled deeply, held the breath long, then released it in a giant *whoosh*, his shoulders sagging. "Well, that settles that."

"Paul, I'm terribly sorry. And if it's any consolation, mother is furious with me. She isn't even talking to me." Winn reached out and touched the back of his hand. "Please don't take this in the wrong way, Paul, because I don't mean any disrespect, but it's too bad you and mother aren't closer to the same age. You'd make the most wonderful husband for her." Then she leaned across the table and kissed his cheek while Paul grew totally flustered and seemed unable to meet her eyes. That's when she knew she'd guessed right.

IT WAS shortly after eight-thirty that evening when Winn Gardner stepped onto the back stoop of Joseph Duggan's house. The radio was on in the kitchen. Tammy Wynette was belting out "Stand By Your Man" in her inimitable cracky voice, and water ran for a moment, then was turned off. Winn angled a peek through the screen and saw the left half of a Duggan back, dressed in a gold-and-black baseball uniform, shoeless, with a black cap pushed onto the back of his head, washing dishes. She waited until she was sure which Duggan it was, and when his profile appeared for a second, she smiled, opened the screen door silently and slipped inside. *Even his back turns me on,* she thought, watching as he rinsed a cup, set it on the drain board, then plunged his hands into the soapy water. The stretchy gold fabric of his breeches clung to his legs like an orange rind, displaying each dent and bulge. There was a grass stain on his left bun, and she smiled, picturing him as a boy, though loving him as a man. When at last she spoke, her voice was soft and quavery. "Hiya, Jo-Jo."

He spun around. Detergent bubbles flew from his fingertips and drifted to the floor. His stocking feet, in their black baseball leggings, were braced wide apart, like an outfielder waiting for a fly. There was a puff of dust on his right cheek, and his shirt was filthy, as if he'd managed a beauty of a slider, belly first. His conglomerate appearance was totally incongruous—the soiled virile athlete with his hands in soapsuds. He gaped at her as if she were a ghost, while she tried to act as if every cell in her body wasn't leaping to get at him. In the same trembling voice she asked, "Need somebody to wipe for you?"

"Winn . . . my God . . . Winn."

"Is that all you can say is Winn? After all I've been through today just to get out of one very fast-approaching wedding for you?"

In one leap he slammed against her, nearly knocking her breath out while taking her off her feet and against his chest, with both of his detergent hands leaving wet prints on the back of her yellow cotton blouse. "Really? Oh, babe, really?" But he didn't give her time to answer. His mouth crushed hers, wide and wet and celebratory as he whirled them both in a circle.

Her arms made a nest for his head, knocking the baseball cap askew while they kissed and kissed and kissed, moving their heads in impatient and wondrous circles, yet still unable to satiate themselves fast enough to believe it was real. When at last she drew her mouth back to say, "Yes, really," her smile was as wide as center field, yet his was even wider. His beautiful bedroom eyes sparkled with the smile she loved, the one that half-closed them while his perfect teeth peeked from behind upturned lips. While he still held her aloft, she appropriated his black baseball cap and put it on her own head so she could get her fingers into that wonderful wealth of fine curls she loved so much.

"You really called it off?" he demanded one more time.

"I really called it off. I told mother to cease and desist. I gave my apologies to Paul. I told the realtor to come and get his damned sign out of my yard and sent the buyers packing, then came to you as fast as my car could get me here."

His mouth possessed hers again, and while they kissed, he let her slide down the front of him with very deliberate slowness. Her blouse caught on his uniform buttons and shimmied up her tummy, and his hands slid beneath it to caress her bare back and ribs.

Tommy Duggan, dressed in a uniform matching Jo-

Jo's, turned the corner into the kitchen, came up short at the sight greeting him, folded his arms across his chest and leaned against the archway, smiling.

"Well, well, well," he drawled, "What do we have here?"

Joseph's hands stayed right where they were while he craned around to look at his brother. Winn kept her arms around Jo-Jo's neck, unwilling to release him in spite of the interruption. "What we have here is Killer Gardner, the woman who's made my life pure misery for the last two months."

"She gonna join the team?" Tommy inquired drolly, eyeing Joseph's cap that was too big for Winn's head and thus rested low against her ears.

Jo-Jo grinned down at her. "Whaddya say, Killer, wanna join the Duggan team?"

She kissed him boldly on the mouth, ending with a loud smack. "That depends. Who won tonight?"

Jo-Jo seemed unaware of his brother's presence as he smiled at the woman in his arms and rubbed her spine. "Me."

Tommy's eyes followed Joseph's hands, then he pulled his shoulder away from the doorway and picked up his own black hat from the kitchen table, settled its bill low over his eyes and remarked, "Well, I can see I'm not needed around here. Might as well go join the guys at Dick's Bar."

Then he slammed out the back door, and a minute later they heard his car start.

Alone again, Joseph and Winn gazed lovingly into each other's eyes, standing just where Tommy had left them, only now his hands were inside her waistband, caressing the slope of her spine. "I can't believe you're here," he said in a gruff whisper, letting his eyes caress her face.

"Neither can I. The last four days have been absolute hell."

This kiss was different. Deliberate, measured, beginning with the lazy lowering of Joseph's mouth to Winn's, the gradual intrusion of tongues, building in ardor as their hands started roaming each other's backs, shoulders, buttocks, breasts, until it was a total bodily clinging as they pressed yearningly against each other, as if never would they get enough . . . never.

He tore his mouth from hers long enough to utter, "I was so scared I'd lose you, and there wasn't anything I could do about it."

"I was scared, too." A hot weakening kiss cut her off for several seconds, then Joseph's face was on her neck, his hands releasing the catch of her bra while she went on. "From the night of the wedding practice I've been scared. I fell for you so hard it terrified me. I thought you were a flirt, and flirts always seem insincere. Then I got to know you better and realized I was falling in love with you. . . ." She clung to him harder. "Oh, Joseph, you have no idea how awful it is to be engaged to one man and in love with another."

His palm slid to ensconce her freed breast in its warm curve. "It can't be any worse than being the one on the outside, watching it happen. God, I felt so helpless!"

Again they kissed, allowing their bodies full greed. He caressed and toyed with her nipple until it stood out proudly, then ran his hand down the stomach of her white jeans, slipping down between her legs where it was warm and slightly damp.

Her hand, too, ran down his body. "Mmm . . .I like you in your baseball uniform. You can't hide anything from me in pants this tight."

"Who's trying to hide?"

"Not me."

"Me, either."

She rested her forehead against his nose laughed then and did her Mae West imitation: *"So, uh, tell me, big boy, where's your brother John?"*

"Up at Dick's Bar with the rest of the team, having a few beers."

"Wanna join them?" she teased, stroking him ardently now.

"Yeah, sure, I was thinking about it. Nothing a man loves better than a nice cold beer on a summer evening."

"Well, don't let me . . .uh, stop you." His eyes sparkled and crinkled at the corners. She'd never get enough of his eyes, not if they lived to be seventy. Or of the rest of him, for that matter.

"I'll head over there in a minute. There's something I've got to do first, though." He had her by both buns and was dancing her backward toward the archway and the stairway around the corner.

"How much time before your brothers get home?"

His tongue teased the corner of her mouth. "They'll be gone till midnight." She felt him grin against her lips. "The beer's damn good at Dick's."

Her heels struck the bottom step and brought them both up short. With her arms looped about his neck she ordered huskily, "Hurry up, Jo-Jo Duggan. The past four days have seemed like years. Show me your bedroom."

He bent and picked her up like a sack of potatoes and took the steps at a leisurely pace while she caressed his backside. "I will. But I'll show you my bathroom first. I played a tough game and took a hard slide into home in the eighth inning. I'm dust from one end to the other."

The bathroom was Classic Grandma: no shower, but a tub with a rubber plug on the end of a chain. The room was painted aqua blue and trimmed with white swan decals on one wall, while that behind the vanityless sink was paneled with some marbly gray stuff that looked like plastic. There was a water heater in one corner and a clothes hamper next to the stool, and the floor was covered with pure unadulterated grade-B hardware-store linoleum, its worn spot covered with an aqua blue scatter rug.

But it mattered not in the least, for anywhere Joseph and Winn shared was their own private heaven. She watched him drop his dusty uniform in the hamper. Then the body that had taken a hard slide into home took a soft slide into the tub. And she came to know the texture of his slick, soapy skin both above and below the surface of the water.

Her Joseph. How she loved him. Kneeling beside the tub, with her eyes caught in his, she lifted her wet hand from the water and laid it on his cheek. His eyes were dark, lustrous, close to hers. "Joseph Duggan, I love you," she whispered thickly.

All was silent but for the soft blip of the ancient, dripping tap. Then he brought his hands from the water to her jaws. His wet thumbs caressed her lips before he gently eradicated the space between their mouths, kissing her gently, wonderingly, the touch filled with praise and promise.

"And I love you, Winn Gardner. Marry me."

Her murmured agreement was lost in his kiss, but neither heard nor cared. For it could be no other way: the choice had never been theirs, not from the first night they'd met to walk down an aisle together.

THE WEDDING INVITATIONS numbered twenty-two. Each was handwritten on plain typing paper, but not all in the same pen. Half were written in Winn's neat forward slant and half in Joseph's rather chicken-scratchy semi-legibility. They began with the words, "Joseph Duggan and Winnifred Gardner invite you to join them in Elm Creek Park. . . ."

Joseph and Winn chose a Friday afternoon for their wedding. She wore a white summer dress of airy piqué, and fixed her hair in a Gibson Girl doughnut, trimming it with a simple sprig of baby's breath they found blooming in Joseph's grandma's garden.

Joseph and Winn rode out together in his Haynes a

half hour before the scheduled time of the service to walk through the woods and gather a bouquet of brown-eyed Susans, wild buttercups and fragrant wild roses, conveniently abloom now in this month of roses.

The guests were waiting when they returned from their walk to the chosen spot, a grassy knoll in a break between the trees where birds were their only music and the grass their aisle. Around them were those they loved most dearly, including a surprised Sandy and Mick, Joseph's parents and brothers, as well as Fern Gardner, still in a state of shock, but present nevertheless.

The service lasted seven minutes and thirty-five seconds, approximately one-third the length of time it had taken most of the assembled to drive out from town.

When Winn kissed her mother's cheek, there was a radiant smile upon the bride's face. That smile was reflected upon the faces of several others close enough to hear the following words. "Mother, I'd like you to meet my husband, Joseph Duggan."

The two shook hands while Joseph spoke his first words to Fern. "Mrs. Gardner, I promise to love your daughter and keep her ecstatic at least until we're seventy years old. After that it depends on whether she lets our grandchildren overrun us or not."

MR. AND MRS. JOSEPH DUGGAN honeymooned in a log cabin on Lake Bemidji. On their first afternoon there they went out fishing, something Winn had never tried before. With typical beginner's luck she caught the only fish of the day—a seven-pound walleyed pike. Within an hour, when the lake provided no more action, she lost all interest in the sport and asked Joseph to head the boat back to the cabin. There, inside, Jo-Jo warned, "Hands off, Killer, I have to clean the fish first."

"Throw him away."

"But he's such a big one."

"I caught one big one. I can catch another. . . ." Then she ran her hands down his body and giggled. "Oh-oh! Here comes one now!"

But in the end Joseph cleaned the walleye, and by the time he finished it was time for dinner. They ate at The Seasons, then returned to their private retreat amid the lakeshore pines. When they faced each other at the side of their bed, Winn felt oddly timid. Joseph was dressed in cottom pajama pants and she in a long white nightgown with tiny satin straps and a bow beneath her breasts. Her cheeks were flushed and his eyes sparkly. His callused hand reached for hers and gave one gentle tug.

"Come here, Mrs. Duggan."

She lifted her arms, and his closed about her, bringing their wispily clad bodies close. His neck smelled of the cedar after-shave she now knew so well. She closed her eyes against the warm skin there and slipped her fingers into his soft curls, cradling his head as her eyes drifted closed. "Mrs. Duggan," she repeated rapturously. "I really am." She backed away and found his eyes with her own. "I'm Mrs. Joseph Duggan."

He slipped one satin strap over a narrow shoulder. "From now till you're at least seventy," he replied with gruff tenderness.

Her fingers brushed the hair on his chest, trembling upon it. "And then?"

The second strap fell slack as he pushed it down. "And then. . . ." His eyes dropped to the satin bow as his fingers freed it. The gown shimmied into an ivory puddle at her feet. Just before his lips and arms claimed her Joseph chided raspily, "Don't ask foolish questions, my love."

"In the spring a young man's fancy
lightly turns to thoughts of love...."

Alfred, Lord Tennyson
From the poem, *Locksley Hall*

## THE AUTHOR

Since publication of *The Fulfillment* (1979), LaVyrle Spencer has completed nine novels. Travel and music are favorites of this vivacious native Minnesotan, who lives in Minneapolis with Dan, her husband of twenty-two years, a general contractor's estimator, and their two daughters, Amy and Beth. Guitarists and vocalists, the Spencers hold frequent jam sessions where good music, food and friends keep their happy house ever lively.